I0642432

THE
COINCIDENCE

By

Gabriël Moens

Connor Court Publishing Pty Ltd

PO Box 7257
Redland Bay QLD 4165
sales@connorcourt.com
www.connorcourt.com

ISBN: 9781922449887

Cover design by Maria Giordano

The cover illustration is a figurine sculpted by Joris Van der Mijnsbrugge, a Belgian sculptor who died in 2003. The imaginative and expressive style of his work is admired widely. The cover could represent the fate of the three protagonists of this novel, Coppelli Colone, Desmond Raymond Clarkenson and Charles Roderick Dudley, whose intertwined lives will eventually result in their demise. The illustrations reproduced in this novel have also been drawn by Joris Van der Mijnsbrugge. They capture the main ideas developed in the relevant part of the novel.

Printed in Australia

CONTENTS

PRAISE FOR GABRIËL MOENS'S
THE COINCIDENCE

The author has done it again. The Coincidence, his second, after his successful debut novel, A Twisted Choice, *has all the attributes of an excellent novel. It is an entertaining story set in America, cleverly conceived from contemporary socio-political trends to create a potential future event at the heart of American politics. It describes and illuminates human nature exposing the misguided and the flawed. It highlights social conditions dominated by violence and lawlessness and explores social issues such as ethnic discrimination and racial inequality. Readers are also treated to a short revelatory account of Christopher Columbus, discoverer of the Americas in the 15th century. An unreservedly recommended read.*

Eric Sim, Singapore

✶✶✶✶✶

An enthralling thriller set in the not-too-distant future, involving a US president and a would-be assassin, the story focuses on an extraordinary cluster of coincidences that will keep the reader guessing as to the resolution until the last page.

Peter Gillies, New South Wales

✶✶✶✶✶

This is a delightful book. It has an engaging story with many heart-rending and unexpected plots. I have no doubt that many readers from diverse backgrounds will appreciate the sentiments expressed by the author and his characterisation of the story's protagonists.

The author has successfully introduced the hologram technology in his story. This technology reveals how it can be used in a meaningful way in the music and tourism industries, and even contribute to protecting the President of the United States. A highly recommended read.

Ong Sing Goh, Malaysia

✶✶✶✶✶

This novel has all the ingredients of a first class read; it is fast moving with multiple plots and side issues which contrive to keep the reader's attention. The comments on academia show an uncanny knowledge of the workings of this most Byzantine of institutions.

Rosemary Lucadou-Wells, Tasmania

✶✶✶✶✶

I deeply enjoyed reading Gabriël Moens's new novel, The Coincidence. *His first novel,* A Twisted Choice, *is a fascinating tale of conspiracy involving a government deliberately creating a global pandemic to obtain geo-political advantages. This new novel,* The Coincidence, *addresses corruption in government, the consequences of DNA science, and political activism that promotes the destruction of property, monuments, and statues. The description of the novel's protagonists, who are actively involved in destructive activities, is compelling.* The Coincidence *is tightly and boldly plotted, well-structured, witty, and clever. It is so enthralling, absorbing, and engaging, that I simply could not stop reading it until I finally read everything. Gabriël Moens is a gifted Australian novelist.*

Augusto Zimmermann, Western Australia

This book is dedicated to

Dr Edith Maria Moens
for a lifetime of support and love

Other books by Gabriël Moens

A Twisted Choice, Boolarong Press
Enduring Ideas, Connor Court Publishing

"I've often noticed that when coincidences start happening, they go on happening in the most extraordinary way. I dare say it's some natural law that we haven't found out."

Agatha Christie, *The Secret Adversary*

PART ONE

The Protagonists

chapters 1-5

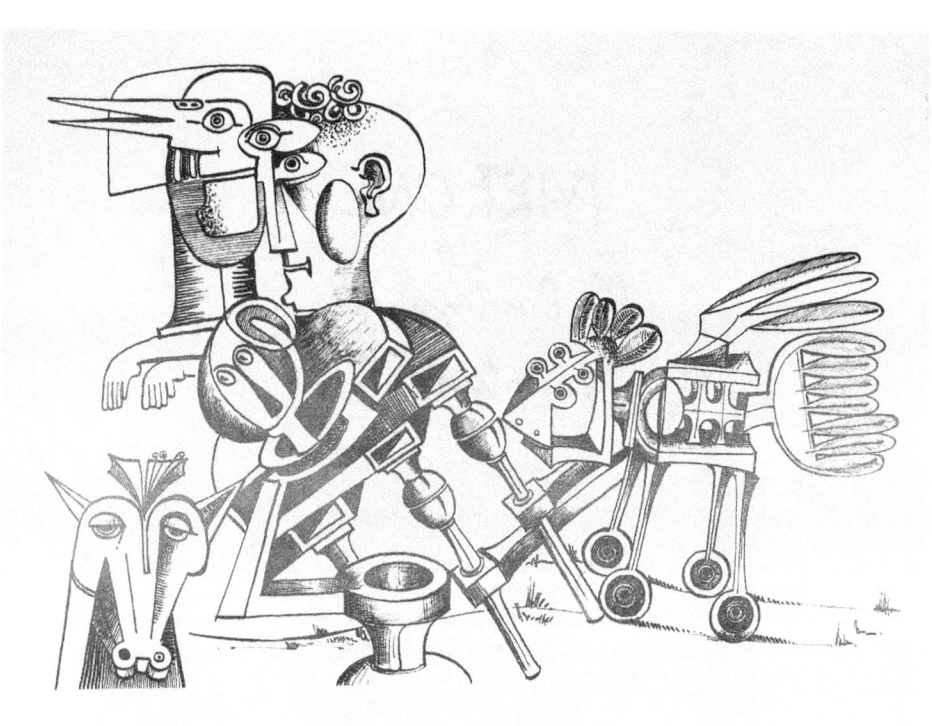

1

I AM RICHARD ANDREAS BENTLEYS, THE PRESS SECRETARY OF
the 47TH President of the United States, Desmond Raymond
Clarkenson. I am an Australian citizen, born and bred in Sydney. I will tell you later how I secured this appointment, usually occupied by an American. My office is located on the third
floor of the West Wing of the White House in Washington DC. It
has beautiful bay windows installed around the time of the Civil
War. When I open the windows, I can step onto a balcony which
provides an excellent view of Pennsylvania Avenue.

Sunday, 16 August 2026, is an idyllic summer day. One would
expect America's wealthy citizens to enjoy a barbeque dinner
with their neighbours, drinking tequilas as a pre-dinner drink
and fine wines with their steaks, preceded by a swim in the Potomac River or swimming pool.

I open the door to my office a few minutes after 7 in the morning, refreshed by an energetic swim in the White House pool,
and some strong coffee. There is always work to be done for the
President, even on Sundays. I know that a major demonstration
has been organised for today and that a bruising confrontation
would soon shatter the tranquil existence of this summer day.
So, I am not surprised to hear loud and chaotic noises coming
from Pennsylvania Avenue. I open the bay windows to observe
the demonstration which is unfolding before my eyes. I retrieve

my binoculars, which I always keep on my desk, to allow me to see what happens on the Avenue and even further away in Union Station Plaza. It is a mesmerizing sight.

A gigantic throng of protestors, waving colourful flags, clogs Pennsylvania Avenue. A cacophony of discordant sounds, emanating from the ceaseless crowd which appears to stretch into the horizon, makes it difficult for journalists to report live on the protest. From the safety of my White House balcony, I can see placards and banners that carry unambiguous messages: 'Down with the racists', 'Equality Now and Forever', 'Sack Republican-appointed Supreme Court judges' and 'Drain the Conservative Swamp'.

Initially, there are only a few hundred people, but the crowd soon swells into the thousands. By nine in the morning, a throng of a quarter of a million people, stretching a few kilometres, strangles the capital's arteries.

What begins as a sedate protest gradually turns into a violent rally. Even before midday, the protestors become riotous and proceed to destroy the shops along the demonstration route. Protective planks, hastily hammered into the wooden frames of shop windows, are crushed effortlessly. The protestors smash their way into the shops and frantically participate in an orgy of looting and destruction. The violence spreads like an uncontrollable virus through the city. It is difficult to distinguish between rioters and those who exercise their right to free speech to promote a more egalitarian American society.

As I am watching the unfolding events, three Secret Service agents entrusted with the protection of the President of the United States, have joined me on the balcony. Their job involves not only the physical protection of the President but also the collection of intelligence to thwart an attack on him. Their collective experience spans slightly more than 40 years. The leader of this little squad is Hayden, a veteran, who has already served three Presidents during his career. The second is his long-term deputy, Lolita, a reliable and capable Mexican American agent with an impeccable pedigree and common sense, and a rookie investigator with limited experience but bountiful ambition and energy, named Jesper.

Television vans are stationed in various places along the route, and reporters are filing live reports for their stations. I switch on my flat-screen television set in my office because my Secret Service friends and I want to know what the commentators have to say about the demonstration. They describe the marchers as African Americans, students, unemployed people, and professional rent-a-crowd agitators imbued with a hatred of American capitalism. Some tell their listeners that the demonstration is a spontaneous eruption of solidarity with African Americans. Others describe it as an orchestrated event to protest America's culture of racial discrimination.

But I know that the demonstration is not a spontaneous outpouring of support for the oppressed.

The 'Demonstrate Now Activist Movement', better-known

simply as the 'DNA Movement' has distributed leaflets inviting people to participate in the demonstration. Announcing the planned march, these leaflets have been widely distributed in shopping malls, and glued to telephone poles and public buildings. The leaflets have also been handed out to students in colleges and universities.

'The leaflets reveal that Charles Roderick Dudley is the organiser of the demonstration. He is apparently the self-proclaimed leader of the DNA Movement,' I inform my Secret Service friends.

Hayden unexpectedly stops my ruminations on the leader of the demonstration.

'Richard, what do you really know about the leader of the DNA Movement, Charles Roderick Dudley?'

'Frankly, I know little about him, but I suspect that among the Movement's sympathisers are people who enjoy the ride of senseless destruction.

'Charles is a professional agitator. I understand this is not his first demonstration?' I respond.

'Quite so, Richard. He has been organizing protests since 2020. Although his family is wealthy, he despises affluent people: they are the enemy.

'He stares at well-to-do people with a hateful gaze on trains and buses, in the park, and cinemas, unsettling even the most robust citizens. For him, they are all despicable members of the bourgeois class.

'Charles has never obtained any qualification because the organization of rallies to advance racial equality has become a full-time obsession. It is an obsession which has prevented him from pursuing an education. In addition to being an organizer for the Movement, he seeks to overthrow the government of the United States by force.

'Charles is soliciting funds from friends to finance his operations.

'He lives on these funds, and he uses the remainder for the organization of DNA Movement demonstrations for racial equality, and the promotion of efforts to redistribute finite resources in society.

'Our Service has applied to a friendly District Court judge to tap Charles's telephone. We have discovered that Charles has invited his friend, Professor Coppelli Colone, to participate in this demonstration, address the crowd and give a rousing speech. They have met and befriended each other at the University of Southern Kansas, where Coppelli is employed as a Professor in the History of Ideas and Jurisprudence Department. Charles has attended some of Coppelli's philosophy lectures and likes the Professor's rhetoric,' Hayden explains.

'You are an excellent speaker, Coppelli, although you have a funny Italian accent. You are the only one who has ever inspired me,' Charles is heard to say in a telephone call.

Coppelli is easily convinced. 'When do we march?' he asks.

'Soon, the march is scheduled to take place on 16 August.

Of course, you will need to travel from Kansas City to Washington DC and the Movement will not reimburse you for the costs of your airline ticket or any other expenses. Your audience will consist of African Americans, students, and young unemployed people, who hate older people who cling to their jobs as if they are precious personal possessions. We are going to bring down the racist regime of the United States,' Charles responds.

Hayden looks at his two Secret Service colleagues and then turns his gaze on me to ensure that we are listening attentively to his revelations. In nodding, Lolita, Jesper and I confirm that we are listening to Hayden's information on the DNA Movement and its self-appointed leader, Charles. This is enough to encourage Hayden to continue with his story.

'Coppelli willingly cancels his classes and prepares for a day of protest and confrontation. He relishes the idea of confrontation which, for him, is a necessary precursor to social change. He has invited his students to join him in Washington DC because he wants them to witness an important event – a game-changer, no doubt.

'He tells his students that he will be giving a riveting speech during the demonstration. He expresses his expectation that his students will support this endeavour because the future of America hinges upon it.

'This is Coppelli's reaction – an enthusiastic reaction I might add – to Charles' invitation to participate in the demonstration,'

Hayden concludes his summary of what his Service has learned about Coppelli.

*****

Quite coincidentally, I do not have to rely on the intelligence of my Secret Service friends to obtain information about Professor Coppelli Colone because, as it happens, I have been his colleague at the University of Southern Kansas before the President invited me to become his Press Secretary. I know Coppelli very well – and I am very worried.

We observe the progress of the demonstration and the ensuing violence from my office on the third floor of the White House. I notice that Coppelli is one of the leaders of the demonstration. He shrieks in Italian and in English.

Coppelli, a 62-years-old academic, has the appearance of a vagabond. He has long tresses of blonde, unwashed hair that dangle from his head. He sports a goatee which is a good nesting place for bugs and insects. His crumpled blue jeans covering his legs have big holes in it at knee level.

In the afternoon, the demonstration turns into a rancorous orgy of violence. As the afternoon progresses, the protestors become restless and some even pick up implements, like fallen tree branches, and rocks, to attack some courageous, but foolish counter protestors.

The police department has sent a sizable delegation of officers to contain the demonstration, but they do nothing to control the boisterous crowd. Police officers merely observe the rowdy activities and conveniently ignore the senseless violence. Some officers applaud enthusiastically when listening to the speakers who address the protestors. Others cross their arms over their bellies as if they are observing a bicycle race or watch a baseball game. They are in combat gear with goggles and face masks that protect their eyes and faces. All officers have shields, not unlike those worn or used by the Romans more than two thousand years ago – not much development there – but their rifles that fire rubber bullets, clubs and tear gas could be used to attack rioting protestors.

In their live reports, reporters insatiably describe the chaotic situation, the rowdy crowd, the speeches, the violence, and the destruction of shops. It makes for excellent television, riveting really, in every corner of the world.

Foreign politicians and analysts also provide a running commentary. The German Chancellor and the Prime Ministers of the United Kingdom and of Australia condemn the violence and plead for a peaceful resolution of the demonstrators' concerns. In contrast, a representative of the Chinese Ministry of Foreign Affairs has difficulty hiding her delight at the unfolding events.

'The chaos and violence in Washington DC confirm the superiority of China's Communist regime which effectively prevents such protests from taking place. China has demonstrated that the adoption of a well-directed security law, like the one adopted in Hong Kong in July 2020, is capable of preventing these calamitous events,' she says. No doubt, as an afterthought, she adds that China's 'well-directed security law' does not constitute a violation of the United Nations registered 'One country, two legal systems' Treaty with the United Kingdom.

*****

An ocean of flags of all colours and sizes provide shade to the demonstrators. They enthusiastically wave them above the rowdy crowd. Some flags whip back and forth on flagpoles.

Coppelli screams slogans into a megaphone as if he wants to be the loudest demonstrator. 'Down with the racists,' Coppelli yells ever so loud.

'American history is a history of murderers,' he exclaims.

Angry men and women with distorted faces shout jarring messages. After each sentence, the crowd repeatedly yells 'Down with the racists' and 'American history is a history of murderers,' slavishly repeating the slogans barked in megaphones.

I observe that the organizer, Charles Dudley, when he is not shrieking into a megaphone, chats amiably with Coppelli Colone. They walk together shoulder to shoulder during the march, while waving at their comrades. When they arrive at a makeshift platform, hastily erected by a few would-be carpenters, Coppelli climbs its few stairs to secure a better view of the sea of angry protestors. He repeatedly raises and lowers both hands to seek the attention of the protesting crowd and to defuse the heated atmosphere. He is ready to address the demonstrators. He gives a fascinating speech, which only people closest to the platform can hear – it appears that a few technicians still frantically try to install a workable audio system, capable of amplifying Coppelli's and the other speakers' diatribes so that the speeches could be heard in the White House. Demonstrators enthusiastically applaud when Coppelli finishes his speech – a venomous invective that is an incitement to hatred and violence which, on other occasions, would be a punishable crime. But not now.

The demonstrators' animated response to his speech emboldens Coppelli. He looks at his megaphone and continues his harangue.

'Let's go to the Columbus Memorial Fountain located in front of the Union Station Plaza to destroy the statue of Christopher Columbus.

'On the Memorial, made by Lorado Taft, is in inscription that glorifies Columbus "whose high faith and indomitable courage gave to mankind a new world."

'This is a grotesque lie. Columbus was not courageous. If there was anything he gave to humankind, it was disease, destitution, misery, and occupation. He was a monster who killed thousands of indigenous people when he landed on the American islands. He was the father of genocide and a child rapist.

'Such a person should not be honoured in America. Let's destroy his statue and the statues of tyrants and criminals who participated in racist activities. Their statues must be demolished,' Coppelli exhorts the demonstrators. The exhortation drains all rationality from the protestors who become restless and combative.

'Christopher Columbus was a criminal who slaughtered thousands of people indiscriminately and stole their country. He should not be feted as the discoverer of America.

'Columbus was not the discoverer anyway because some five hundred years before he arrived at the American islands, the Norse people had already visited this continent. Americans should not celebrate Columbus Day on 12 October because it is a day of infamy and despair.

'As an Italian American, I am ashamed that Columbus was born in Genoa.

'The Memorial Columbus Fountain stands three metres high in front of the Union Station Plaza. Let's march to the Plaza and destroy the statue. Follow me, comrades. Let's dance on the corpse of a murderer and dump him in the river,' he urges his followers.

A scream of approval swells up from the protestors and becomes an oral Mexican wave. The inspired crowd erupts into a vortex of violence. They advance on the statue as if they are advancing into the trenches of the enemy during the First World War. It is, however, an enemy that could not fight back and there is no need to be courageous or daring.

When you are in a crowd, nobody is individually guilty of anything and you can always blame others, I mumble to myself.

The four of us observe the protestors meandering on Pennsylvania Avenue. The crowd is moving slowly but, not unlike a venomous snake slithering in the bushes, it pursues its intention with dogged determination. Their destination is the Christopher Columbus Memorial Fountain in Union Station Plaza. When they finally arrive at the Memorial, unexpectedly, a strong and sturdy rope appears – nobody would later be able to tell where it came from – and it is thrown over the head of the unfortunate Columbus. A group of ardent protestors proceeds to pull the granite statue from its stone pedestal. If he were alive, Columbus would be fruitlessly begging for mercy. But, on this occasion, Columbus does not reply, which enrages the crowd even more. Suddenly, the statue leaves its pedestal and crashes to the ground where it splits in several pieces.

Without warning, an axe materializes, as sharp as a guillotine, and protestors decapitate Columbus, and female demonstrators remove their bras and dance on his corpse. They take the decapitated body and the head to the Potomac River and dump the remains of the historical figure in the water. Police officers, who observe the carnage, even form a line to expedite the dumping of the toppled statue in the river.

'This is where a genocidal murderer belongs,' the protestors scream endlessly.

The protestors, using a megaphone, proceed to list all the crimes that Columbus is guilty of, as if they are in a court where the prosecutor reads the allegations against the accused. They describe Columbus as a symbol of racism, a genocidal murderer, guilty of ethnic cleansing, and other heinous crimes against Native Americans.

Patrol troopers in helmets, who provide security in the Capital, observe the disturbances but do not try to stop the protestors, who celebrate afterwards with Native Americans, singing and dancing. A makeshift podium is built hastily, and musicians who want to promote their seditious songs treat the demonstrators to an impromptu concert.

Columbus is decapitated in America on 16 August 2026.

I wonder whether 12 October would still be named 'Christopher Columbus Day'.

✶✶✶✶✶

A police investigation later revealed that the trigger for the protest was a fatal altercation between police officers and an African American, Alex Flothersam, which occurred a week earlier, on 7 August in Chicago. Alex was born into an impoverished family. His parents were often unemployed, and his mother became an alcoholic soon after Alex was born. Her drinking was a direct response to the poverty and destitution that surrounded her at home and the inability of the family to find work. Alex contributed to the household budget by stealing from grocery shops, petrol stations, and public service buildings. He had also already attempted a few burglaries with some unsavoury friends.

Alex had been caught, red-handed, stealing a bicycle from a department store. He'd verbally abused the officers when he was ordered to produce his social security card and disclose his address. A police spokesperson claimed that Alex had threatened the officers, brandishing a knife in front of them. One of the officers had taken his pistol and shot Alex, murdering him in cold blood.

Alex's senseless killing had provided Charles and his DNA Movement with a convenient opportunity to organize a huge demonstration in Washington DC. Charles had already organized a dozen protests since 2020 when the Movement first came to prominence following the killing of an African American who had died from asphyxiation when a police officer planted his knee on the victim's neck for eight minutes. But more violence was still to come to the land of the free, America.

2

THE FLOTHERSAM PROTEST ON 16 AUGUST WAS THE FIRST SALVO in a sustained campaign of violence which raged in America during the summer and fall of 2026.

I stepped onto the balcony of my office each time a demonstration was held to observe the unfolding of an important event in American history.

'The pent-up frustration of many Americans, and not just African Americans, needs to be addressed if ever there will be reconciliation in this country,' I reassured myself.

I followed the progress of the DNA Movement protests with great interest.

The demonstrators would clog Pennsylvania Avenue which would be transformed into a sea of irate people waving flags and screaming obscenities.

Most of the time, the three Secret Service agents would join me to watch the disturbances.

'Is it not horrible that so many protestors scream obscenities?' Lolita asked, obviously seeking support for her view.

'Well, Lolita, I am also disturbed by the vile language that some of the demonstrators use during the protests. But screaming obscenities is not illegal in America. There is freedom of speech in this country, enshrined in the Constitution. People's behaviour may be regarded as uncivilized, yet protected by our legal system,' I replied. Lolita did not respond. Her facial expression indicated that she did not agree with my comment. I understood that, for her, use of vile language is an indicator of what people might do in the future – like attempting to assassinate the President of the United States. It was her job to prevent this from happening.

During one of the demonstrations, in October 2026, – I cannot remember the precise date – Hayden must have listened carefully to my Australian accent because he unexpectedly said: 'Richard, your preparation for the position of the President's Press Secretary is most unconventional because your accent reveals that you may not even be an American citizen.'

'But, Hayden, I could still hold American citizenship even if I speak with an Australian accent. This country is full of people who speak in different languages and dialects and, yet, are American nationals,' I retorted.

'But as it happens, I have maintained my Australian citizenship and I am proud of it. Indeed, Hayden, I am an Australian who has grown up in Sydney.' I added.

'It is not really that important, Richard. There is no doubt that you are a great Press Secretary. One of the best, really. The media vultures are eating out of your hands,' Hayden said, trying to defuse the relevance of his comment.

'How did the President find you?' he inquired.

'I would like to hear more. I find it fascinating that an Australian could become the Press Secretary of the American President.

'And it is a coincidence that you know Professor Coppelli Colone,' Hayden remarked.

'Well, Hayden, I will tell you the story of my life. It is a story that took me from Sydney, Australia, to Chicago, Kansas City, and Washington DC in the United States.

'I do not remember very much about my childhood. In any event, at the best of times, memory is nothing else but a string of disconnected patches of lucidity that sear through the body like a brainwave,' I pompously said endeavouring to sound erudite and debonair.

*****

'In primary school in Sydney, my days were uneventful and dull. I played soccer on Wednesday afternoon, but I was not good at it, and I was soon dropped from the school team. My father was a stockbroker, and through sheer luck or careful planning, he became very wealthy. My mother had a language teaching qualification from the University of Southern Sydney, majoring in English literature, specializing in American novels of the 20th century. She taught in the local high school for a while, but she abandoned full-time work when my father's business became successful. She later became interested in archaeology and ancient history. On trips to Europe and the United States, my parents would stop-over in the Mediterranean and the Middle East to enable my mother to admire the ruins of ancient civilizations.

'When I finished year 6 of primary school, my parents enrolled me in a Catholic boys-only boarding school in Chicago, Illinois, which my father had also attended. My father's parents – my grandparents – had been in the diplomatic service and worked in the Australian Consulate-General in Chicago for six years. My father wanted me to benefit from the same excellent education he had enjoyed in this boarding school in Chicago.

'I admit that I was not thrilled when I first heard about my parents' plan to send me to the United States. It looked to me as if they were abandoning me when I needed their help the most.' I confessed to my Secret Service friends.

'Do I really have to attend high school in the United States?', I asked my mother.

'Well, Richard, look at your dad,' my mother said. 'He has done very well in his career, and he attended this high school in Chicago. Surely you want to do as well as your dad?'

'But, mum, what about my friends, here in Sydney? There are many good schools, right here in Sydney. And I will be away from both of you for lengthy periods of time,' I responded.

'Do not worry, darling, we will telephone you every second day, and during the holidays, you can come home. Dad and I will also visit you in Chicago as often as we can,' my mother promised.

The matter was settled and so, it happened that a few weeks before my 12th birthday, my parents took me to the United States where I became a boarder in *The Loyola Catholic Academy*, located in a posh Chicago suburb.

'Our boy will learn to be independent and look after himself. This is the greatest gift we could possibly give him,' my father said at the time.

Hayden's eyes carefully observed my every gesture and betrayed his keen interest in my life's story. The demonstration which was going on just a few hundred metres away was an unwelcome inconvenience which deprived him of all the juicy details he hoped to extract from my story.

'Yes, it would have been a frightening gift. You were only 12 years old. But it made you into the man you are,' Hayden remarked while watching the unfolding dramas on Pennsylvania Avenue.

'When my parents left, I cried uncontrollably for several hours because I had never felt so abandoned in my life. And the opulence of the school and its surroundings could not dull the pain I felt for a few months,' I admitted.

'The school had been built on the top of a forested hill. An impressively paved driveway with beautiful oak trees on either side led to a metal gate. A guard operated the gate remotely from within a gatehouse located in the school grounds. A wall snaked around the school which had a chapel, a swimming pool, tennis courts, a gym, a library, a conference centre used for student performances, assemblies and graduations, and several computer labs, more appropriately described today as "computer museums". As the students were surrounded by affluence, one could have been forgiven for thinking that it was a monastery for rich monks. But for all its opulence, the boarders regarded the school as an expensive jail where every inmate had a luxury cell with all modern amenities, except a television set. A set of oppressive rules regulated the everyday lives of the boarders. Especially, leave applications submitted by them were subject to a convoluted process, and the success rate was extremely low. Exemptions from the School's oppressive rules were as rare as exemptions granted in 2020 and 2021 to Australians who wanted to travel overseas during the Covid-19 pandemic or cross the border from Victoria into New South Wales,' I told Hayden.

'A Catholic girls-only school, with tiled walkways crisscrossing its four-hectares site, was located next to the boys' school. It could as well have been on the other side of the world because male and female students rarely had opportunities to meet informally.

'I developed into the school's best public speaker. I was interested in debating the major political and social issues of the day and whenever there was a speaking competition, I would win it. However, my teachers did not see debating and speaking skills as a substitute for studying mathematics, chemistry, and physics.

'My interest in public speaking may well be a consequence of an altercation that took place in my second year of high school. My history teacher confidently asserted that we were fortunate to live in the wealthiest, happiest, most powerful, and best country in the world. As an Australian, such a wide and sweeping claim stirred up sentimental emotions within me. As the teacher had previously admitted that he had not yet visited any other country, I was mystified how he could make such a definite assertion. When I timidly, but audaciously, asked how it is possible to compare countries that one has not visited, the teacher stated confidently that, "There is no need to compare the United States with any other country, because the statistics speak for themselves".

'I did not know which statistics the teacher referred to, but I assumed they related to the longevity of Americans, American economic power, entrepreneurial achievements, the size of national parks, the opulence of department stores, the wealth of their banks and big companies, the rate of home ownership, and the number of cars owned by Americans, among others. I wanted to point out that the United States statistics are among the worst in the world in the field of health service delivery and crime rates. During my first two years of high school, there already had been four mass shootings that killed many innocent victims. And the United States continued to execute criminals at a rate comparably higher than in other countries, except Iran and China.

'I looked around the classroom and I saw beaming and smiling students, secure in their knowledge that they were living in the best country in the world. For them, I was a loser, a loner, a foreign imposter, and an ignorant troublemaker. I decided not to challenge the teacher because it is pointless to start a war that one cannot win. However, I am convinced that the teacher wrongly interpreted my reticence and timidity as backwardness. Later, I would prove him wrong, terribly wrong.

'There was one event that is firmly embedded in my mind. I was a disinterested member of my high school's photography club. In retrospect, most members were disinterested and did not even own a camera. However, the club's mentor, the teacher of chemistry and physics, was a proficient photographer who took pictures, usually black and white, and he would allocate them to the members of the club, who were directed to enter them in a national photography competition. The winners were rewarded with valuable prizes, including holidays, trips, meals in restaurants, books, and precious goods, like bicycles. The students would then be expected "to donate" their prizes to the school and any touristic prizes would be transferred, voluntarily and willingly, to the school's principal or the teacher.

'The photo, which the teacher allocated to me, depicted an ebullient gondolier in traditional attire with a sash around his waist on a Venice canal, looking after a couple of lovers. The photo won first prize and I was rewarded with a business class flight from Chicago to Washington DC and three days' accommodation in the upmarket Willard InterContinental Hotel. As part of the prize, a tour guide would introduce me to the nation's monuments, the White House, the Capitol, the Supreme Court, the Lincoln Memorial, the Smithsonian Museum, the Columbus Memorial Fountain, and many more.

'Rather than transferring my trip to the principal or teacher, as I was expected to do, I decided to expose the school's scam by going on the trip myself. It was my first introduction to the nation's capital and a welcome opportunity to see the historical monuments and statues in Washington DC.

'A few weeks later, after I had already left to study at a college, an airline investigator contacted my parents, who were visiting me in the United States at the time, to ascertain the circumstances surrounding my trip to the capital.'

'We have received a complaint from your school that we are investigating. The school principal claims that the photo you sent in was not taken by you,' the airline investigator said.

'That is correct, apart from the United States, I have never been to any other country and, so, I could not have taken the photo in Venice,' I confirmed.

My parents and I then told the investigator about the fraud, the school's deceptive behaviour, and the arrogance and bullying that was a part of it.

'Do not worry,' he told us.

'This is the last time you will hear about the school's complaint. My office will deal with this fraud. I am sure we will no longer sponsor the school,' he stated.

'The investigator may have been an atheist because he relentlessly proceeded to criticize, directly, the obnoxiously dishonest behaviour of the club's mentor and the school's immoral deception.

'A few weeks later, I received a note in the mail from the principal. It was as shocking as it was unbelievable. It stated: "You have behaved in a dishonest way. We in the School try to educate our pupils in the best traditions of the Catholic Church but you have decided to demean the education you have received in our school which is founded on the principles of honesty, integrity, and morality. You may think that, from a legal point of view, you are in the clear. Even if that is the case, I will see to it that you will never get an undergraduate degree. When you were at our school, you expressed the hope to become a lawyer one day. You will never be a lawyer. We have connections and the school's tentacles reach deep into the higher education sector. We will ensure that your studies will result in failure. You should go back to Australia because you do not belong here." The note had the name of the principal under it, but he had not signed it. Until this day, I do not understand how the principal dared to complain to the airline about the school's scam without expecting retribution.' *When arrogance has embedded itself as a way of life, and when people and institutions get away with it for a long time, it becomes difficult to distinguish between morality and immorality,* I thought.

'After completing high school, and with the encouragement of my parents, I decided to enrol in the Hillsdale College in Michigan, a fine liberal arts institution. The high school principal's threats never eventuated because I thrived in college. I especially enjoyed the readings of the Great Books of Western Civilization, and the many visits to historical places connected with the history of the United States. One of the highlights was a privately sponsored trip organized by the College to Europe visiting the Roman, Greek, and Turkish archaeological treasures from antiquity. My mother was delighted when I decided to join this archaeological odyssey. I spent many hours admiring the Forum Romanum in Rome, the Parthenon in Athens and the ancient statues that are reflections of European history.

'While in college, I also became a paid-up member of the Republican Party and did volunteer work during local and state elections for candidates selected by the Party. I was attracted by the Party's focus on "law-and-order" issues, protection of our cultural heritage, small business, and social conservatism.

'When I finished college, I applied to five top law schools, and I was admitted to the Pritzker School of Law of Northwestern University in Chicago. At the law school, I felt that, as a registered Republican, I was a member of a dwindling minority. Most of my colleagues and law professors blindly followed the fallacious ideas promulgated by the Democratic Party. Northwestern is, however, an outstanding law school where I received an excellent education. I am proud to call myself a Northwestern graduate. After getting my Juris Doctor degree, I sat for, and I passed, the bar examination in Illinois and in New York, but I never practised as an attorney. My first job was as a Lecturer in the History of Ideas and Jurisprudence Department at the University of Southern Kansas, teaching legal history.

'My parents were not impressed with my first job.'

'Surely, you would be able to make much more money if you

worked for a big city law firm. Law teachers are not well-paid and are not highly regarded, not even by their students. Teaching is not really a job for ambitious people, who want to get somewhere in life,' my father said.

'I agreed with my father's sentiment. I promised myself that my tenure in the Department would merely be a stepping-stone to something more exciting and rewarding.

'But, in retrospect, my time at the University of Southern Kansas enabled me to get to know Professor Coppelli Colone, who took a leading role in the DNA Movement demonstrations.'

'I am confident that your knowledge of Coppelli will provide the Secret Service with invaluable insights into the murky world of this enigmatic Italian-American scholar and will enrich our knowledge of the DNA Movement,' Hayden remarked.

'Hopefully so. The teaching of legal history also prepared me well for my present role as Press Secretary because it required me to delve into the pursuit by presidents of the American dream, and their contributions to the development of a mature legal system.

'Hayden, you are aware that, philosophically, my views are certainly aligned with those of Desmond. One could say that I am a fellow traveller who believes in the soundness of the President's vision for America.

'I took a leading part in the presidential election campaign and effectively promoted the interests, views and vision of the candidate who now occupies the White House. I knew I would be rewarded for my arduous work on behalf of the candidate,' I added.

I looked at the faces of the three Secret Service agents; they still betrayed unfamiliarity with my story. My explanation as to how I met the President and why I was offered the position of Press Secretary still seemed incredible to them.

'Look, Hayden, you recall that very few people believed that Desmond would be elected President of the United States, even though he had been selected – unexpectedly I might say – as the presidential candidate for the Republican party. Consequently, he had difficulty finding suitably qualified and loyal spokespersons to work on his campaign. Indeed, most offered their services to the opposing candidate from the Democratic Party. But I offered my services to him because I was available, at the right time, with the right kind of motivation, so he hired me to serve as his campaign spokesperson,' I explained.

Hayden did not respond. I am certain that he wanted to maintain the aura of non-partisanship which was required of the Secret Service. He and his colleagues were there to protect the President, not to dabble in politics.

'Following his election victory, the President appointed me to the coveted position of Press Secretary.

'As you know, I am the President's spokesperson and I address the concerns of the media, almost daily. I have been the Press Secretary to the President since the inauguration of the new Administration in January 2025.

'I have to admit, though, that it is a difficult, sensitive, and demanding job which is relentlessly scrutinized by the press looking for intrigue, conspiracies, juicy scandals, backstabbing episodes, and potential troubles.

'I know that my job tenure depends on my ability to reconcile the conflicting needs of the President. I am expected to satisfy his legitimate expectations. I see myself as an in-house, well-paid tutor who looks after the prosperity and welfare of his pupil. Like all tutors, I hope that my pupil is a quick learner. After the first eighteen months of this Administration, I have not yet made up my mind about this.

'As you well know, Hayden, my job is to portray the President as a leader who is confidently in charge of his Administration and fully in command of the government's policies and decisions. I see it as my job to ensure that the President is able to operate as an adept negotiator in his dealings with Congress, especially now that the House of Representatives and the Senate are unfortunately in the hands of the Democratic Party.'

'Richard, your use of the word "unfortunately" obviously reveals that you are partisan. In contrast, my friends in the Secret Service and I are non-partisan; I would like to remind you that we protect the President, regardless of the colour of his stripes,' Hayden said.

'Of course, I know that the Service is apolitical. But as the Press Secretary, I am a member of the President's inner circle, so I guess I could be described as "partisan". I keep the President informed about everything that happens in Congress, the White House and beyond.

'I ensure the President is able to answer all questions that members of the press corps ask of him.

'The President's predecessor suffered great embarrassment when he could not answer questions about his Administration's inability to address the concerns of the DNA Movement. Blood-thirsty journalists labelled the President "indecisive". My pupil exploited the former President's indecisiveness with great benefit during the election campaign. He now occupies the Oval Office.

'The President was always my greatest supporter. Do you remember what he said when he appointed me?' I asked Hayden.

'Yes, of course. I was standing just a few metres away when he announced your appointment. He said: "Mr. Bentleys' appointment is a victory for those who are interested in effective communication and rational thinking."'

'Your memory is serving you well,' I said admiringly.

'Nevertheless, the President's adversaries questioned the soundness of his decision. "After all," they said, "Mr. Bentleys is an Australian citizen. How could a foreigner represent the interests of the President of the United States and be a voice for America in the world?" they asked.'

'The President's reply was determined and unequivocal: "I appoint people on their merits. Mr. Bentleys is a capable professional who has been in the United States for more than 20 years now. He is the best person for the job. Period."'

'It was the "Period" that ended this little charade, and my story, as the President's Press Secretary, was ready to unfold.

'Well, there you have it, Hayden. You are now au fait with my history and the journey that took me to this office.' I concluded.

'This is a most interesting and extraordinary journey,' Hayden commented. He was keen to ask for further details, but he managed to restrain himself. *I am sure I will have other opportunities to tease out later more details about the extraordinary journey that has taken Richard from Sydney to his third level office with a balcony in the White House*, he thought.

He looked out over Pennsylvania Avenue where the demonstrators chanted their slogans which penetrated the walls of the White House, so loud were they. The agents regarded these slogans as disturbing and potentially troublesome; they were responsible for the physical safety of the President.

✶✶✶✶✶

The DNA Movement organized a wave of protests on Pennsylvania Avenue from August to late November 2026. On several occasions, members of the Movement abused law-abiding white citizens and demanded that they surrender their houses because they were living in previously black neighbourhoods.

The demonstrations were defining moments in my tenure as the President's Press Secretary. Ironically, they made my job easier than expected because I knew that, in my daily briefing for the Press, there would be endless questions about the proposed response of the White House to the demonstrations. So, I was prepared for the onslaught.

'Mr. Bentleys,' a prominent journalist asked during one of the press briefings, 'how come that so little has been done even though the DNA Movement, since its inception in 2020, provided evidence of continuing racial discrimination?'

'The President regrets instances of racial discrimination and is aware of the existence of an endemic problem which needs to be addressed in this country. The President's predecessor also tried to improve the plight of our African American citizens, but his proposed remedies were declared unconstitutional by our courts,' I said.

'Yes, this is because the 45th American President, a Republican stacked the Supreme Court with conservative judges,' the journalist retorted.

'The judicial branch of government is independent of the political branches. This independence should be respected. In any event, all appointees were well-qualified lawyers, and the American Bar Association supported their nomination. The candidates were confirmed by the Senate.

'It is important right now for all people of goodwill to work together to alleviate the pressing problems generated by centuries of racial discrimination. I can assure you that the President is taking this task very seriously. Indeed, this is what the President has done thus far ...'.

I was interrupted by another accredited reporter who said:

'Surely, the President realizes that the destruction of statues and monuments which glorify racial superiority and condone prejudice are a legitimate and proportionate response to centuries of discrimination?'

'May I please ask not to interrupt me when I am speaking? I never interrupt when you are asking your questions and I hope you might extend the same courtesy to me? To answer your question, let me say that destruction of public statues and monuments is illegal. The President's view is that reconciliation will only be achieved when we honestly face our history, with its achievements and failures, and address our shortcomings with determination.'

'Isn't that a recipe for doing nothing?' the journalist persisted.

'No, reconciliation requires all parties to work out solutions that commend themselves to all. Now, returning to the initiatives that have been taken by this Administration to lift Americans out of the poverty trap to enable them to enjoy the promise of freedom and equality ...' .

There would also be questions on how to respond to future DNA Movement demonstrations which, inevitably, would be planned by the Movement in the months to come.

Indeed, Charles Roderick Dudley had already announced that more protests would be organized in 2027, starting in the spring. A campaign would be waged to demolish the statues of those who had opposed the creation of an egalitarian society and perpetrated racial discrimination, like Confederate generals and degenerate and corrupt politicians. Alex Flothersam's case was merely a pretext which provided progressive forces with a convenient opportunity to rail against perceived injustices existing in American society.

'This Movement will succeed where others have failed,' Charles was quoted in a leaflet.

*****

The DNA Movement demonstrations were not limited to America. The Movement inspired the establishment of similar organisations in many other countries. The Movement became a phenomenon throughout the Western world which, according to the demonstrators, was infested with the diseases of racial superiority and white supremacy. Charles Roderick Dudley and Professor Colone called for a radical redistribution of wealth in society, and the equal treatment of all people regardless of race. It was a movement that blamed racial discrimination and inequality for the disadvantages, victimization, and lack of opportunities of oppressed people.

There is little doubt that the Movement occupied the mind of the President and his Administration. During the last months of 2026, he constantly sought the advice of his minders about initiatives his Administration could take to abate the situation.

'What can be done by this Administration to improve the plight of African Americas and to ensure that "equality" will exist, not just in name, but in practice as well?' he would ask the members of his Cabinet. Often, he would not wait for an answer, but would make suggestions himself.

'We need to work with the States to provide better education, to increase citizens' ability to read and write and to foster entrepreneurship among the disadvantaged communities. Government-sponsored programs should enable the disadvantaged to help themselves. Please bring specific proposals to the table,' he requested.

In my view, the President was genuinely interested in improving the plight of all Americans, especially the downtrodden.

The leaders of the Movement suspended the demonstrations during the winter months, but I knew that this was merely a temporary stay. I was certain that worse was to come. The President would have to deal with a spring and summer in 2027 full of violence and hate.

3

WASHINGTON, DC, LATE JANUARY 2027.

The sentinels who guarded the entrance to the White House were dressed for a reception at the North Pole and, even then, they constantly lifted their legs and moved their feet to pump some warmth into their bodies.

They looked at the arriving limousine which deposited the Chief of Staff, the austere David Lockermee, the President's National Security Advisor, Amanda Rosaria Rutledge, who was regarded by the media as a stout and hawkish member of the President's entourage, and me. It stopped in front of the main entrance to the White House.

The Chief of Staff greeted the sentinels when he entered the White House. 'Are they not supposed to stand still?' he asked Amanda. 'Their leg movements constitute a violation of the Guards' Protocol. But I guess that, on a day like this, I could not criticize them,' he added, acknowledging the severe cold that had gripped the city. Amanda merely nodded her approval of the Chief of Staff's comment.

When they entered the Oval Office, they were greeted by the President, two secretaries, and the Chief Valet responsible for the appearance, grooming and clothing of the President. 'Welcome to the Oval Office, my friends,' he said jovially. 'We have a few things to discuss on this chilly day,' he added.

Desmond unceremoniously dumped his matching coat on the seat of his presidential swivel chair, and he shifted its two movable armrests to the side. He was resting his right hand, with outstretched fingers and manicured nails, on his huge teak desk. He removed his wedding ring from his left ring finger and placed it on the desk in front of the telephone. He found it easier to work without the ring because it cut into his flesh and, especially on hot, but also on cold, days, he had difficulty removing it from his finger. The other hand was casually tucked away in the left-hand pocket of his neatly pressed trousers which were held up by suspenders.

A knitted sweater partially covered his tailor-made blue shirt that already displayed a coffee stain, a poignant reminder of breakfast. A tie, which depicted the American flag hung lifelessly from the collar of his shirt. He removed his cufflinks and he placed them next to the wedding ring. He started to roll up his sleeves because he wanted to make himself a tuna and mayo sandwich in the kitchen of the White House – something he enjoyed doing, much to the chagrin of his minders who labelled this practice as unpresidential behaviour.

An arctic weather front had rolled in from the Midwest. It planted its icy claws in Washington DC which was now in the grip of an unfeeling vicious winter that enveloped the city. Until then, the weather had been spring-like and pleasant. People even had continued to walk their dogs in the idyllic meadows outside the capital and enjoyed picnics surrounded by cows and sheep who were quietly munching on grass. A few racing horses heart-ily wandered on the meadows and were waiting to be taken to the racetrack. Birds had been chirping noisily in the mistaken belief that spring had arrived.

But, in late January, the weather changed as if it had been reprimanded by the Weather God for its laxity. And when it changed, it recouped the lost time by unleashing bitterly cold temperatures and transforming the landscape in a lily-white snowy carpet. Winter well and truly invaded the capital city and behaved like an occupying force of ruthless enemy soldiers, who cruelly oppressed a conquered people. The savagery of the winter brutally confined people to their homes where fireplaces were burning at full capacity and heaters did overtime. The streets were deserted – it was as if the oppressive occupier had imposed a curfew. Occasionally, some courageous children ventured out-side to play in the snow or construct a snowman. A few cross-country skiers with caps that covered their half-frozen red ears bravely traversed the desolate landscape in their polished skis.

The gauge indicated a temperature of 5 degrees Fahrenheit, or minus 15 degrees Celsius – seriously cold. The temperature was in freefall and, according to the weather forecasters, it would get colder in the days to come. 'The "Polar Vortex" is moving south', they said.

Snowstorms slowed down significantly the traffic in the capi-tal. Huge snowploughs were in action to make the roads pass-able for the convoy of government and corporate vehicles that were expected to sweep through the city in the next couple of hours. The trees along the wide boulevards, leading to the White House and the Capitol, were bereft of leaves and sat lonely, like rejected nude statues, in their allocated spots. An occasional jogger passed by, tantalizing the sub-zero temperatures, and looking all the time at the White House as if they expected to be invited into the warm embraces of this symbol of power.

The heavy crimson drapes of the expansive windows of the Oval Office were closed to keep the heat inside, preventing people from looking at the White House's lawns. In the Oval Office, the central heating hummed its regular beat and distributed its warmth throughout the Office. A peek through the windows would have revealed that the lawns had been converted into an idyllic Christmas-like landscape – without the dashing lights and the tastefully decorated Christmas tree with its magnificent illuminations which had delighted visitors to the White House only a month earlier. The flagpole at the entrance to the White House felt cold, miserable, and abandoned; it seemed as if it only reluctantly continued to fly the flag which whipped back and forth brought on by fierce winds nurtured by the arctic cold front.

*****

I looked disapprovingly at the President's appearance. He seemed fatigued.

The stain on his shirt surely is an unforgiveable transgression of presidential discretion, I thought.

The President's minders – and that included me – always insisted that he be dressed attractively and neatly.

'A person's appearance is important,' they said.

The attire of the President was always a matter of concern. It was also a matter of constant friction in the White House. The President's Chief Valet, a most knowledgeable African American, who had already served six presidents, repeatedly reminded us that it was his job to look after the President's appearance and clothing. 'When making suggestions for improving the President's appearance, you are trespassing on my domain,' he told us repeatedly.

Of course, I knew that the White House machine has many cogs, all of which are expected to do their allocated jobs without intruding in the sphere of responsibility of other staff members. But this was more an aspirational objective than the reality, an insight that had struck me quite recently, in a humorous but embarrassing way, I guess. A few months ago, the President presided over a lengthy news conference, which dealt with the Administration's plan to curb the violent demonstrations in the United States and to halt the destruction of America's national statues and monuments, but he had forgotten to close the zipper of his trousers. Usually, this would never happen, but on this occasion the Valet had failed to check this part of the President's attire before he appeared in public. A big hole had appeared in the trousers that revealed the grey flannel underwear of the President. A photo of the President's underwear was printed in the local papers the next day. I thought he was extremely lucky that his penis did not protrude out of the underwear.

'If you cannot look after your own zipper, you cannot look

after the country,' a journalist wrote pompously and satirically in an early morning newspaper. I was disturbed by this comment because the journalist was usually sympathetic to the President and his Administration. I did not look forward to reading the afternoon newspapers.

Fortunately, most readers of the newspaper article thought that it was a hilarious story, but the President and his minders were not amused. While this mishap did not affect his ratings – indeed, it may have increased his popularity because he had displayed a human frailty – it was certainly an unwelcome embarrassment he could have done without.

The Valet was most apologetic since he was afraid to lose his job. But I knew there was no need for him to be concerned because the President would never sack a staff member who, for many years, provided excellent and loyal service to the President.

'Mr. President, please accept my apologies. I overlooked that part of your clothing. I hope you are able to forgive my oversight,' the Valet implored.

'There is no need to worry. It is fine, really,' the President answered magnanimously. The face of the Valet visibly brightened when the President exonerated him.

I impetuously decided to butt in, overstepping my role. I said: 'Mr. President, in a news conference, you want journalists to concentrate on the message you seek to convey. You do not want them to focus on your appearance.

'You can do something about your appearance, but you cannot completely control how your message will be received by the pack of insatiable journalists looking for intrigue, embarrassment, and scandal.

'A politician who does not look after his appearance will not be electable,' I warned him, not for the first time.

The President found this repeated message about appearances tiresome and an example of bullying. Surely, it was a form of harassment which had not yet been made illegal by any law. Perhaps he should sign an Executive Order prohibiting his subordinates from commenting on his appearance? He found this thought as amusing as it was unrealistic and light-hearted.

*****

A few months ago, during the summer and fall of 2026, most questions asked of the President had dealt with the Administration's response to the continuing protests organized by the DNA Movement and the destruction of monuments and statues throughout the United States by marauding gangs. Over time, these protests had become increasingly violent and threatened the fabric of American society.

During a protest, held in November 2026, a rowdy mob had targeted the White House, climbing over metal fences, and invading the grounds. The riot almost made the President take shelter in the bunker beneath the mansion. It reminded me of the storming of the Bastille on 14 July 1789, in Paris when riotous hordes of protestors murdered the Director of the jail and freed all inmates. Fortunately, the guards were able to prevent the crowd from entering the White House, so it was not necessary for the President to shelter in the bunker. But the scary event certainly served as an admonition.

At the demonstration, a small group of hecklers who opposed the unruly behaviour of the rioters was pounced upon by the marchers and brutally beaten until their battered and bloodied faces became unrecognizable. They could not get up because their ribs had been broken in several places.

Unfortunately, in his daily press briefings, the President advocated different, and incompatible, strategies. Sometimes, he strongly supported a law-and-order approach to stop the rioting, whereas at other times he was more conciliatory and recommended the adoption of remedial legislation which would improve the opportunities of oppressed people. This incompatibility fed the voracious appetites of the accredited White House journalists who exploited any inconsistency in the answers provided by the President during his press briefings. To minimize adverse impact on the electorate, the President's minders recommended that the President stick to a well-prepared script which, if implemented, might result in electoral benefits at the next election.

His minders had learned a lot from the previous presidential campaign. At the beginning of that campaign, Desmond was painted by the media as the underdog, a no-hoper who miraculously gained nomination by the Republican Party to represent it at the election. But as the campaign progressed, he effectively communicated a vision which turned the electorate around, just in time for election day.

I provided the President with appropriate and factual advice, a defensible and realistic vision, and a straightforward mission statement. Although the law-and-order issue was always debated by the candidates during the previous election campaign, I had encouraged him to promote equality of opportunity for all Americans, stress the importance of traditional family values, instil a sense of pride in America's history, heritage, and achievements, and support the establishment of small businesses which he described as the 'arteries of American prosperity'.

The President's vision of an independent, self-reliable America with prosperity and welfare for every citizen, and promotion of the small business and agricultural sectors, registered with the electorate. I recommended that he communicate his vision to his audience several times in each rally as if it were part of a Hail Mary rosary, until all attendees were able to recite it themselves.

I may be blowing my own trumpet here – indeed, I hope I do not sound too narcissistic – but my communication skills con tributed to the electoral success of the President. It got him over the line in his campaign. It was certainly a narrow victory; some of the early morning papers even predicted that our opponent would have enough votes in the Electoral College to claim victory. But Desmond Raymond Clarkenson scraped through to become the 47th President of the United States.

*****

I looked at the stain on the President's shirt while pretending to consult the President's Valet by raising my eyebrows. I courageously decided to address this issue.

'Mr. President, do you want to freshen up before meeting your next visitor? You might also want to change your shirt?'

The Chief of Staff understood where I was heading, and he took over from me.

'Mr. President, you have an appointment with the Ambassador of the People's Republic of China in less than two hours. It may be a contentious meeting since you are planning to discuss the current aggressive militarism displayed by that country,' said the Chief of Staff. The Security Advisor nodded when he referred to the aggressiveness of China. She had instigated the meeting with the Chinese Ambassador by demonstrating, and lamenting, the measurable loss of American influence in the South China Sea and Africa, and China's demonstrated desire for world domination.

'And after your meeting with the Ambassador, there is a luncheon meeting with the Australian Prime Minister, Benjamin Adhemar, one of our esteemed friends. On the agenda for the meeting is a discussion on the conclusion of a wide-ranging bilateral trade agreement between the United States and Australia,' he reminded him.

'And later, at 4 pm, there is a meeting with your Cabinet to consider the Administration's response to the continuing violence, instigated by the DNA Movement. This meeting will be followed by a press meeting,' he concluded his overview of the day.

The President did not reply immediately. He was seething inside because he interpreted our comments about his appearance as another attempt to yet reduce his own decision-making facilities. He looked around the room, he lifted his right hand from the desk, and stroked the back of his swivel chair as if it were the President's family dog who responded to the name 'Louis'. I observed the President obliquely admiring the portrait of his predecessor on the wall of the Office and figured that one day he would also be immortalized on this very wall.

I looked expectantly at the President waiting for an answer, although I knew I would be waiting for a long time.

The President finally decided to harp about his treatment.

'It is one thing to have to listen to the First Lady about how to be dressed, it is an entirely different matter if other people, my Press Secretary, Chief of Staff, the Chief Valet and other minders, were to interfere with my dressing habits,' the President mumbled to himself, but loud enough for all to hear. But invariably, he followed our advice because there was no alternative that the President could fall back on.

'The President of the United States lives in a gilded cage, surrounded at the same time by material opulence and emotional poverty. Everything you do is monitored by some person or committee that considers the impact of your actions on the electorate,' the President remarked ruefully.

His face became sad when he recognized the inescapable truth of his comment. He wondered why he had pursued a political career. Was it a burning ambition to help people? Or to make America great again? Or was it merely an ambitious exercise in seeking raw power? Even though the Office of the President is deemed to be the most powerful Office in the Free World, he did not seem to have any decision-making power over his own circumstances, even what he would wear or where he would eat! His life was like the tax code, highly regulated and complex, and for every circumstance he found himself in, there were rules and incomprehensible exceptions.

I noticed that the President again planted his right hand on his desk. In my experience, this was a sign that he had an important message for his assembled minders.

The secretaries were waiting patiently, armed with their writing pads. Their unctuous smile revealed a sense of edginess because they wanted to know about their assignment for the day. The Security Advisor looked at her watch. She was keen to brief the President on China's attempt at world domination. The Chief of Staff visibly disclosed his impatience by looking indifferently at the paintings on the wall and pretending he owned the place.

'I will take a quick shower now and change my shirt. I assume this will make my Press Secretary happy. I should also select another tie. Do I have a tie with a hammer and sickle on it? the President asked his Valet facetiously.

'And there is still enough time for a Chinese briefing,' he told his Security Advisor.

4

THE BRUTAL WINTER WHICH INVADED WASHINGTON DC IN January 2027 was oddly short. The snow had melted by the end of February and temperatures started to rise in the beginning of March. And the lawlessness returned to the capital and other American cities each time the Movement organized demonstrations.

On a lovely day in March in that early spring of 2027, Desmond was pacing up and down the Oval Office with his clenched hands behind his back. He occasionally stretched his fingers to prevent getting a cramp. He stared through the window of the Office to seek solace in the green garden, with its beautifully maintained flower beds, which snaked around the White House. The presidential First Dog was running around, wagging his tail constantly, playing with the multi-coloured leaves that had fallen from the trees, and chasing the squirrels that made the President's lawn their hunting ground. In the distance, one could see tourists waving at the White House and pointing in the direction of the West Wing. Some leaned on the fence surrounding the grounds of the White House to have a better look and were reprimanded by the guards. '*These tourists are very courageous. They are still intent on visiting the White House in times of uncertainty and danger,*' I thought.

As he was fuming, the President looked at the assembled members of his staff, his eyes wide-open and eyebrows raised. A small stream of saliva had escaped from his mouth, and he collected it with a tissue that one of his secretaries discreetly passed to him. It was obvious that he was visibly enraged about the lawlessness that engulfed his country. The rage within him drained his face of blood. He looked like a scary ghost, dressed in bedsheets, with a grotesque face and big white ears.

'The gratuitous violence in Washington DC and other cities that we witness on television, almost daily, is making me mad. I lament the destruction of property and businesses, the vandalism, the desecration of national monuments and defilement of historical statues, the decapitation of Christopher Columbus, the attempt to obliterate American history.

'This is not what you would expect to happen in a civilized society,' he told his entourage.

I reflected on the President's remark. *Surely, the destruction of monuments and statues might well happen in a civilized society, indeed especially in 'civilized' societies where people are still free to protest on the streets*, I thought. But I let it go. There was an interview coming up on the Public Broadcasting Service, or PBS for short, with Professor Coppelli Colone, one of the leaders of the DNA Movement and I wanted the President and members of his Cabinet assembled in the Oval Office to watch it.

'Mr. President, may I suggest we watch the interview with Professor Colone that is scheduled to be screened on PBS soon. Perhaps we will get a few pointers about the future of the DNA Movement by watching the interview?' I suggested. As the President nodded, I switched on the television and, after a few moments, the host of the show *Meet the movers and shakers of today*, David Andrea Rothermere, came into view. He was already seated in a chair with a bunch of papers on his lap. A television technician fixed a microphone to David's shirt; a Director conveyed last-minute instructions to the program's host. Across from him, was another chair where his interviewee would be sitting. A small table, placed next to the chair with a glass of water on it, completed the austere scene. When the familiar introductory jingle finished, David turned his face to the camera:

'Ladies and gentlemen, this morning we feature one of the leaders of the DNA Movement, Professor Coppelli Colone. Professor Colone hails from Florence, Italy, but has, for many years, been the Professor of the History of Ideas and Jurisprudence at the University of Southern Kansas,' he said.

Professor Colone walked on-stage, a microphone visibly sticking out from under his shirt.

'Professor Colone, please take a seat and welcome to the program this morning,' David said.

The President's eyes were glued to the television set. It was the first time that he saw Coppelli. 'He looks like a derelict, who lives under a railway bridge and begs for a living. I am surprised they would allow him to appear in such a disgusting state,' he mumbled to himself but loud enough for his entourage to hear.

'Professor Colone, what is the DNA Movement and what are its objectives?' the interviewer asked.

'Well, David, the establishment of the Movement is a spontaneous response to the history of discrimination in this country,' Coppelli said in accented English. 'Since well before Independence, African Americans were enslaved, and even after emancipation, they were systematically excluded from meaningful participation in the affairs of this Republic. Their life expectancy, on average, is four years less than that of white citizens, and twelve years less than Asian Americans. This is an issue involving lack of access to affordable medical facilities. African Americans were excluded from quality education, even after the Supreme Court declared segregation illegal. For too long, they have been confined to their own segregated educational facilities, which were never properly resourced, and ...'.

'These statistics are well known, Professor Colone, but surely the President and his Predecessor have significantly improved the plight of African Americans?' the interviewer interrupted.

'It is a case of too little, too late. In my view, drastic action is needed to bring about meaningful change. And that is precisely what the DNA Movement aims to achieve. It is a necessary game changer, desperately needed in this country.

'In any event, the number of African Americans who die because of police brutality is increasing rapidly. The Movement calls for a proportionate response to the indiscriminate cruelty suffered by African Americans and the downtrodden,' Coppelli said.

'But is it necessary for the Movement to foment strife and to encourage demonstrators to destroy shops and to pull down monuments and statues?' David asked.

'The Movement never condones violence, but occasionally it is not possible to control a million demonstrators. Changes are rarely achieved without collateral damage. But I do not personally approve of violence. However, it is legitimate to remove offending statues and monuments that glorify the misdeeds of Americans who have sodomized groups of people and destroyed their dignity and freedom. The DNA Movement will continue to promote the removal, even destruction, of monuments and statues that lionize racial discrimination. The continuing discrimination suffered by African Americans calls for retribution and revenge,' Coppelli said belligerently.

'Please, switch off the television. I have seen and heard enough. It is clear the Movement will continue to lengthen the trail of destruction and deny Americans their historical heritage.

'The DNA Movement is clearly not a genealogical movement; it is a domestic terrorist organisation.

'And it has nothing to do with medical science or the extraction of a person's DNA,' the President added.

'Of course, some aspects of our heritage are despicable. Indeed, it is regrettable that white settlers sometimes resorted to violence in the past to maintain their dominance. But I also regret that protestors used violence to respond to decades of discrimination. It is my sincere belief that America will not and will never benefit from uncontrolled and gratuitous violence. This Nation is based on hard work by industrious people who built their lives with little governmental interference, secure in the knowledge they will enjoy the fruits of their labour. America stands for individual freedom, security, and the pursuit of prosperity,' he continued. He left out the promise of equality, realizing that it could not be implemented.

He sounded like he was campaigning for re-election.

'The other day, the crowd even attempted to destroy the Lincoln Memorial here in Washington DC. Lincoln is the President who freed the slaves and yet, that is not enough for the radicals who want to take over this country and destroy what our ancestors have built during the last two hundred years,' the President said.

'These demonstrators probably wanted to achieve what a murder plot in 1861 failed to deliver,' I retorted.

'I have just finished reading a riveting debut novel entitled *The First Assassin* by John J. Miller. It is an excellent historical fiction thriller about a plot to assassinate President-elect Lincoln in 1861. I am certain you would enjoy reading it.'

'If only I had time to read, Richard.

'At one stage, we were afraid that the demonstrators would invade the White House and lynch all those inside. What has become of this country?

'Of course, fortunately, the White House is heavily fortified with missiles in place and snipers on the roof. It is inconceivable protestors would be able to invade the House, even if they got onto the grounds.

'For the demonstrators, the White House must have been

what the Bastille represented to the impoverished Frenchmen in 1789,' the President said.

It is true that the President was ready to seek protection in the below ground bunker to escape the rabble crowd, but the guards prevented the demonstrators from entering the White House. They blocked its entrance with determination and firmness. But it took a few hours to evict all invaders from the grounds surrounding the White House.

'Why do these demonstrators destroy the statues of the Confederate Generals and other Civil War participants? Yes, the Confederacy lost the Civil War, but it is a part of the history of this country. In destroying the statues, we destroy our history.

'They even demanded that all copies of *Gone with the Wind* be destroyed because it depicts a scene about slavery in the South – a historically correct depiction, I might add. This is perhaps the most popular and best movie ever made, an icon of American cinema!' he reminded his entourage.

The President proceeded to give his captive audience in the Oval Office a history lesson.

'Even as a child I learned that history repeats itself. The atrocious mistakes made by our ancestors are likely to be repeated, in a different context, by the present generation. We should learn from history, not destroy it. Students should learn about the glorious achievements and dismal failures of America, including, of course, the appalling history of racial discrimination and slavery.

'There have also been protests in many other parts of the United States. In Boston, a statue of Christopher Columbus located in Waterfront Park was removed a few days ago and beheaded. The corpse and the head were dumped in the Boston Harbour, like the tea during the Boston Tea Party which precipitated the War of Independence,' the President said disgustedly.

'It appears that this unstoppable trend has infected many other countries too. It is also sometimes referred to as the "cancel culture movement", I said.

'How could you cancel a "culture"? Culture is something that evolves over time, hundred even thousands of years. You just can't switch it on and off,' the President said.

'The situation is not any better in the United Kingdom where officials in East London removed a statue of the 18th century merchant and slave owner Robert Milligan from its place in the city's docklands. And protestors in Bristol knocked down a monument erected to honour the legacy of slave trader Edward Colston. This happened the day after the Mayor of London announced that more statues of colonial figures could be removed from Britain's streets. The Mayor tweeted that, "It's a sad truth that much of our wealth was derived from the slave trade – but this does not have to be celebrated in our public spaces."

'The Mayor announced the establishment of a Commission, to advise on which statues should be removed. So, the Diversity Commission – a pedestrian name for this Commission – would decide which legacies the United Kingdom will be allowed to celebrate,' the President commented.

'In my home country, Australia, statues of Captain James Cook, the great navigator, were graffitied in several cities,' I said.

The President frowned. He expected better from me because I somehow felt that he regarded my contributions on a par with schoolboy level arguments, not sophisticated enough for the White House.

'This is just horrible. Where did you get this information?' the President asked.

'*The Daily Telegraph*,' I said, referring to a local Sydney-based newspaper.

'That would be right! I assume there is never any fake news in daily newspapers, isn't that the case?', the President retorted laconically.

As I was about to confirm the President's assumption, the Secretary of State, Murray Oliver Pompo, a graduate of Oxford University, entered the Oval Office. He had obviously overheard the last part of the discussion. He was keen to add to it.

'The unfortunate events are moving fast in the United Kingdom,' he said.

'There have been calls for Oxford University to remove a statue of Cecil Rhodes, a Victorian imperialist in southern Africa who made a fortune from mines and endowed Oxford University's Rhodes scholarships. Oxford University itself recommended the removal of the statue even though Rhodes is invariably connected with the history of this once great University. Just the other day, hundreds of supporters of the "Rhodes Must Fall Movement" congregated near the statue chanting "Take it Down", he explained sadly.

'Yes, I am aware of that sordid episode. The reality is that historical figures have a complex history. Take, for example, Winston Churchill, who is revered as the Prime Minister who defeated Nazi Germany in the Second World War. He was, however, a staunch supporter of the British Empire and may have expressed views which our progressive intellectual elites find disgusting. They accuse the great Man of having made offensive and racially charged comments in the context of denouncing the independence movements in South Asia,' I retorted.

The President and the Secretary of State pondered my contribution to the debate. They wondered whether they too would become historical figures with a complex history. They were pensive for a few long minutes, lost in their own thoughts and simmering inside, thinking about what could be done by the Oval Office to stem the tide of history.

Destruction and desecration of monuments is as old as humankind, I thought.

I reminded the President and the Secretary of State of the destruction by the Taliban of the magnificent Buddhas of Bamyan in Afghanistan. These had been carved into the side of a cliff, 2,000 years ago and were destroyed in March 2001 because they depicted faces. The government deemed such depiction to be incompatible with its version of the Islamic religion. This fanatical event also prompted me to reflect on the destruction of the ancient site of Palmyra in war-torn Syria by Islamic State, and the Temple of Baalshamin dedicated to the ancient God Baal. Marauding gangs of Islamic thugs had also rampaged through the Archaeology Museum of Mosul in Iraq with sledgehammers and axes, to destroy what they regarded as idolatry. I noticed that these movements violently agitated against archaeology as an academic discipline.

'Sure, but these movements were religiously inspired, not motivated by racial discrimination, as in the United States. In any event, the issue of iconoclasm has a long history in Christianity as well', the Secretary of State remarked.

'There is often an overlap between race and religion, Mr. Pompo. Fanatics often select easy targets, like churches, where congregations expect to listen to the words of God, not the terrifying noise of bullets.

'A climate of intolerance and destruction is engulfing the world. As I see it, America, and like-minded nations, like Australia, have a moral duty to protect the world's heritage', I said.

I also reminded the President of the graphically challenging television pictures of Saddam Hussain's statue in Baghdad, being toppled by an enraged and liberated crowd. People danced on the statue of the dictator and used sledgehammers to pulverise it to pieces. I pointed out that this raised an interesting conundrum: Saddam was clearly a modern-day despot, who undoubtedly facilitated the murder of many people. Was it justifiable to destroy his statue, but not the statue of Christopher Columbus?

Was it the case that, with the passage of time, statues gain a protective veneer which somehow hid the horrible crimes committed by these historical figures? At what point in time did a statue become a historical relic and a part of the history and culture of a country? These were tough questions to answer, I told the President.

I continued my history lesson.

'There are statues of villainous historical figures which, for one reason or another, most likely ignorance and the passage of time, have not been touched by the current generation of protestors. For example, Emperor Napoleon Bonaparte, who subjugated many European nations, is now typically described as a visionary who introduced the Civil Code in the countries his armies conquered.

'The history books are full of lies, or do not accurately describe what happened in the world. So, the best we can say is that the DNA Movement's protests are well-intentioned but misconceived attempts to rewrite the history books. History is often nothing else than fiction,' I said.

'I know that history does not necessarily point in one direction, Richard,' the President said.

'History as it is taught in schools and universities is incomplete at best, and fictitious at worst.

'It is truly deplorable that, in our high schools, colleges and universities, students are often exposed to a potted history of discrimination, displacement, slavery, greed, and exploitation. History does not appear to be studied in a meaningful way. I need to do something about this unfortunate situation.

'This Administration has an obligation to ensure that the teaching of history provides students with a balanced understanding of America's past achievements and failures. It is regrettable that the teaching of the history of America often caters to the political correctness movement. The teaching of history should be as factual as is possible and encourage students to consider the causes and consequences of historical events.

'The greatness of this country and its documented protection of freedom around the world is frequently forgotten. Too many citizens display a staggering ignorance of even the most basic facts of history. I am not sure that these protestors – and not just the protestors, mind you – know the basics of American history. How many of them would know which Presidents have been assassinated while they were in office? Would they know anything at all about the War of Independence, Watergate, the floating of the American dollar, our contribution to the execution of the First and Second World Wars, Pearl Harbor, the Civil War, Monica Lewinsky, the two impeachment trials of President Trump, and even our exploration of space?

'I am only mentioning American historical events. Once we discuss the history of the world, even greater ignorance would be exhibited.

'Of course, I do not want to live in the past, but it is always important for the past to live in us.

'What I find worrying is that ignorant people are amenable to intimidation by those who peddle false concepts and principles which appear reasonable, but on reflection are deceptively simple and duplicitous.'

'Mr. President, I could not agree more. The study of history is a valuable tool in the maintenance of a healthy democracy because it reminds our Nation of the sacrifices that our ancestors have made to ensure that people enjoy the freedoms which we take for granted,' the Secretary of State said pompously.

'Unfortunately, it appears that nothing can be taken for granted anymore. It is ironic that some people use their constitution-protected rights as a sword to frustrate the legitimate expectations of other people who merely want to exercise their rights in a peaceful manner,' the President said.

'Of course, under no circumstances could I possibly condone the destruction of public or private property. I need to draft an Executive Order that criminalizes the destruction of our historical monuments and statues and penalizes those who resort to violence to change our way of life,' the President announced.

'Right now, I will draft an Executive Order. I can't stand the lawlessness and I must protect our cultural heritage, and our statues and monuments,'

*****

The Executive Order was signed on 26 April 2027. In it, the President lamented the rewriting of history, not just in America but in other countries as well. He wrote that, 'Over the last 9 months, there has been a sustained assault on the life and property of civilians, law enforcement officers, government property, and revered American statues and monuments such as the Lincoln Memorial and the Columbus Memorial. Many of the rioters, arsonists and extremists who have carried out and supported these acts have explicitly identified themselves with ideologies that call for the destruction of the United States system of government.' The Order also provided for heavy fines to be imposed on anyone who destroyed historical monuments and statues.

The Executive Order was signed by the President in the Oval Office. He was surrounded by most members of his Administration. As his Press Secretary, I stood right behind him as if to reassure him of the importance of his Order for the maintenance of American Civilization. In his oral statement, the President indicated that he could not condone the violence that had occurred in America and that he had to act to safeguard the rights and freedom of Americans, of all races. And historical treasures, monuments and statues were to be protected – it was the American way of life.

5

PROFESSOR COPPELLI COLONE SAT IN HIS SMALL BUT COM-
fortable office at the University of Southern Kansas. His office,
located on the left-hand side of the main quadrangle of the
University, offered good views of the expansive lawn dotted with
trees, a few walkways, and wooden benches. The building was a
solid structure, erected in the 1930s, with gargoyles of beastly creatures on its façade. During the Second World War, it was used as
a barracks for soldiers destined to fight in the Pacific. When the
building was renovated in the 1990s, renovators found that a room
had been hermetically soundproofed during the War. Presumably,
some secret meetings had been held in that room during the war. A
bell tower stood in the middle of the quadrangle; it chimed during
orientation week, graduations, and it heralded the beginning and
end of the examination periods.

Books and papers were strewn everywhere, covering the floor,
two chairs and a desk of Coppelli's office. A telephone sat atop a
metal drawer in the corner of his office as there was no room left
for it on his desk. The laptop was kept on his lap or stored in his
briefcase.

An unusual mix of good intentions, unkept promises, and
contempt of authority exemplified Coppelli's attitude to his university position. As an academic in America, he enjoyed a good
salary and some desirable perks, such as a sabbatical every six

years, and an opportunity to think and contribute to the exciting world of ideas and literature. Coppelli certainly never expected when he was a child, living in a small village in Italy, to ever visit the United States, let alone become a professor in the history of ideas and jurisprudence in a respected institution.

Coppelli's long blonde hair, inquisitive blue eyes, and goatee gave him an almost Germanic appearance. An upturned nose looked like an elfin addition to his face, an afterthought when the contours of his frame had already been settled. Coppelli's yellow teeth revealed that he was a chain smoker; the toxic smoke contaminated his malodorous breath. His muscular arms swung inanely around him and served as a clothesline for his garments. A shirt which would have been lily-white at one time, was glued to his belly and, on a sweltering day, would be difficult to remove. It was tucked into his pants which were held together by a cord rather than a belt.

'Belts are expensive and reflect bourgeois attitudes to life,' he told his colleagues, who regarded Coppelli's comment as 'irrational' in the extreme.

His listeners started to gossip behind his back, belittling his appearance and accusing him of narcissism, egotism, and overbearingness. 'He pretends to know everything because he is a professor. He sees his job at the University as a license to pursue his idiosyncratic lifestyle,' they said.

At the University of Southern Kansas, Coppelli had a personal assistant, called Debbie. It was rumoured that she had been allocated to Coppelli's office to enforce the University rule which prohibited smoking in academic offices. However, Coppelli either did not hear about this rule or was determined to ignore it, regardless of the cost. Nevertheless, Debbie regularly reminded him of the existence of this rule.

'Coppelli, the University prohibits smoking in academic offices. I received a phone call from the University's health and safety officer, asking to remind you of this rule,' said Debbie.

'Well, they do not seem to have the courage to contact me personally. Unless I hear from them directly, I will do as I please. And Debbie, if the safety officer rings you, tell her that I am not in my office. I have no time for these bureaucratic apparatchiks whose only job is to harass other people into complying with irrational and discretionary rules,' Coppelli remarked.

'Do I make myself clear, or do you need more information on what I expect you to do?' he said gruffly but not impolitely.

Debbie merely nodded. She had decided, a long time ago, that no reply was the best reply. *How do you change the behaviour of a chain smoker anyway?* she asked herself.

'Coppelli, the Provost is also unhappy that you have a habit of cancelling your classes when there is a DNA Movement demonstration. Some students have complained to her and insist they have paid for lectures that should not be cancelled.

'Students have also complained that you are inciting people into violence, leading to destruction of property and the removal of historical statues. If you are not careful, Coppelli, you will get into serious trouble.

'Your detractors say you intimidate students into accepting your version of human rights. Might it not be sensible to tone down your advocacy of these sensitive issues?' Debbie asked.

'Debbie, a person should stand up for their beliefs. It is important to act upon your beliefs if you want to contribute to the making of a better America. There is nothing the Provost, or any other university bureaucrat, can do to make me change my views or alter my relationships with students. They can all get lost,' Coppelli answered combatively.

Debbie's approaches, however, made Coppelli reflect on his involvement with the DNA Movement. For months now, he had been at the forefront of the demonstrations which had taken him all over the country. He had almost reached the limit of what he could do for the Movement without losing his job. All the leave which he could legally take had been used, and it would be difficult to engineer further absences from the University to take part in the demonstrations. Yet, he was ideologically committed to what he called 'The Great Struggle'. The President's Executive Order was on his desk. He read it several times and underlined the provisions he disagreed with. Most articles of the Order had been underlined because, for him, the document was a worthless ideological diatribe.

'How far could I go without upsetting the University's apparatchiks?', he wondered.

✶✶✶✶✶

Coppelli's unorthodox career provides an insight into his strident defence of the Movement. His unusual journey from Italy to the United States is a confluence of coincidences and luck.

Soon after his arrival at the University of Southern Kansas, he told me how he ended up in the United States. Of course, what I am recounting happened some years ago and my memory is not as strong as it used to be. I was able to recall the price of bread and milk in the early 1990s, no doubt a gift from my mother who had a phenomenal memory, especially for prices, but I would be unable to tell you what I ate for breakfast, unless I probed my mind vigorously to recall this recent, but to me, irrelevant occurrence. I am regularly unable to recall some words like 'pomegranate' and 'testimonial' which I had no difficulty using when I was younger. In any event, history is 'a mess of memories and impressions scattered, clotted and pasted together like a mulch of fallen leaves on a damp autumn pavement' as George Johnston reminded us in his award-winning book *My Brother Jack*. Thus, while I do my best to recall the details as best I can, some may be more fictitious than others. But it will give you a useful insight into Coppelli's mind and his fanatical pursuit of the Movement's interests.

*****

His youth was unremarkable, dominated as it was by predictable routines, going to church on Sundays, attending the local primary school during weekdays, and helping his father in the grocery store on weekends. He knew everybody in the village, the rich and famous, the poor and downtrodden, the local priest, the chemist and the doctor, and the teachers, and they knew him as a polite down-to-earth, but potentially mischievous, boy.

The boredom and drudgery of his youth stifled his imagination. He longed for freedom and independence, away from his parents and village. He was a baby-boomer, born after the Second World War in 1964. In his village's primary school, he developed an early interest in literature and history which was to stay with him throughout his life. This interest was also stimulated by his mother who encouraged him to draft stories at an early age, and to read good books. She reminded him often of a quote attributed to the noted English 18th century historian, Edward Gibbon, who wrote that, 'Books are those faithful mirrors that reflect to our mind the minds of sages and heroes'.

His primary school teacher, a former member of Benito Mussolini's party, tried to instil a keen sense of law-and-order into his pupils. This did not deter Coppelli from stealing from the local co-op shop and cheating on his homework and examinations – he was a rebel in the making.

In high school, he showed an ability to write well and his essays on civic duties, which students were expected to write, were erudite but indicative of his critical views on society. He was left-handed at a time when children were still encouraged to become right-handed.

His high school was located some ten kilometres from his house. As his mind developed, he became more critical, argumentative, and rebellious. He did not accept the social order that came into existence after the War. He also had a penchant for violence; he would get into boxing fights with other boys who disagreed with his views. He rode a bike to and from high school. On rainy days, and there were many of them, the bike ride became an inconvenient, even a despised activity which often resulted in Coppelli getting a cold. But his parents, although they were not paupers, did not have the money to buy a car and drive him to school, so Coppelli had to go to school on a bike.

'Your choice is between biking to school, or working at home in the business,' his father had told him. He chose the bike because working in his father's grocery store was an unappealing prospect that would dull his brain and stifle his prospects.

After finishing high school, Coppelli attended the University of Macerata in Italy in the early 1980s studying law and philosophy. The '80s was a time of rebellion and sexual liberation, not just in Italy. Immature, but idealistic, students railed against the established order for a variety of reasons, most of which were irrational or infantile expressions of freedom of expression. They channelled their youthful enthusiasm into opposing the policies and decisions made by their governments.

Coppelli was a loner, and he certainly did not have a cheer squad of youthful, attractive, and available girls to applaud his actions. He envied the lifestyle of his more sexually astute, adventurous, and successful colleagues in the University. It was not so much that it would be impossible for him to get a girlfriend. He was intelligent, knowledgeable, and he could be very sociable. But, in fact, girls did not want to socialize with him because of his hygiene problems. His parents were never attuned to dental or physical hygiene and their house did not have a bathroom; it was a three-room medieval cottage in the main piazza of the village, above a grocery shop. He somehow blended in because it was not unusual for people to disregard their hygienic needs. His disregard of basic hygiene had obviously followed him all to the way to the United States because his appearance was truly confronting – something I pointed out before. His unwashed clothes, unkempt hair, goatee, smelly body, and probing eyes terrified female students.

While he studied at the University of Macerata, Coppelli also trained to become a professional boxer. He entered a few boxing competitions and he either won them or was highly ranked. He saw boxing as an outlet which substituted for the absence of a satisfying love life.

He was also a capable, eloquent student and an indefatigable rabble rouser. He gave speeches and when he did, his yellow teeth flashed, and everyone knew that he smoked which was still the in-thing to do in those days, something I was reminded of the other day when I saw *The King's Speech*. The Duke of York told his therapist that his doctors had indicated to him that smoking relaxes you. The therapist, an Australian citizen who had helped shell-shocked returned soldiers after the First World War, however, always reprimanded the Duke when he lit a cigarette. Not surprisingly, the Duke, then King George VI, died prematurely of lung cancer. Smoking was always part of the Hollywood movies of the '30s, '40s, and even '50s because it proved that the protagonist was a successful, debonair character, a role model for other people. Coppelli's smoking habit antagonized his more enlightened colleagues because they knew it was an unhealthy,

even gross, habit. But for Coppelli, freedom and smoking cigarettes were inseparable, like Churchill and cigars.

'Did you ever see Churchill portrayed without a cigar in his
hands?' I asked my own assistant, a recent graduate of the University of Southern Sydney.

'No, not really,' he answered indifferently, returning to his
work of writing a draft of a speech.

An afterthought occurred to my assistant. 'Isn't Churchill the
politician who said that in victory I deserve cigars and whiskey,
and in defeat I need cigars and whiskey?' he asked, not expecting
a reply.

In his university town of Macerata, there were streets paved
with cobblestones, which romantically adorned the streets and
squares of this medieval university town. One day in the rebellious early '80s, when every year Italy appeared to have a new
government, even sometimes in coalition with the Communists,
he challenged his colleagues to break up the cobblestones.

'We want to prevent the carabenieri from reaching the law
school where I will be delivering a mesmeric speech this afternoon on the ancient Roman Empire which was drenched in the
blood of slaves. It is a union-sponsored talk which will be followed by a pizza party. Many students are expected to attend the
talk,' he said.

His exhortation to his colleagues was, of course, a pointless
exercise in grandstanding, but it certainly served as a pointer to
the rebellious behaviour he exhibited while teaching at the Uni-

versity of Southern Kansas and participating in the Movement as a firebrand.

On another occasion, Coppelli and some other bodacious students went into their constitutional law classroom, and they took the professor by the arms and legs and unceremoniously dumped him in the gutter outside on the street. They strongly objected to the philistine views of the professor and his support of capitalism and the established democratic legal system.

'That is where a bourgeois professor belongs, in the gutter,' they said.

They were never convicted of assault. The professor showed leniency and justified the behaviour of the students as an enthusiastic, but mis-conceived, expression of freedom of expression by well-intentioned scholars. He would forgive their indiscretion because experience told him that students, if not properly guided, embrace risky activities which might potentially impact on their prospects in the future. But, under these circumstances, it was still a miracle that the students passed the constitutional law examination. This is because the names of the students were recorded on the examination paper and, hence, the professor would have known that the paper had been written by one of his attackers. Coppelli looked at his examination results with incredulity.

'I never expected to pass this examination.

'I can only applaud the professor's academic objectivity,' he said.

After obtaining his Italian law degree, Coppelli was not invited to join a law firm, one of the few of his class who failed to get a job once they got their degrees. Also, although he was undeniably a talented scholar, he never really had a position at an institute of advanced learning either, apart from some casual tutoring which was poorly paid and could be changed without recourse at any time, and often it was.

But his situation changed when Professor Paul Boscombe, a Professor at the University of Southern Sydney, came to his rescue, some seven years after Coppelli graduated with his law and humanities degrees. Coppelli obtained a visiting role in that University in 1992 where Paul was an influential shaker and mover. It is still a bit of a mystery how Paul got to know Coppelli, but the most obvious explanation is that Paul must have read a few articles written by Coppelli, in Italian, and was impressed by their quality.

In Sydney, Coppelli, however, did not use the opportunity to improve his knowledge of the English language. Although he had enough knowledge to engage in conversational English, he conversed with Paul in Italian. But he did what all visitors do in that great city: he visited the Opera House, the historical Rocks area, and went on a camping trip to the Blue Mountains and, also, stayed at the Carrington Hotel in Katoomba for one night during this trip. He capably assisted Paul with whom he co-authored three articles for publication in Italian journals. He also gave a few lectures in the Italian Department of the University, using

Italian as the language of instruction. They were well received by keen students, hungry for knowledge and Italian magic. They were curious about this unusual professor from Italy who had been invited by Paul. Paul, against the wishes of his wife, even leased a room in his house to Coppelli. He was able to walk to campus because Paul's house was close to the University. The students thought that they were an odd couple, but a formidable bastion of erudition and scholarship.

After that year in Sydney, his mentor by whom he had been invited, Professor Paul Boscombe, became a Professor in the Department of the History of Ideas and Jurisprudence at the University of Southern Kansas. This appointment was not really a promotion, but it would have involved a significant pay rise, something that Paul was interested in. As it happened, I was working in that Department after finishing my law studies at Northwestern University and taking the Bar examination. It was my first job before I became politically involved with the President. So, as I was employed in this Department, I was most familiar with the circumstances surrounding Boscombe's appointment.

Paul, unlike Coppelli, was married. His wife was supportive and, as they did not have any children, the move to Kansas City was not too complicated. As she was a homemaker and did not have a paying job, she encouraged her husband to embark on this American adventure. As far as she was concerned, the risk of failure was minimal. Indeed, when Paul left the University of

Southern Sydney, he was able to take a three-year period of leave without pay from the University, which guaranteed that he could return whenever he wanted during that period.

Nevertheless, the Southern Kansas appointment was a most unusual appointment because Paul, being an Australian, was expected to teach American constitutional law and run the School's History of Ideas and Jurisprudence Department. I never understood why he even accepted the job because it was clear to any keen observer that the Department was in the final stages of decline. It was underfunded by the school for a long time, which was a consequence of two feuding law professors over a twenty-year period. One of these was the Dean, and the other was the former Director of the Department of the History of Ideas and Jurisprudence. Staff members placed bets to predict who would win the long war between these two antagonistic and formidable characters, a war that was played out in official meetings of the School and University. The school needed to find an easy and gullible victim, preferably non-American, who could be blamed for the Department's demise. Paul was the perfect candidate to activate this solution. However, within a year of accepting the job, Paul managed to turn around the fortunes of the Department by convincing an army of foreign students to study in his school which he irreverently referred to as the 'Mecca of Jurisprudence' – and they came in substantial numbers to study for a Master of Laws, specializing in Jurisprudence and the History of Ideas.

He succeeded because he spoke several languages and was able to converse in them with foreign students on his many trips – he was irreverently called Professor Tarmac by his detractors, of which there were many. I never discovered where Paul first learned his languages, but he spoke German impeccably, like a local, and Italian. My research revealed that in the sixties, he completed a doctorate in Heidelberg and later had been a Visiting Professor at the University of Florence. His doctoral dissertation was written in German and had been hailed as a rare and exciting contribution to the world of jurisprudence, including legal logic. Interestingly, even though he wrote about logic, his life's endeavours were not dictated by logic.

One day, Paul asked me to drive to his house, located in the country some forty kilometres from Kansas City, during the winter when there was still a lot of snow on the roads. He instructed me to tell his wife that she should return to Australia. She had become an alcoholic and started to drink early in the day. She was not gainfully employed, and she was unable to accomplish anything at all because she was bereft of social contacts. Encouraging her husband to relocate to the United States misfired badly.

I drove to the sleepy hamlet, in my old Volkswagen. It took me over ninety minutes to get there because the roads were slippery and dangerous in the middle of winter. When I arrived, I told her the unwelcome news and I handed over some Australian coins, spare money, amounting to a few dollars which could be used in Australia. I also told her that Paul had decided not to return to his house, but to stay in a cheap hotel for a few weeks. He expected his wife to vacate the house during that time. On my return to the University of Southern Kansas, I discovered that the brakes of the Volkswagen were defective and did not work. I had to constantly use the handbrakes. The trip took more than two hours to complete. But I had successfully undertaken the task which Paul had given me.

After his wife had been evicted and left for Sydney, I visited Paul at his home for a debriefing, and the question arose what we would eat for lunch. I suggested that we could make pancakes. It was about the only thing I was comfortable preparing! There was flour, eggs, sugar, and milk in the house. Paul was deliriously happy with my proposal, and he provided all the ingredients necessary to bake pancakes. On that occasion, I became a pancake hero and Paul's best friend.

*****

Sometime, in the middle of the '90s, Paul decided to offer Coppelli a job as a Lecturer in his Department. I played a key role in Coppelli's appointment because I was a member of the appointments and interviewing committee. Paul made it clear to me that he only wanted to appoint Coppelli Colone, and I should not consider any other candidates.

'Do you understand what I am asking you to do, Richard? Have I made myself clear?' he asked.

'No problem, Paul, I will most certainly support you to secure the services of Coppelli,' I confirmed.

I was, at that stage, not aware as to why Paul wanted to appoint him and nobody else. I was confident I would find out later, but right now my job was to ensure that Coppelli would be the successful appointee. But there was a problem. There is inevitably a University Appointments Committee, which consists of the Dean of the School of Law, a member of a cognate discipline, the University's Equal Opportunity and Equity Officer, and the Human Resources representative. In my experience, if a committee is involved, you never get the person you want. This is because the appointee is necessarily a compromise because some people on the committee have only an interest in the procedural aspect of the process or want to ensure that the appointee is a member of an unrepresented or under-represented minority. I called it the "diversity curse".

'How can we ensure that as few people as possible will apply for this position?' Paul asked.

'Well, why don't we stipulate in the advertisement that the successful applicant will be expected to teach Italian jurisprudence? Surely that should decrease the number of Americans who will apply for this position. Not many would fancy themselves as experts in Italian jurisprudence,' I offered helpfully as a suggestion to Paul.

'Is there such a thing as Italian Jurisprudence?', Paul asked.

'Of course not. But does it matter? Surely, nobody on the committee will question our understanding of the needs of the Jurisprudence Department,' I predicted confidently.

'In any event, there is huge diaspora of Italians here in Kansas. They arrived from Italy in the 19th century to settle in this part of America. Surely, this could lend credence to our request to teach Italian Jurisprudence?' I added.

'You may well be right, there. Very well, let's do this,' Paul replied.

'However, this is not enough, Paul. We also need to stipulate that, as the successful applicant is going to teach Italian jurisprudence, the appointee must have a perfect command of the Italian language. That will eliminate all Americans who otherwise would have wanted to apply for this position,' I said.

'This is an excellent idea. Hopefully, we will get away with it. I am happy to have you in the Department, Richard. You are a brilliant ideas man, are you not?', he said.

'Umh, just trying to be of assistance, Paul,' I retorted modestly.

My recommended strategy was most successful. Only one person applied for the position, Coppelli Colone. However, this created another problem because the University regulations required an interview regardless of the number of applicants. Our candidate did not know English well and, therefore, would fail to impress an interviewing committee. I wryly explained to Paul that it is 'useful' to know a little bit of professional English if you propose to teach in a university where the language of instruction is English!

'How did Coppelli manage to work at the University of Southern Sydney for one long year with only a limited knowledge of English?' I asked.

'He was mainly employed by me to co-author articles in Italian on the history of ideas, suitable for publication in Italian journals,' Paul said.

'Be that as it may, here in Southern Kansas, he will have to teach – in English!', I answered.

I came to Paul's rescue again; it accelerated my exalted status as an ideas man.

'We should send a letter to the President of the University, explaining that, although we did our utmost to find applicants, we only received one application.'

'Indeed, we went to the four corners of the world, and most unfortunately, we only ended up with one credible applicant,' Paul repeated what I had said, using different words.

'We should ask the President for permission to appoint the applicant without an interview. As the only candidate is certainly supremely qualified, could we not just appoint him without an interview, especially since the candidate resides in Italy?'

The President of the University either did not see the trap or decided to ignore it because he readily agreed to the proposal. Paul later intimated that he knew the secretary of the President and he had asked her to put the letter of appointment, together with other correspondence, on his desk for signature. I suspected that Paul and the secretary maintained an intimate relationship – his comments certainly revealed his infatuation for her. *That may have precipitated the separation from his wife*, I thought. I kept my views to myself, but I was of course interested in the result of this strategy. As it happens, the President received many requests, and it may well be that he signed the letter without knowing what he was signing. His secretary simply put it in front of him and he signed without knowing the contents of the letters? Or the secretary forged the signature of the President on the letter? I decided not to think about the different scenarios that could have played out here.

Following his appointment, Coppelli could not teach a class with an inquisitive student body because his knowledge of the English language was deficient. So, Coppelli agreed to work tirelessly in a small, windowless cubicle for six months surrounded by English-language books, video and audio tapes and we told him to tidy up his English. His colleagues would supply food and water, but we expected him to be proficient in English after the appointed time. Nowadays, this treatment would constitute an example of false imprisonment and might lead to serious legal complications. But in those days, it was not a problem yet. In any event, Coppelli willingly submitted himself to this ordeal and studied as I have never seen a student study in my life. He was obsessed with the English language and traumatized if he did not understand something.

But after six months, he emerged from his self-imposed incarceration and he started to speak impeccable, though accented, English certainly well enough to entertain a class of demanding English-speaking students.

This is how Coppelli came to be at the University of Southern Kansas. There was no doubt that he was a man with a brilliant mind. However, at the time of his appointment, I was not aware of the darker side to Coppelli's character. That manifested itself when he became involved with the DNA Movement.

PART TWO
The Attack
chapters 6-14

6

CHARLES RODERICK DUDLEY SAT IN THE ONLY CHAIR IN HIS apartment. It was a huge chair which he picked up very cheaply in an auction. It took him an eternity to transport it from the auction house to his apartment because he did not want to pay the $40 which the auctioneer demanded for the transport.

'This is an example of daylight robbery,' he protested. But the auctioneer already walked away after receiving $20 for the chair.

Charles was interested in the origins of language, and he exhibited traces of intellectual curiosity in his everyday actions. He looked up the meaning of 'daylight robbery' on his laptop when he returned to his apartment and found that it referred to a tax levied by the United Kingdom in the early part of the 19th century on the number of windows of a house. The more windows, the higher the tax payable to the Treasury.

'That's incredible, this is another example of a greedy capitalist government that is not concerned about the health of people, who are not even allowed to enjoy daylight and sunshine in their homes,' he said disgustedly to himself.

He had just read the Executive Order of the President on the Internet. He was happy he missed the televised signing of the Order because he would have smashed his laptop and his battered decrepit furniture.

'This is an outrage. This Executive Order directly targets the

DNA Movement. Its general tone is merely a smokescreen to hide the real intentions of this despicable Administration.

'The President is directly attacking our right to freedom of expression. The Executive Order's emphasis on violence and destruction of property is a gimmick to justify this attack on the Movement and to implement policies that divide the nation and its people. He wants to eliminate this Movement,' Charles concluded.

In his view, a vicious, but still powerful, President, and an Administration bent on silencing all opposition to their rule attacked his freedom of expression.

Charles contemplated the consequences of this Executive Order for his Movement. He jumped out of his chair and brusquely left his apartment, slamming the door shut with his right foot. He strode up and down the wide public balcony outside the apartments, keeping his arms behind his back, fuming like a rhinoceros. Plastic glass windows separated the enclosed balcony from the outside world. They were difficult to look through because grime covered their scratched surface. It was obvious that the building's management did not regularly clean the windows.

Charles looked in disgust at the dilapidated apartment building where he lived. The paint was peeling away from the doors of the apartments. Wallpaper covered the outside walls, but it was now impossible to ascertain the pattern of the paper. When he looked outside through the plastic glass window, he saw people walking their dogs. He tried to open one of the windows to have a better look, but it would not budge because the rust had cemented the frame into the cement wall of the apartment building. He strained his eyes and observed that sometimes the dogs, who were all on a leash – no doubt yet another insane municipal requirement – walked well ahead of their masters, sometimes they were behind. He wondered whether the dog took his master walking, or the master took the dog walking. *The reality favoured the former interpretation*, he thought amusingly.

Green moss had foisted itself on the apartment doors, alerting visitors that, when the rains came, the apartments would be damp. The doorknobs were rickety and gave the appearance they could fall off at any time. A few of the other inhabitants of the building passed by, acknowledging the existence of Charles with a curt 'hi'. They were all shabbily dressed, heads buried in poverty, and they shuffled away, out of sight.

Charles expected his friend, Coppelli, to appear any time. They had met when he attended a few of Coppelli's history of ideas lectures at the University of Southern Kansas. He also conversed with Coppelli in Chicago where the esteemed professor had given a few guest lectures which Charles attended. Charles enjoyed listening to Coppelli's lectures because he found them to be lucid and captivating. Their friendship was a most unlikely occurrence: the intellectual and the radical found areas of common interest and concern.

Their friendship had thrived also because neither had a steady girlfriend and indeed, never had one in the past. Both were haggard looking and would have had a challenging time appealing to the opposite sex. However, they were certainly not gay. They speculated about the other sex and, occasionally, they had watched hard porn together, which merely stimulated their prurient interest in sexual matters. From time to time, they sought to expand the horizons of their minds by using stimulants, like cocaine, that Charles was able to acquire on the black market.

'You should see what the Internet has to offer by way of porn,' he would tell Coppelli.

'The other day, I swear I saw one of my acquaintances having sex with a good-looking girl I have never seen. Would you like me to describe what they did, or would you rather watch it yourself?' he asked.

'Not sure I want to know. In any event, I have enough imagination to know what would have occurred. Right now, I am not interested in your graphic descriptions of their activity. Later perhaps? I will seek your professional pornographic and sexual advice when I need it,' Coppelli retorted sarcastically.

Both certainly were a couple of societal rejects who were looking for retribution and revenge. Revenge needed to happen soon.

'Someone has to pay for America's history of displacement and racism. There is a need to rectify this endemic problem.

'Revenge is a basic human instinct and a great motivator, like love, compassion, and courage. Psychologists do not pay enough attention to this trait. Yet, it would explain many occurrences in society,' Charles said. Coppelli agreed.

*****

Coppelli arrived at the appointed time. He was always on time, which Charles found unusual as well as amusing because, in his experience, Italians always had a relaxed attitude about time.

'Is Italy not the country that invented the long afternoon siesta and the quarter of the hour a professor would wait for his students to turn up at the lecture? Italians are notorious for being late which frustrates the organizers of a feast, like a wedding or music recital or a play, or other activity,' he mumbled.

'I once attended a concert in open air in Italy and it started more than one hour after the advertised starting time. Even Italians started to get upset with the delay,' he said.

'Surely, your description of Italians is nothing else but an odious and inaccurate stereotype,' Coppelli retorted.

'But Coppelli, it is based on my experience, and it is what common wisdom tells us: Italians have no understanding of time. If you want them to be on time, you impose a non-extendable deadline. But you are different, my friend. You are an honorary American,' Charles said.

'I thought you don't like America and Americans, and you want me to behave like an honorary American?

'Forget it, will you? What counts is that you are always on time. Shall we go inside?', Charles insisted.

He retraced his steps to his apartment followed by Coppelli who felt like an obedient child following its father.

'Ah, Coppelli, it is so good to see you. Have a seat,' Charles motioned to his only chair in the apartment.

'I will sit on the bed. Would you like some tea? I bought some tea. Let me repeat this, I "acquired" some tea yesterday in the local food shop. It comes from Indonesia, and I have chocolates with hazelnuts produced in Belgium,' he said.

Coppelli realized that Charles's use of the verb 'to acquire' indicated that he had stolen the tea and chocolates from the shop. It is something he routinely did, and thus far the police had not arrested him. Coppelli was sure that one day the police would swoop on him and drag him in chains to the dungeon. *His activism and destruction of the property of law-abiding citizens also would not help*, he thought.

'Sure, that is fine, I like chocolates,' Coppelli answered. They stared at each other for a while without saying anything. Their reticence disclosed that they were thinking about the President's Executive Order.

'What shall we do about this Executive Order?' Charles finally asked.

'I have not yet digested the ramifications of this document. I should read it again, the fine print that is. I understand that huge fines will be imposed on people who pull down the statues of murderers, slave drivers and genocidal tyrants?' Coppelli said. His question sounded more like an assertion than a question.

'Yes, but more. It makes illegal the destruction of property of white supremacists. Well, of course, it was always illegal, but the penalties have increased substantially, and the Order even provides for imprisonment,' Charles explained.

'What can we do? We cannot very well repeal the Executive Order, can we? Unless I am the President of the United States or I have enough support in Congress, none of which is going to materialize soon or ever,' Coppelli stated sarcastically.

'There is another way, Coppelli. What if something were to happen to the President?'

'What exactly do you have in mind? Like the President having an accident or mysteriously having been dispatched by an enemy, by a Putin-sponsored assassin who spikes his tea with an untraceable poison, a nerve agent? Even so, the Executive Order would remain in force, would it not?' he retorted.

'Yes, the Order would still be enforceable, but as there would be a new President, the Order may be modified or repealed. I understand that the Vice-President is more philosophically aligned with our way of thinking than the President, although he would not admit to it, right now, of course,' Charles answered.

'In any event, Coppelli, whether the Order is repealed is ultimately irrelevant. This is about revenge, mate. Revenge for all the nasty things that this despicable Administration, the predecessor Administrations, and the capitalist system of the United States have heaped upon us. Revenge is the important motivating factor in this business of ours. That is what I am after: revenge.

Revenge may well lead to social changes and the eradication of racist attitudes and ideas, but revenge would be the main aim of our project,' he further explained.

'What you have in mind, Charles, cannot be done. Be realistic. An army of guards protects the President. It is like an impregnable fort surrounded by a moat of sour-looking but well-armed and well-trained determined guards who have taken an oath to protect the President with their own lives, you know.'

'I know about that ridiculous custom. But Coppelli, you are an ideas man. That is why I wanted you to visit me right now. I am not interested when people tell me that something cannot be done. I want to know only how something can be done,' Charles said.

'Right! What you are asking me to do is not as easy as playing chess. But if I were able to get close to the President, then perhaps I could do something.'

'There is an annual academic awards ceremony coming up. The President will give awards to deserving academics nominated by their universities. The awards ceremony will take place in the White House. And you, as a prominent academic, could engineer an invitation. Perhaps you could convince your university to select you for the purpose of representing it at the ceremony?' Charles suggested.

'It won't work, Charles. For one thing, it is most unlikely that the University would nominate me for this purpose. There are too many competitors who are friendly with the University's President. That includes Cindy Lamarre who is rumoured to have something in common with the President. They maybe watch porn together.

'However, leave it to me. I have an idea how to remove the President. But it may take several months before I am able to discuss any specific ideas with you further,' Coppelli said.

'A plan that will enable you to get close to the President?' Charles asked.

'Yes, of course, if you want him … how shall I say it, to be neutralized, it would be necessary to get awfully close to him, would it not, Charles?'

'I am an ideas man, Charles!', Coppelli said.

'Well, this is the best news I have heard all day,' Charles mused.

'The key is finding a pattern in the President's lifestyle and observing how he responds to catastrophes,' Coppelli added slightly mysteriously.

'I'll get back to you with further details, soon, but it may take a few months – as I said. So have patience, my friend.

'Now, where is the tea that you have promised? And the chocolates? Are they Leonidas chocolates – they are my favourites? I ate a truckload of them when I was in Ghent a few years ago,' Coppelli said.

'No, it is not Leonidas. I can't remember now what kind of chocolates they are. I'll have to look at the packaging. Maybe Godiva? Ferrero Rocher isn't bad either. It comes from Italy,' Charles answered.

They both sounded like a capitalist couple enjoying the fruits of their exploitative behaviour. They both laughed, but they did not know what they were laughing about.

Coppelli was indeed a brilliant ideas man.

✶✶✶✶✶

I knew, based on personal experience, that Coppelli was immensely intelligent and that his claim to be an ideas man was not an exaggeration.

Coppelli was simply the most intelligent person I have ever met in my whole life and will ever meet. Let me give you an example of his genius. One day I was asked to author a paper about a recently deceased history of ideas scholar. The journal gave me two months to accomplish the job. However, I had never read any published papers of the deceased and therefore it would have been difficult, at the best of times, to finish the article in the appointed timeframe. I told Coppelli about my quandary.

'This is not a problem, Richard. I will dictate the essay to you. Just sit down and start writing,' he said.

I was so perplexed that I could not formulate a reply. But I did as he told me, and I started to write down everything that he dictated over four hours. Sometimes, he would revise badly constructed sentences and dictate improved versions of these sentences. The four-hour ordeal totally exhausted me.

'Now, just give it to Maria, our departmental secretary, with a request to type it up and correct any grammatical mistakes. Then send it to the publisher and see what happens,' he said.

'Oh, thank you for your valuable assistance. I very much appreciate your help. I'll put your name down as the co-author of the paper,' I indicated to Coppelli.

'No need to do that, Richard. In fact, I prefer it if you were not to mention my involvement with this paper at all. It is your achievement,' Coppelli answered mysteriously.

I proceeded as requested by Coppelli. Fourteen days later, I received a letter from the Journal's Editor, congratulating me on a splendid article and asking me if I wanted to submit more papers to the Journal.

I went to see Coppelli.

'I know that your contribution was minor,' I said untruthfully and sheepishly, 'but I would still have liked you to be the co-author of this paper. Why did you not want to be named as the co-author of the paper?' I asked.

'No, I would never have agreed to be a co author of the paper because it is the worst paper that I have ever dictated,' he said.

I was as surprised by his answer as I was intrigued. Obviously, he had 'dictated' papers to other people! He was the only person who could author an article without doing scholarly research and yet give the impression that the paper was the result of months of intense scholarly research. He was simply a genius.

However, *la genie touche la folie*, as the French would say. There was a fine line between geniality and insanity. This line was a discernible thread in Coppelli's life because he only took a bath or a shower occasionally and, therefore, he stank. He lacked elementary hygiene which made it difficult for him to function in society. He stank like a rotting rat that lay hidden in the attic because he bathed or showered only once or twice a month. It was revolting.

A few years later, when I did a visiting teaching stint at the University of Florence, I was promenading on one of the beautiful boulevards of this magnificent medieval city one day and, as I was about to turn a corner, a familiar smell wafted through the air.

'It is him. It is him!' I exclaimed.

'It is Coppelli,' I mumbled to myself. I could recognize the smell from a mile away.

And indeed, it was. I was careful enough not to embrace him. I took him to a café. We conversed in a remote corner of the establishment, as far away as possible from other people, because the smell was terribly inconvenient for other people.

*****

Soon after meeting Charles, Coppelli Colone decided to get to work enthusiastically. An important job had to be done and Charles relied upon him for its successful execution. Coppelli was an ideas man.

7

'WHAT IS BEHIND ALL THIS?' THE THREE SECRET SERVICE AGENTS said simultaneously. They were sitting around a conference table in the office of their team leader in the White House, Washington DC.

They had been listening to the conversation between Charles and Coppelli. A few days earlier, when Charles was in the local grocery store to buy, or steal, his weekly supply of food, they had installed a listening device in his apartment because they were concerned about plans by the DNA Movement to disrupt the traffic on Pennsylvania Avenue, which could potentially threaten the safety of the President and result in the destruction of property. The bug's installation was legal. Hayden had applied to a sympathetic District Court Judge for permission to install this device. The whole operation took less than half an hour. If Charles had returned to his apartment earlier than expected, Jesper would have been responsible for delaying him.

'Coppelli is an ideas man. He said so himself. So, what has he got in mind?' Hayden asked.

Hayden was a burly man with imposingly broad shoulders, a receding hairline, a forehead that protruded slightly and a chin that pointed upwards. A bulging stomach overhung his belly, he had hands as big as a shovel, and a booming, authoritative voice. It was impossible to ignore him because he had a commanding presence. He was made for this job. And he liked it; for him this was a dream job, full of adventure and unexpected thrills.

'He said that the key is finding a pattern in the President's lifestyle and observing how he responds to catastrophes.'

'Coppelli also railed against the Executive Order,' Lolita added. Jesper merely nodded his approval.

'But I have no idea what he has in mind *specifically*, considering that a potential attacker could never come near the President because he is guarded by an army of well-trained and devoted guards.

'Coppelli also said that he would find out how it is possible to come close to the President.

'Really, we must find out what these two plotters have in mind. That is our job, and we are good at it, are we not?' Hayden asked for confirmation.

'We also need to coordinate our response with the President's Press Secretary, Richard Bentleys. The Oval Office needs to know what is happening.

'Richard has asked to be informed daily and he has expressed a wish to be actively involved in our plans and strategies to protect the American President,' Hayden explained.

'Sure, we will keep Richard in the loop,' Lolita confirmed.

'I have an idea I would like to share with you,' she said.

'Coppelli is an academic. He teaches jurisprudence and the history of ideas at the University of Southern Kansas.

'The President is scheduled to present academic awards to scholars in the White House at the end of next month. Is it possible that Coppelli is engineering a nomination by his university for a teaching award, thereby also securing an invitation to visit the White House and meet with the President?' Lolita asked.

'Yes, Charles and Coppelli also discussed and rejected this possibility. It is a long stretch, Lolita, but good lateral thinking, nevertheless. First, the University would need to nominate him. That is not a straightforward process. It may in fact be difficult because it is a comparative and competitive process. Didn't he say that Ms. Lamarre has a better chance of being nominated by the University? She obviously has something that Coppelli can't compete with? Second, even if he were to be successfully nominated and invited to the awards ceremony in the White House, he would still be expected to go through our sophisticated X-ray machine that picks up any items that could be used as a weapon, or that could be utilized in the construction of a weapon. Third, during the ceremony, officers of the secret service squad and the President's guard would observe the awardees like hawks. As I see it, there is no way there is anything he could do', Jesper explained proudly, showing off his reasoning skills.

'And, in any event, if we want to ensure that Coppelli is not nominated, all we need to do is to request the President of the University not to nominate Coppelli for the White House visit.'

'I am not sure that such an approach would be successful. The University President who, incidentally, is a registered Democrat, might well argue that the Administration can't interfere with the academic freedom enjoyed by its academics. A direct approach to the University President could easily be interpreted as interference with the affairs of the University – such an approach could backfire. As we know, universities often hide behind academic freedom when it suits them, and reject it when it is not convenient,' Hayden reminded his two colleagues.

'However, on the balance of probabilities, I agree that an attempt to seek a university nomination is not a ready option for Coppelli,' Hayden concluded.

'But even assuming he manages to gain access to the White House and the Awards Ceremony, how could he possibly get close enough to the President to harm him? He would not have any weapons because these would have been discovered by the X-ray machine,' Lolita reasoned.

'Yes, that is a good point. Without weapons, it would appear to be difficult to harm the President. We need to carefully consider this issue. It is a challenge to ascertain Coppelli's options in this situation,' Hayden responded.

'Do you think he would jump on the President, wrestle him to the floor of the auditorium and proceed to strangle him?' Jesper asked.

'I assume this is a rhetorical question?' Hayden responded.

This knock back by his team leader visibly dismayed Jesper. He thought that his suggestion was worthy of consideration.

'But, Hayden, we should not dismiss my suggestion out of

hand. Do you remember that Coppelli was an amateur boxer, a good one, when he was still in Italy? He even won a few local competitions in Macerata. He could easily grasp the neck of the President, wrestle him to the ground, if necessary, and strangle him with his experienced killer hands. It would probably take only 30 seconds for Coppelli to assassinate the President,' Jesper commented in an exasperated tone.

'Oh yes, I have overlooked that detail. The boxing skills of Coppelli may indeed be relevant. Good that you reminded us of this, Jesper'. Jesper, his dignity restored, smiled victoriously.

'Apart from the academic awards ceremony, the President is scheduled to personally inspect the flooding in New Orleans where he will be meeting community leaders, and victims affected by the atrocious weather conditions.

'Coppelli is obviously not a victim of flooding. And I cannot see him going to New Orleans without any prospect of getting close to the President,' Lolita surmised.

'Obviously, we have a job to do – some snooping around. Let's get cracking,' Hayden said.

*****

Meanwhile, hundreds of miles away in his comfortable office in the University of Southern Kansas, Coppelli was about to start his research on the domestic travels and itineraries of the American President. He made himself a cup of percolated Lavazza coffee on the only hotplate in the school's kitchen and grabbed three biscuits from the tin which his colleagues regularly raided. He felt that his intellectual abilities were most productive when drafting a written plan of action, which he could constantly revise.

'I will start by reviewing all the public events attended by the President since his inauguration in January 2025, slightly more than two years ago. I will look for a common denominator. Specifically, I need to know how he interacted with the people he met,' he said to himself. He diligently collected all the information he found and he ordered and re-ordered this material to find what he was looking for in his research. He drafted a plan of action as his research developed.

On the first day of his research, Coppelli worked for twelve hours without a break. When he eventually decided to take a break, he looked at his written plan of action and ruminated about how he became an accomplished writer. He liked writing and literature and recalled that his mother stimulated his interest in books and history. She had started to read to him when he was two years old. He still remembered her comforting, sweet voice, and beautifully accented readings of Winnie the Pooh, and the Lazy Tortoise, in Italian, of course. Since then, he read most of the great American classics of the English language, in English. Recently he read, and enjoyed, Donna Tartt's iconic novel *The Secret History* about some eccentric students, studying classical Greek, at a Vermont college – he could relate to these undisciplined misfits – and John Williams's classic novel on university life, *Stoner*.

In his spare time, mostly at night, because he only needed about four hours of sleep, he authored murder and mystery stories. These stories had not been published – in fact, Coppelli had never submitted any of his stories to a publisher – but he was certain that, once he became famous, publishers would be keen to obtain the right to print his fiction. Coppelli was convinced that his stories were page-turners you do not want to put down once you start reading.

'I specialise in stories that are stranger than fiction,' he told his students and colleagues.

He commenced writing when he was still a student at the University of Macerata in Italy. Now he wrote in English; he asked some colleagues, who had expressed a willingness to become his beta readers, to give him feedback about the content of his stories and the characterisations of the protagonists.

'Please, send your manuscript to us, and we will start turning the pages,' they promised.

Coppelli told his readers that he was modelling himself on the writings of Georges Simenon, the famous Belgian writer.

'I hope Simenon only stimulates your imagination,' they jokingly warned him. 'Because the *modus operandi* of the Belgian author will kill you,' they predicted.

Indeed, Simenon wrote hundreds of popular books, around five hundred, about the iconic Inspector Jules Maigret. Simenon would get an idea for a story and work furiously throughout the day and night until the book was written. After that, he would go to the bathroom and vomit. Such was the pressure and stress of getting the idea of his novel out of his brain onto paper.

'If you do not relax from time to time, you will feel the need to visit the bathroom and vomit,' they warned him.

These recollections caused Coppelli to visit the bathroom at the end of the corridor where his office was located. He looked at his worried face in the mirror above the wash basin. During the last year, wrinkles that looked like the furrows of a potato field had appeared and criss-crossed his face.

'So, Coppelli Colone, do you have a more painless technique when you draft and revise your plan of action?' he asked himself rhetorically.

He then returned to the task before him. For weeks, Coppelli studied the movements of the President throughout the United States and focused on visits to places where a catastrophe had taken place. He became an undisputed expert in the comings and goings of the American President. He knew where the President had been during the last two years and whom he had seen, and how many people came to see him, whom he embraced, how he was protected, and what needed to be done to come close to the President.

After about four weeks of intense study, he thought he knew what to do. But to be sure of the soundness of his analysis, he needed to wait until there was a mass shooting in the United States.

'Well, I am never going to be "absolutely" certain what to do, even if there is a mass shooting, but keeping in mind the best evidence available, I would like to be in a position to predict how the President will respond to a disastrous situation, for example, a shooting that results in many casualties,' he said to himself.

He knew he would not have to wait for a long time. This was the United States, where guns are cheap, and people are even cheaper.

However, he did not know that the three Secret Service officers were keeping an eye on him and followed his every move.

8

THE SECRET SERVICE OFFICERS OBSERVED, FROM A SAFE distance, the two conspirators and listened attentively to their discussions. Most of their conversations were boring dialogues, Marxian claptrap spiced up with Marcuse quotes. Their lives were as mundane as their conversations, but from time to time, they snorted cocaine to achieve ecstasy, transforming their lives into a frenzied and trance-like state in the process. Sometimes, they moved Charles's sparse furniture around in a futile attempt at creating a more liveable space, and at other times they commented upon a few novels which they had recently read. They speculated how they would fare if they were protagonists in a murder story. Occasionally, they watched porn movies together.

The weeks crept into the fall of 2027 with a determination that was remarkably irreversible. The trees started to lose their leaves on time, as expected. While the days were still sunny and the sunsets spectacular, the nights and mornings were cool harbingers of colder days to come. It was also the rainy season which created an unwelcome problem because of a leak in Charles's bathroom which allowed water to drip into his wash basin. He had contacted his capitalist landlord a few weeks earlier about this problem, but he had not yet acted upon Charles's complaint, noting that the rent hardly covered the costs of maintaining the apartment. Charles had some umbrellas permanently positioned outside his door to be used when he went outside.

'Is there any indication they were homosexual lovers?' Lolita asked.

'No, I don't think they were lovers.

'In fact, we observed a steady stream of available girls who visited Charles's apartment. Many of these were young virgins keen to secure their first sexual experience,' Jesper said.

'How do you know they were virgins?' Lolita asked.

Jesper was too stumped to answer Lolita's question. He gathered that he was not an "expert" in the deflowering of girls!

Charles would welcome the girls to his apartment and ask whether they wanted to drink something. He had an impressive supply of expensive drinks in his kitchen – it was his only serious investment – which could be used for the purpose of impressing or seducing his female visitors. He would then ask the girls to remove their clothing and accompany him to his bedroom for whatever they had in mind – deflowering could have been part of it but may not have been the only purpose of visiting his bedroom.

'We heard the moaning and light screaming – of joy, no doubt,' Hayden remarked.

Charles was heard to say: 'There you are, you are now cured. and you will be able to service your boyfriend without losing face,'

'So, he was a gigolo?' Lolita wanted to know.

'Kind of, but he never charged any money, at least not that we are aware of,' Hayden answered.

'We did not learn a lot, really, about any plot or conspiracy. They were obviously careful not to discuss their plans in the apartment.

'Charles and Coppelli went on long walks and probably discussed their plans in detail during that time.'

'Do you think they expected the phone to be bugged?' Jesper wanted to know.

'Charles must have known, or at least suspected, that his apartment had been bugged by the authorities, but we can't be sure. In any case, they played it safe and, if something of importance had to be discussed, it was done outside on their walks when we could not hear the discussion.'

'Did you follow them?' Lolita inquired.

'Yes, Jesper and I took turns. We followed them all right, leaving a very respectable distance between them and us, of course.

'On a few occasions, they went to a French creamery to buy butter and ice-cream; they stopped at a bottle shop a few times. They sat on a bench in the park for an interminable period. Sometimes, they stole a copy of Kansas's morning paper *The Star* from the local news agency, and they would each read a different part of the paper and then switch – things like that, not interesting, I would assume,' Hayden explained.

'However, what is curious is the discovery that nearly every week, Charles was visited by an attractive blonde girl whose wavy hair flowed elegantly to her shoulders. She was always conservatively dressed, with a fashionable skirt below her knees, a shawl with a bull fighter on it to protect her against the wind, a few rings which looked expensive from a distance, little make-up, very presentable' he said.

'Wow, it appears you enjoyed your "observation duties", Lolita said jokingly.

'Umh, don't know about that. But, on one occasion, we followed her home. She lives in a middle class, well-to-do suburb. She does not appear to be Charles's girlfriend – he hasn't got any girlfriend. She is a high-class hooker, available to the wealthy,' he said.

'Is Charles wealthy? He does not strike me as a logical candidate to be considered a regular client of a VIP hooker,' Jesper opined.

'Yes, you got me there. I do not know, but somehow we will find out later what the story is,' Hayden surmised.

'So, we have already established that there is a close link between the two conspirators. Presumably, what they discussed on their long walks is part of Coppelli's preparation in ascertaining a pattern in the President's lifestyle and in observing how he responds to calamities,' Lolita said.

A calamity happened a few days later, in late September 2027.

9

DURHAM, NORTH CAROLINA.

It was devastation on a grand scale. The attacker had stormed an Episcopal Church when the overwhelmingly black congregation was seated, and the church was full. The pastor stood at the altar with outstretched hands and was about to start his weekly sermon when the attacker burst into the church in combat gear. He had exchanged his casual attire for combat gear in his car, parked across the road with the key still in the ignition switch. After the carnage, police found that the attacker had two revolvers, a rapid-fire Kalashnikov rifle, two grenades and several sharp knives. He was armed for war. For him, it was a war and he considered himself to be a soldier, or a mercenary.

When bursting into the church, the attacker started to shoot indiscriminately. The first person killed was the pastor who stood exposed at the altar. A cacophony of terrible screams ripped through the Church and people started to run in all directions. Some worshippers even ran in the direction of the attacker, and they were mowed down instantly. Blood was smeared on the walls of the Church and dripped from the cross of Jesus Christ that hung above the altar. It formed a rivulet of dirty wax-like substance that zig zagged its way like a snake on the paved granite stones of the church.

One of the parishioners had been able to send a mobile

phone message to the local police station and within a matter of minutes, the sirens could be heard across the city. The attacker continued to fire. When he heard the sirens, he went systematically from pew to pew to see if anyone pretended to be dead. He would shoot them if they showed any sign of life. But some parishioners were able to save themselves that way and would later recall the horror to the police, the television journalists, and the world. When the sirens stopped, a battalion of police officers stormed the church and fired wildly at the attacker, who calmly took a revolver from its holster and committed suicide. Before doing so, he surveyed his work, and he was satisfied with the carnage for which he was responsible. Before he committed suicide, he had started to count the dead, but could not finish the job.

He had murdered thirty-seven people and an additional 46 were wounded badly, some would still die, increasing the fatality rate. Television vans arrived not long after the police, and journalists commenced to interview bystanders and a few survivors, who commented upon the horror. It would be the top news story for a few weeks, but not much longer because shootings are regular events in the United States.

To say that the city and the nation were in shock is an understatement. The church was a crime scene for a long time. A police tape cordoned off the scene of the crime, but people had been allowed to place flowers at the entrance to the church. Within a few hours of the attack, the steps leading to the nave and chancel of the church were covered with flowers, and photos of the victims were displayed on the fence that separated the church from the street. A quartet played funeral music nearby to console the souls of the victims and to placate the anger of the survivors.

✶✶✶✶✶

Within five minutes of the suicide of the attacker, I received a phone call from the senior police officer at the scene.

'Mr. Bentleys, there has been a shooting in an Episcopal Church in Durham, North Carolina. Most victims are African Americans. I have decided to ring you because you may want to inform the President. We do not want him to find out about this from the television or some obnoxious journalist. The killer appears to be a white supremacist,' he said.

'My God, not another shooting! Thank you for informing me. I will contact the President immediately,' I said, and terminated the call. I soon realized that I did not even ask the officer about the identity of the murderer and the number of people killed in the massacre.

I hurried to the Oval Office to inform the President of this dreadful news.

'Mr. President, there has been another shooting. A white supremacist murdered many parishioners in an Episcopal Church in Durham, North Carolina, which is frequented by African Americans. You need to address the nation soon. There will be many demands to curb the use and possession of guns.'

The President, visibly shocked, immediately called a meeting of his speech writers and told them to jot down a few thoughts. He asked his secretaries to contact the police department in Durham to find out more information about the shooting.

A few hours later, the President addressed the nation.

'My fellow Americans, I am very saddened by the unspeakable horrific event that took place earlier today in an Episcopal Church in Durham, North Carolina. The families of the victims are understandably devastated, and I would like to offer them my condolences. I know that, in doing so, I will not be able to lessen their pain and anger. I completely understand if they are tortured with feelings of revenge, but right now the best thing I can do is to comfort them. The federal government will do whatever needs to be done to provide solace and assistance to these families and the city where this atrocity took pace.

'I expect that now there will be renewed calls for gun control. It is a perennial issue that comes up each time we endure a major calamity like this one. I fully favour proposals to make substantial changes to the weapons registration system. It is a problem that has plagued this country for a long time, and now politicians need to do something substantial because the memory of these victims will otherwise haunt us forever. As responsible citizens, we can no longer turn a blind eye and rely on the Constitution to continue as in the past. At the very least, substantial changes should be made to our gun laws to honour the victims of this tragedy. I repeat that these changes should not be cosmetic but must represent real progress in this area. I will be sending a proposal to Congress in the next couple of days. And while I am not able right now to share the details of my proposals with you, I want to assure you that change is definitively on the way.

'On Thursday of next week, I will travel to Durham, North Carolina and visit the scene of this massacre. I will have meetings with the city's representatives to convey our intention to assist in any way we can. I also want to meet the families of the victims and embrace their loved ones to give them courage and strength in these tough times and to share in their loss. It is the only way to grieve in this country.

'I would like to ask all Americans to join me in a prayer to beg the Almighty to alleviate the pain that has been caused by the attacker. There is no room for extremists in this country that is based on the promise of freedom and equality for all citizens,' the President said.

Apart from the Atheist Association, which objected to the President's invocation of the Almighty, the speech was warmly received, even though the most critical commentators regarded it as not much more than a string of platitudes. But they were welcome platitudes, and the President knew how to offer them to the American public and to make them palatable.

*****

Durham's police commissioner, flanked by the Mayor and his Deputy and the Governor of North Carolina, gave a long press conference a few hours after the massacre, and he answered most of the questions of the assembled journalists, at least as far as the information was available to him. The commissioner revealed that the murderer, whose name was Petrov, served as a former devoted member of the Ku Klux Klan. He was a known white supremacist, who had already spent some time in jail for attacks on African American citizens. But he was not deemed to be a major risk to the community, and he had been released only six months before the shooting on a good behaviour bond. The police, ruling out terrorism, expressed the opinion that it was a racially charged attack on a group of peaceful people who were serving the God of their choice on a Sunday morning, a bright day in late September 2027. It was another horrible story in the history of the United States. A stain on the reputation of a great nation!

One of the journalists, an expert in the judicial enforcement system, asked whether the State's parole system was broken, and what the politicians intended to do about this.

The police commissioner yielded the floor to the Governor, who also took part in the press conference.

'The system is not broken, but it certainly failed our citizens on this occasion. I propose to first establish a committee to review the terrible events that happened here today, and I will ask it to make appropriate recommendations, also with regards to the parole system. If the system needs to be strengthened to prevent such massacres in the future, I will recommend the

State legislature adopt the committee's proposed changes,' he said.

*****

In the days after the attack, there were more DNA Movement protests throughout the country, some more violent than others, and it became an unstoppable wave that swept over the Nation. Many statues of historical figures who profited from discrimination against African Americans were destroyed in the process. Charles had never been busier. The catastrophe in North Carolina hardened his resolve to seek revenge to punish the United States for its divisive and discriminatory racial policies.

10

CHARLES DUDLEY DID NOT HAVE A GIRLFRIEND, AT LEAST NOT that I am aware of. By that I mean that he did not have a *steady* girlfriend, because he was no stranger to the art of lovemaking and the pursuit of available girls. However, although he was blatantly promiscuous – something that the three Secret Service officers were well familiar with – he had a special girl on "call". The girl was always available and ready to pamper him, and look after his sexual needs, when he approached her. Her name was Martha – I prefer not to disclose her surname – and while she visited Charles from time to time in his derelict apartment, she preferred to service him in her own luxury apartment. It was the girl the Secret Service officers had observed visiting Charles in his apartment.

Martha was a VIP escort. Politicians, businesspeople, professional people, even priests hired her to provide them with specialized massage services, and more. Although she charged a lot of money for her services, she always had a steady stream of wealthy clients, and admirers, willing to pay a decent price for quality service.

About a year ago, she had been hired by Charles to provide him with her special and sought-after services. Of course, Charles did not fit the profile of her wealthy clientele. He was a brash young man with radical ideas and even bigger aspirations. It is precisely this trait that attracted her to him. Charles became a regular visitor, and he was still seeing her a year after his first visit.

Martha was an attractive, good-looking girl who exuded the appearance of innocence. When young people, like university students, boisterously boasted about their sexual exploits as if it were the only topic of interest, she exhibited reserve and restraint. She did not laugh hysterically, like most people present, when a male student told a dirty joke or described a successful pursuit of a female student. She would smile but did not take part in the brouhaha that inevitably followed the lurid revelations of her friends. In matters of love and sex, she was discreet, and she never gave the impression that she was an experienced provider of sexual services for hire.

She got into this industry by accident or design, whatever interpretation you favour. She certainly was a willing participant in this industry because she craved money to buy the best things in life, like diamonds, luxury handbags, fine clothes, gourmet meals, exotic holidays, plays, concerts, and opera performances. She liked opera and classical concerts; she enjoyed the robust performances of the opera singers, especially The Three Tenors, and she admired the skills of the musicians. She particularly liked to listen to the New Year's Concert from Vienna which focuses on the magnificent music of the Strauss family. Although she preferred classical music, she would also listen to, and enjoy, the European Song Contest, a gateway to the world of modern pop. She played the piano as a child, but she was clearly not good enough to take it further. When she was ten years old, her parents even suggested that she might want to become a luthier because this profession would at least enable her to maintain an interest in the world of music. Instead, she reluctantly finished high school, but she had no intention to remain a pauper for another three years or more by going to college. She did, however, retain her interest in music and she became knowledgeable about classical music, musical performances, and instruments. She would later discover that music was an excellent accompaniment to her chosen business activities.

Her parents could not sustain Martha's extravagant lifestyle and fulfill her insatiable desires. They did not have the necessary financial resources to purchase the expensive luxury goods which she wanted to buy during her frequent shopping sprees. Her father was a public servant in a boring and uninteresting accounting job, and her mother worked as a Senior Teacher's Aide in the local high school. They were middle class, not too poor, but also not rich enough to spend it on luxury.

In her final year of high school, unbeknownst to her parents, Martha secretly visited a nearby warehouse, which had been converted into a movie set for a porn production. She had observed the activities of the porn stars for some time, and she thought she could do their song and dance routines even better than them. She considered that she possessed the physical qualities and emotional charms to make an impact in the industry. The production's Director granted her an interview and an audition.

When the Director asked about her parents, upbringing, school, and sexual prowess, Martha reluctantly admitted that she had no experience in sexual matters at all. A promiscuous lifestyle was not promoted, or condoned, in the Catholic convent school that she attended. When the interviewer suggested it was necessary to engage in sex acts with him to ascertain her ability and willingness to succumb to lust and basic needs, she admitted that she was still a virgin. The interviewer, although he feigned surprise, was excited to be able to deflower this available girl. Martha was asked to take off her clothes slowly, leaving only her bra and underpants which would be removed at the right time by the interviewer. She happily auditioned for a part in a porn movie, provisionally entitled *The Horny Homemaker*, but she never got an offer for a role. The interviewer told her that she lacked passion, enthusiasm and seduction skills and was therefore not suitable for a role in the movie. Martha did not dwell on this rejection for long. She was entrepreneurial and determined to succeed in her chosen occupation.

She was a blonde beauty who rarely used any make-up products. Her teeth were pearly white; it was obvious she had never found the need to visit a dentist's chair. Her blue eyes sparkled like a diamond; her long legs were her main asset that immediately attracted a bevy of customers willing to pay good money to spend a few hours with her. She made a decent living. However, she was not willing to succumb to the demands and pursuits of just anyone. She would carefully select her customers. And she had chosen Charles as one of her clients. It was his enthusiasm, his desire to change the world for the better, his willingness to sacrifice himself for the greater good, and his intellectual prowess that mesmerized her. She saw in him a good prospect for the future. He was an insurance project and she wanted to invest in it.

*****

She had received a phone call from Charles who summoned her for his weekly check-up.

Charles always uses this medical language, like a physical "check-up". Surely, this is a sentimental and inaccurate description of the service she would provide, she thought.

Although she was not a medical practitioner, she certainly intended to examine Charles's physical treasures, not for the purpose of curing a disease or making a diagnosis, but to stimulate him into an exciting sexual adventure.

'Yes, Charles, I am available, but I would like you to come to my apartment. You know I am not comfortable in your place. You really need to do some spring cleaning if you want me to visit you there. I will be waiting for you in my apartment. Shall we say at 5 in the afternoon, today?' she suggested.

'I'll be there at that time. See you then,' he replied, and he disconnected the call.

Martha's apartment was in an appealing, safe neighbourhood, opposite a park. To the left of the park was a science museum which boasted a skeleton of an extinct dinosaur. A heated swimming pool had recently been built in the righthand corner of the park. In summer, it would become a beehive of activity with screaming children and anxious yelling parents. There would be a congregation of prams and babbling parents who proudly showed off their babies. They would complain about the prohibitive cost of baby nappies and talk amongst themselves about the best baby formula. There was also a swing nearby which was constantly in use, and a sand pit for infants to get dirty in.

The apartment was nicely decorated with lots of plants. A solitary palm tree which proudly exhibited its green fronds was standing in a corner of the living room, waiting to be joined by a companion. A bunch of pink orchids luxuriated in a vase on the dinner table, covered with a red tablecloth which depicted a Persian wedding. The furnishings were of the chic shabby variety. The dishes were stacked neatly in the dishwasher where they would be washed later in the night. The kitchen area had been sanitized thoroughly with Glen20; the bottle was still in the washbasin. Charles did not realize that this product was available in Kansas City. He had seen it on sale everywhere in Australia when he visited that country a few years ago after he finished high school. But it was the first time he saw it in the United States. He made a note to ascertain the name of the company that imported this product. The sofa had been newly upholstered just a few weeks before. A dry-cleaning company had recently cleaned all other furniture.

There was a huge portrait of Ernesto "Che" Guevara on the wall. Che was grinning and enjoying his grand tour of Colombia trying to incite people into a revolution. Martha was fully conversant with Che's story. She had been an intelligent high school student in a girls-only Catholic convent school, where she did not learn a lot about religion, but more about things which were never discussed in class, like sex, communist infiltrations in South-East Asian and South American countries, revolutions, and Guevara. On several occasions, she had tried to sneak out of the convent during the day to rendezvous with a couple of boys who looked promising, but she was always apprehended by a school security guard who returned her to the classroom where she had to endure a sermon of complaints.

She decided not to attend college, but to invest in a business which she called *Beating Hearts* and promoted it locally in Kansas in community newspapers. In advertisements, she described the business as an up-market counselling and support service that would go the extra mile to ensure the happiness of its clients. Satisfaction would be guaranteed and the hygiene standards in her salon – which she did not have since she used her bedroom as her office – would exceed industry expectations and standards.

She had a crude screening process to keep undesirable clients away from the business. Anyone with a tattoo, irrespective where it had been painted on the body, was an "undesirable" applicant for her. An applicant with decayed teeth was also not welcome. Her clients needed to have at least a high school education, if not higher education, and be polite, considerate, and well-mannered. She would always organize a Skype session to evaluate the applicant before taking him as a client. It was a one-person business, and she regarded herself as a classy escort, intelligent, knowledgeable, witty, and willing to accompany well-educated and wealthy men to dazzling receptions, followed by adventurous sex which would usually last until after breakfast the next day, when they would be asked to leave, because she had to prepare herself for the next client. She was, of course, willing to consider repeat business, and Charles was a repeat client.

Over the period of one year, Martha got attached to Charles and she stopped asking for payment. She would be willing to provide her services for free when he needed a check-up. He needed a check-up tonight.

✶✶✶✶✶

Charles parked his rundown car in the carpark of her building and climbed the stairs to the third floor. There was no elevator, which kept the corporate strata fees low. This was welcomed by most of the residents, but some of the older residents had expressed a wish to move to another apartment building with an elevator because, as they got older, climbing became a difficult and arduous chore. Some residents had discovered the unusual comings and goings in Martha's apartment, at odd hours of the day and night, and suspected, without being able to provide proof, that she was involved in a lucrative business, selling herself to well-to-do clients. What prevented them from seeking alternative accommodation, was the exorbitant cost of moving.

Charles knocked on the door and took a step back. He wanted to have a long look at Martha when she opened the door. When he visited her the first time, America was still recovering from the deadly Covid-19 pandemic, when everyone had been indoctrinated to practise social distancing but, on this occasion, taking a step backwards had nothing to do with the pandemic, and everything to do with the anticipated joy he would derive from looking at her attire, which he expected to be sexy, hopefully see-through, and always captivating.

Martha opened the door, first ajar with the security lock still in place. From experience, she knew that unwelcome visitors sometimes took the liberty to invade her private domain. When she saw Charles, a smile formed on her face and her teeth started to flash. She was already dressed in a blue negligée; it would not be difficult for Charles to remove her clothing and secure her services quickly. He felt his penis stiffen in his pants.

'Welcome Charles, I assume you want your usual service?' she said.

'Yes, the usual. Thank you,' he retorted.

'You look lovely, as always,' he said. Charles started to undress. He removed first his trousers, then his shirt and finally his underwear except his underpants, which was Martha's job. Martha climbed on him and caressed him from top to toe. Her fine fingers disappeared into his luxurious long hairdo, which resembled a dense forest of thin and tall trees, and she withdrew them occasionally to kiss him softly and gently on the eyes, ears, cheeks, and stomach. When she arrived at his private parts, she grasped his penis with her left hand and took it out of his pants as if it was a big trophy. She worked her way down and removed his underpants in one swoop. She rolled over and he kissed her lovely breasts gently and played with her hair. She opened her legs, and he inserted his penis into her vagina, and they passionately started to make love. It only ended when Charles was satisfied. They stayed in bed for a while longer and looked at each other as a couple of satisfied teenagers who just experienced sex for the first time.

'What do you think of the DNA Movement?' he asked.

'Why would you like to know what I think about it?' she inquired.

'If something were to happen to me, you should contact a friend of mine, he is an Italian American, Coppelli Colone. He teaches the history of ideas and jurisprudence courses in the University of Southern Kansas'.

'What is jurisprudence?' she asked.

'Uhm, don't ask tough questions, Martha,' he answered dejectedly.

'I would also like you to give him an envelope.

'It is in my pants. I'll get it for you. It is confidential, of course. Will you give it to him if something were to happen to me?' he asked insistently.

'Nothing is going to happen to you,' she said emphatically.

'Do not bet on it,' he replied.

'I promise. I promise. I promise, Mr. Charles Roderick Dudley,' she affirmed. She turned to him and kissed him passionately on the lips.

'There is something else, Martha, if something happens to me, would you also please inform the President of the United States?', he asked.

'You mean, Desmond Raymond Clarkenson?'

'Yes, that's him.'

'But Charles, I do not have a bee-line to the President of the United States. I am just a luxury hooker, as you well know.'

'Just promise you will do it,' he said.

'Sure, I will do it. Anything else?', she asked exasperatingly.

He did not reply but he started to kiss her in preparation for another check-up session.

11

THE THREE SECRET SERVICE AGENTS AND I WERE WAITING impatiently at the check-out counter of a food store. We were on our way to Martha's apartment who had agreed to grant us an interview. We had not disclosed what we wanted to talk about but had offered to provide proof of our professional roles, which Martha decided to check before agreeing to meet with us. She rang the United States Federal Civil Service information number – it was not the first time!

'My name is Martha. Three Secret Service Officers want to interview me this afternoon. Is it possible for you to confirm that they are indeed officers of the Service? Their names are ...', she asked the receptionist before he interrupted her.

'I am sorry, Martha, but we do not comment upon the identity of Secret Service agents over the phone. The best way forward is for you to sight their accreditation papers. It is a serious offence for anyone to falsely claim to be a member of the Secret Service. The offence is compounded if false identity papers are used to gain access to you,' he helpfully commented.

But a simple telephone call to the switchboard of the White House revealed my identity as the Press Secretary to the President.

Following her telephone calls, Martha sighted our accreditations during a video Skype session and, also, decided to check our credentials upon arrival at her apartment. We had told her we would arrive around three in the afternoon, but it could be later because of the inclement weather conditions.

My decision to stopover at a food store was as impulsive as it was unwise. I wanted to buy some donuts which I would share with my Secret Service friends. Our patience was severely tested because in front of us at the check-out counter was an elderly gentleman who behaved in accordance with his own rules of purchase.

'It is difficult and frustrating to be patient when you are impatient,' I said to my friends.

The older man in front of us had a trolley full of groceries. The man carefully inspected every product and slowly put it on the belt. He methodically arranged the groceries on the belt: the dairy products and meat were placed in one corner, and bread, cereals, biscuits, and grain in another. He designated a place for the vegetables, fish, and the tin cans of assorted sizes, small, large, thin, and thick. The daily newspaper was placed on top of the groceries to protect them against imaginable and unimaginable diseases that otherwise would spoil his groceries.

'It is as if the man is organizing a display in a recently built custom-made kitchen,' I said to the Secret Service team.

'Yes, shall we arrest him for obstruction?' Hayden asked.

'Very funny. I think we'll suffer for a while. It is always the same sorry story. None of the other counters have a checkout person and a queue is rapidly building up here. I think we should arrest the manager of the store,' I said jokingly.

The belt moved and a divider was placed behind the elderly

man's groceries. The checkout person scanned every product and then threw it into a plastic bag, supplied by the customer. The old man immediately rearranged the groceries in the bag in accordance with a well-rehearsed strategy. The checkout person, observing this phobia, then tried to ensure that goods of the same family would stay together, but she could obviously not guarantee that this would occur. When the loading had finished, the elderly customer took out a thick wallet full of credit cards and coins. The wallet also contained a discount voucher which he had forgotten to give to the checkout person. Unfortunately, he was told that it could not be used anymore because the transaction had already been finalized. Disappointed he put it back into his wallet. He then took out a credit card, fumbled a bit with it and inserted it into the designated slot in the banking machine. Somehow, there was a problem. It was taken out, cleaned, and inserted again. But again, to no avail because it did not work. My colleagues and I counted three credit cards before one worked in the store's banking device.

Our patience was almost exhausted, when the man started to talk incoherently about the procedure involved in getting money out of the store's banking device. The checkout person politely answered the man's questions without demonstrating how the device would work for this purpose.

'So, do you need some money, sir?' she asked. 'No,' he replied. 'I was simply curious how it worked because I have seen other people asking for money. I thought you have to visit a bank to get money,' he said.

Finally, his hands clasped the handle of the trolley and he moved away.

I expected that, when we finished shopping, the shop's manager would send a request to fill in a survey about our shopping experience. I was not enthused about this because, these days, when buying a service or goods, it is likely that the buyer will receive such a request to complete a survey. While the survey might indicate that it will take only 5 minutes of your time, my experience showed it could easily take half an hour. Thus, if customers were to complete the survey for all services they received or goods bought, they could spend the better part of the day working for businesses that were unlikely to read or heed the results of the survey anyway. Indeed, there would be no time anymore to shop in the first place. At worst, these requests were window-dressing exercises and at best, they indicated the existence of incompetent management. I was frustrated.

The checkout person gawked at us, and she obviously read our mind.

'I am sorry it took so long, sir,' she said.

'Never mind,' I retorted.

*****

It was just after 4 in the afternoon when we arrived at Martha's apartment. It was already getting darker and soon the tepid afternoon sun would disappear behind the grey clouds that congregated in the skies above Washington DC like soldiers, in their green battle gear, returning to their barracks. The clouds formed a disciplined battalion of fighter planes with outstretched wings to protect the city. The trip which we thought would take no more than half an hour turned out to be a 90-minute ordeal. During the last three days, it had snowed heavily and now it started to melt, leaving the roads slippery and dangerous to navigate. A few erratic drivers terrorized the road. They revved up their engines to make deafening and screeching noises that disturbed the afternoon peace and made the few winter birds fly away. The cars ploughed into the remaining snow and sleet with unstoppable zeal. I was afraid that they would hit my new service car that came with my job. If something were to happen, the insurance, of course, would reimburse the White House's carpool, and I would get a replacement car. It was the time that would be lost filling in forms and phoning around that worried me. I regretted not having requested a driver from the pool to take me to Martha's apartment, but it was too late now. In any event, I was on a mission that required secrecy and privacy.

The three Secret Service agents and I finally arrived at the apartment building which appeared to be well maintained. In front of us was a low-rise building which three floors. All apartments were separated from each other with a flexi glass separator like those you find on a cruise ship to separate the cabins. I counted a total of twenty-four apartments. A few of the residents were already arriving home from their shopping trips, and some returned from a day's work in their offices or businesses. The residents were middle class Americans, well-to-do but not excessively rich. Most residents, I expected, cared for their properties which they owned, and all appeared to be middle-aged in their fifties or sixties. I could only see two young people entering one of the apartments.

They are probably the children of the people who live in the apartment, I thought.

It was an apartment block without an elevator, but when I walked around the building to familiarize myself with the place, I discovered it also boasted a heated swimming pool at the back, so it would be possible for residents to swim most of the year. I also noticed that a hot spa was sitting invitingly on one of the sides of the swimming pool. An elderly man with a young boy, probably a grandchild, were luxuriating in the spa, but their features were hazy because they were partially hidden by the emitted steam. The man's arms were lovingly spread out to protect the boy. I observed that there was also a swimming pool complex in the park opposite the apartment building, which the residents of the apartment block would not have to use because they had their own heated pool.

Martha's apartment was on the third floor, which was the top floor. From her balcony at the back, with one small table and two chairs, one could see the park and its maze where children would play hide and seek. A small pond nestled snugly in the middle of the park. A few arctic ground squirrels were playing on the shore of the pond.

'This is an unusual sight because the only arctic ground squir-

rels I had recently observed dillydallied in southwestern Alaska,' I thought. I made a mental note to find out how the squirrels migrated to Kansas City.

I first knocked on the door, but then I saw a bell knob on the right which I pushed. The sound reminded me of a Bell Tower concert in a medieval Tuscan village in Italy. It was pleasant and effective, and its tone lovingly embraced the apartment filling it inside with warmth. I immediately heard a person rummaging in the apartment followed by an energetic run to the door.

The door opened and Martha stood in front of us.

'You are the Press Secretary of the President. And you must be the Secret Service guys – you are spies, aren't you? Welcome. It is the first time that I see you in the flesh, so to say. Richard is your name? You look surprisingly like the person who, every second day, sings the praises of the President during these news conferences in the White House,' she said.

'Indeed, I am that person, Ms. Martha. May we come in to have a chat with you?'

She did not immediately reply. She looked me over carefully.

'Do you honestly believe all these things you tell people about the President in your media meetings?' she asked.

'Of course, my job is to tell people accurately and correctly what is on the President's mind and what policies are pursued by the Administration,' I reassured her.

My reassurance somehow did not convince her because disbelief was written all over her face. She thought that my answer was nothing else but a white lie, but she refrained from taking the matter further.

'Please come in and make yourself comfortable. Would you like some Lavazza coffee and special Oreo cookies bought today? I also made an apple strudel, and that would go well with some fabulous ice cream. What do you think?' she asked graciously.

I felt as if I was in a restaurant and the waiter asked me to sample the products sold by the establishment.

'Just some coffee will be fine,' I said. But the three Secret Service agents opted for coffee, apple strudel and ice cream.

Martha hastily rearranged five chairs around the dinner table. We did not wait to be invited to sit down and immediately occupied four chairs.

I took an immediate liking to Martha. I thought she was friendly, vivacious, and inquisitive.

'What can I do for you, Mr. President-Minder?' she asked politely.

She was attractively dressed, in a yellow skirt depicting African elephants; the dress modestly covered her knees.

Martha took the only remaining seat at the window. She observed my interest in her skirt, or was it the elephants?

'I bought this when I went on an African safari last year. It was my second overseas trip. I enjoyed watching the animals in their natural habitat, the ambiance and the freedom that goes with searching for the big game animals that roam in the wild. My only other overseas trip was a compulsory coming-of-age trip to Europe with perfunctory visits to London and Paris,' she said.

She failed to mention that the trip was financed by one of her admirers, Richard thought.

'And this sweater,' she explained proudly, 'I have knitted myself.'

'It goes very well with the blouse.'

I reminded myself that I was not here for a fashion parade, but it was necessary to listen to her for a while to thaw her reluctance to speak. I looked at her shoes; they had high heels which were made from red cows' leather. Her lipstick suited her appearance and blended in well with her face. Her lips became redder when she smiled, but that must certainly be an optical illusion. The attraction was reciprocated because she flashed her teeth and smiled when she talked to me. Or was she surveying a potential client?

On another occasion, I would have invited her to dinner. It is always nice to get to know a person, their history, and aspirations. But not now because I had a job to do.

'Any hint of improper behaviour, even if untrue, would ruin or certainly diminish the President's chances for re-election,' I reminded myself.

There was no way I was going to jettison the Rules Book because it would result in the media devouring me and the President, like a hungry crocodile prowling in the river looking for a good supper.

Of course, I was aware that Martha was a hooker, indeed a high-class hooker, and it was necessary to keep an appropriate distance from her.

I reminded myself of the story of General Joseph Hooker, who during the American Civil War commanded the armies of the Union, unsuccessfully. He is remembered as an indecisive General who was decisively defeated by a smaller army led by General Robert E Lee at the Battle of Chancellorsville in the first week of May 1863. But there is another reason for Hooker's notoriety. To improve the morale of his troops he encouraged an army of girls, known as the 'Hooker's Brigade' to follow his army. During weekends, he would invite this army to the barracks and organize an orgy as a reward for the hard work of his soldiers. It was an egregious example of depraved morality. It is no wonder that, soon after his disastrous military defeat, Hooker was replaced by President Abraham Lincoln. So, the General lent his name to a slang word that describes a prostitute.

'Well, he clearly contributed to the development of the English language. And it appears to have been a lasting contribution,' I remarked to myself.

'Martha, do you know a person by the name of Charles?' I asked.

'You mean Charles Roderick Dudley?'

'Aha.'

'Yes, why do you want to know? she asked.

'I am here on official government business, and I would like to discuss something of the greatest importance to this country with you. Do you think you are able to keep secrets even if they pertain to Charles?'

'Is he in trouble?'

'Not yet, but you know that he is involved in the DNA Movement. That is, of course, not a crime, but incitement to hatred is, including encouraging people to destroy monuments and statues, like they did right here in Washington DC, in Minneapolis and Boston, and other cities where a statue of Christopher Columbus was decapitated, and his head thrown in a river.'

'Did Charles ever mention a person by the name of Coppelli to you?' Hayden asked.

'As a matter of fact, yes, he mentioned that name to me,' she answered.

'We need to know what Charles and Coppelli discussed and what their plans are. Are you willing to help us find out?'

'Why would I want to do that? What is in it for me?'

'Martha, you know that your business is an escort business, but it has not been registered for that purpose. It could be shut down immediately. Obviously, we do not want to do that,' I said.

I did not feel happy about my threat, but it had to be done.

'You do not have to disclose any confidential information about Charles. Right now, I merely want to know what Charles told you about Coppelli. I know Charles is a compassionate person, and it would be good for us to know who he wants to help. Perhaps the government could also contribute to his cause.'

Martha did not feel comfortable in the company of these four important government people. She was out of her league.

'Well, Charles asked me to give an envelope to Coppelli if something were to happen to him,'

'… if something were to happen to Charles?'

'Yes,'

'Do you still have that envelope?'

'Yes, I assume you want it. If I give it to you, I will be left in peace?' she asked.

'Absolutely, Martha,'

Deception always works, especially if you are backed up by authority, I thought.

She went into her bedroom and withdrew an envelope from one of the drawers.

'Here it is,' she said.

'Charles is a compassionate person, and extremely loyal and good-natured. He is obviously concerned about Coppelli Colonc. He wants to protect him.

'Coppelli?'

'Yes, Coppelli'.

'Thank you, Martha, you have been an immense help. You have a lovely place here,' I said.

Martha relaxed a bit, and she became loquacious as if a great burden had been lifted from her body.

'There is more. Charles also asked me to contact the President of the United States if something were to happen to him,'

'You mean, contact Desmond Raymond Clarkenson?'

'Sure, he is the President of the United States,' she said.

'What are you supposed to say to the President?' I asked.

'I have no idea. Charles just asked me to communicate his demise to the President.'

'Is it really your intention to honour your promise to Charles to contact the President, if something were to happen to him?'

'Of course not, but it was the only way to pacify Charles, so I promised to do this for him,' Martha said.

The Secret Service agents and I pretended not to be too interested in this disclosure, but we knew instinctively that Martha had just told us an important piece of information. But the information was still a jigsaw puzzle because we did not fathom the reason for Charles's unusual request.

The Secret Service agents and I thanked Martha for her co-operation and for the delicious coffee, apple strudel and ice-cream. I wished I would be able to take Martha out to dinner, one day.

'I hope to see you again, Richard,' she said as we parted.

We pensively walked back to our limousine. The weather was changing, and it started to drizzle. This made the return trip to the White House hazardous, but our thoughts were on the information we had just received from Martha.

'If something were to happen to Charles, this envelope – which we have not yet opened – is to be given to Coppelli, and Martha is expected to contact the President of the United States,' I said loudly.

'Lolita and gentlemen, we have work to do when we get back to the office,' I announced.

12

COPPELLI'S LECTURE THEATRE WAS ONLY A SHORT WALK FROM his office to the left of the main quadrangle, in a purpose-built block with lecture rooms on the sides, accommodating up to a hundred students, and an in-door garden in the middle. The garden provided a peaceful oasis for students to reflect on their studies and for couples to smooth over any problems in their relationships.

Coppelli never wore a tie when instructing his students. When he started his academic career in the '90s, most academics wore a tie, typically the tie of the institution or college that employed them. Some even had their academic regalia on when teaching or seeing students. They saw themselves as the university equivalent of these pompous-looking barristers who walk the streets of the city in their black robes and grey wigs, carrying heavy files, on their way to the courthouse.

Eight weeks after the attack on the Episcopal Church in Durham, North Carolina, towards the end of November 2027, Coppelli was giving a lecture on Marxism and the Law to thirty-five students in his lecture theatre.

Some of his students interacted with the professor and his ideas and asked questions of him and made comments. Others looked terribly bored; their minds were already focusing on the winter holidays in the warm embraces of the Bahamas. The islands of the Bahamas were a traditional playground for adventurous students who wanted to get away from the tedious boredom sometimes encountered in universities. The students' union had organized a cheap getaway, chartering a few planes to take them to the playground paradise. It was the perfect tonic to shake off the stressful examination period which usually preceded trips to these idyllic islands.

Professor Colone always kept the door of the lecture theatre open. He mumbled something about air circulation, but his students suspected that their professor was vain because he was visibly enthralled when passers-by stopped to listen to his Socratic way of teaching.

Suddenly, a stranger brusquely appeared at the open door of the lecture theatre. A student later reported that the stranger looked disoriented. His face was not covered with a mask. His frightening eyes surveyed the room methodically and quickly.

'The intruder first looked at Coppelli as if he wanted to be certain he had selected the right lecture theatre,' the student reported.

'In his hands, he carried a rifle which the intruder nervously moved from one hand to the other as if he were involved in a marching band dancing routine.

'I saw that his waist was unusually thick. He may have had a suicide belt around his waist. His waist was casually covered with a stained blouse. I noticed at least three daggers and two pistols which had been securely positioned on a belt that held up his jeans. The stranger grinned as he was looking at our professor, Coppelli.

'For a fleeting moment, I thought the two knew each other, but I could be wrong about that,' the student said.

'There was a door at the opposite side of the lecture theatre, leading into the building's in-door garden. I decided to make a run for it. Happily, I am still alive. It may have been the best decision that I have made thus far,' the student told investigating police.

At the time of the intrusion, there was a heated debate between Coppelli and two students.

'Marxism predicts that, in an ideal society, law will disappear because there will be no need any longer for law in a classless society,' Coppelli argued. The two students disagreed with the Professor's prediction that, in an ideal society, law would disappear because it would not be needed anymore.

Most students were listening intently because the conversation had been going on for at least a quarter of an hour and there was no victor in sight. But when they saw the stranger at the door, a soul-destroying scream of anxiety went through the room, and it stopped Coppelli in mid-sentence.

'… he predicted a proletarian … What is happening?' he asked a student who was sitting in the front row. He had obviously not yet seen the stranger at the door. The student had the face of a dead pharaoh, already embalmed and ready for burial. He pointed anxiously to the door and remained glued to his chair.

Coppelli looked at the stranger and the formidable weapons in his hands and around his waist.

'What are you doing here? Is there anything we can do for you?' enquired a frightened Coppelli. He was trying to think of a way to pacify the stranger and abate this alarming situation.

While addressing the intruder, he indicated to the students, by waving his hands, that they should take shelter wherever they could find it. Coppelli pointed feverishly to the opposite door of the classroom as it provided an opportunity to flee from this potential calamity.

He later explained to the police, during the debriefing, that he remained polite because, when someone is threatening you with a rifle, it does not pay to be unfriendly or antagonistic.

The stranger at the door hesitated for a moment when he heard steps in the corridor. He turned around to see where the noise came from. Some students used this moment of hesitation to run to the opposite door of the lecture theatre. Their attempt at escaping became a stampede which hindered their objective of fleeing. The noise in the corridor became louder and louder and came closer and closer. There were screaming voices and telephones started to ring everywhere. Pandemonium was taking over the building. Soon the police would be here, and there was a job to be done before that time.

The stranger started his killing spree. He fired at any student who was moving or dared to flee. Surprisingly, Coppelli, not really knowing what to do, was not hit in the pandemic orgy of violence that surrounded him. But he was not waiting to be slaughtered. When the stranger reviewed his killing progress, Coppelli jumped onto him and frantically started to struggle with the intruder, always trying to ensure that the rifle would be pointed upwards and away from him and the students. He implored some frightened staff members who had reached the lecture theatre to help him, but they all fled in horror, disoriented and afraid for their life. No one wanted to become a hero. Coppelli valiantly tried to wrestle the rifle from the stranger's hand. The stranger pushed and shoved and directed his rifle at the fleeing students. The steps in the corridor became louder; snipers took up their positions in the corridor of the building, and soon the police would reach the lecture theatre. Suddenly, a fatal shot was fired, and the intruder collapsed. He let out a terrible scream and died on the spot.

There was blood everywhere, on the walls, on students' clothes, on the furniture. Tables were upturned, and papers strewn everywhere. Some survivors made gurgling noises, and some were begging for help. The room looked like the living room left behind by the Manson family who murdered actor Sharon Tate and a few other people in 1969 in California – but on a bigger scale.

Soon after the final shots were fired, police and staff stormed into the lecture theatre which resembled a warzone and started the process of investigation and recovery. The ambulance services had been called and appeared at the door of the building within 15 minutes of the start of the killing spree. A huge crowd gathered on campus, students, and staff, but also retired people who wanted to be close to the developing story, and the parents of university students. Within a few minutes of the massacre, television stations in Kansas and throughout the United States were reporting on this calamity, the 7th mass shooting of the year.

A student in Coppelli's classroom, who miraculously had not been hit, told the police and the television station that their professor, Coppelli Colone, had disregarded his own welfare and safety by tackling the stranger and heroically protecting his students. Coppelli was immediately hailed as a hero who had saved most of his students from an ignominious death. The television reporter praised the academic who had his picture taken, looking haggard and fatigued. It was a riveting piece of television which was replayed many times during the week following the shooting. Coppelli was invited to a formal live interview on Sixty Minutes to be held on the following Sunday. When the University heard about this interview, the Dean of his Faculty had been able to convince Coppelli to take a bath and dress conservatively.

'Once you have taken a hot bath, you will be able to think more logically after this terrible ordeal,' he had said.

It was the first time in a month that Coppelli felt the water warming his body. It felt surprisingly good and soothing. He promised himself that he would do it more often but, if experience was an indication, his promises were not always acted upon. But on this occasion, Coppelli looked presentable during the interview, and any imperfections could easily be attributed to the massacre and the near-death experience.

The President, Desmond Raymond Clarkenson, sent his personal condolences to the families of the victims and expressed his gratitude to the police and all those who helped contain this calamity. On television, he indicated he would visit the University in the coming days to comfort the parents of those who had died. In total, fifteen students lost their lives, and seven were injured badly, with three in intensive care. But for the actions of Coppelli, the whole class would have been slaughtered.

The President indicated that he and the Secretary of State intended to personally thank the heroic professor who saved so many students. He said he had instructed the Secretary to bestow the highest Bravery Medal of the United States on the professor during their visit to the University. The courage of the professor became the talking point in the households of the United States. Coppelli was also feted as a hero in the Tuscan village where he was born in Italy and a street was named after him. He would receive the keys to the City of Florence whenever he decided to return to Italy.

'The actions of the professor are a permanent and visible reminder of the greatness of the American character,' the President said in a televised interview. The President would address the University community in its Conventions Centre, built five years ago with federal money. He would concentrate on the American traits of courage, selflessness, and compassion. He would celebrate all those heroes who are willing to make sacrifices to protect the lives of other people. The meeting and visit were organized for the end of the following week, the first week of December 2027.

The police easily identified the attacker as Charles Roderick Dudley, the leader of the DNA Movement. They found a Chase credit card in his wallet. He was an extremist, 31 years of age, who lived in a decrepit apartment building in Kansas City. He was unemployed and he stole food from the big food stores. The police portrayed him as a failed student, a no-hoper with extremely idealistic views of society. His mother had died a few years ago, a victim of leukemia. His father, who was interviewed on television, was visibly shaken and expressed his shame for the actions of his son. He asked for forgiveness and privacy, and he cried uncontrollably.

*****

The adulation and glorification of Coppelli's heroic deeds presented the investigating police team with a few dilemmas and many unanswered questions.

'Why did he attack the Coppelli classroom? In fact, on his way to Coppelli's room, Charles passed four other lecture theatres, all with more than thirty-five students. So, if he wanted to assassinate the greatest number of students, he could have burst into any of the other rooms. But he did not. Isn't that odd?' a police investigator asked.

'Perhaps Charles specifically selected Coppelli's classroom? If so, we need to find the reason for targeting this lecture theatre,' another investigator agreed.

The police investigators continued to speculate.

'According to the surviving students, Charles, before dying, screamed that America's leaders were "racists" and that the day of "revenge" had arrived. Is it possible that Charles, in becoming a martyr, wanted to highlight the pernicious racist nature of American society? But surely, if he wanted to fight racism, it could have been done in other ways, less dramatic, but equally effective?

'What other ways could have been used by the attacker, though? Martyrdom is a powerful, yet final, statement of the martyr. They die in the knowledge that, at least for a few days, the media would work overtime to highlight their vision.

'This has been the case throughout history. A good example of this were the Japanese kamikaze martyrs who committed suicide in return for a fleeting moment of glory. Aren't the Muslim terrorists using the same technique?' a police investigator asked.

'Of course, none of this explains why the Coppelli classroom was targeted.

'It is also a mystery as to why the attacker never shot Coppelli. Yes, he struggled with Charles, but it was Charles who died in the scuffle,' the investigator pointed out.

There were so many questions which the police could not answer.

The police speculated about the motives for the carnage. 'These fanatics have a victim mentality. It is always someone else who is responsible for their problems. They never blame themselves for their own situation.

'Considering Charles's involvement in the DNA Movement, it is likely that he wanted to address the sordid legacy of racial discrimination,' a police officer suggested.

'Yes, this is feasible. But, in any event, discrimination is at the heart of all decisions made by people. Indeed, we all discriminate all the time: what we eat, whom we marry, where to holiday. It is about making choices,' he opined

*****

When I heard about the massacre at the University of Southern Kansas, I decided to fly to Kansas City to help the police in their investigations. The police appreciated my intimate knowledge of Professor Colone and was interested in my views on Charles Dudley. My three Secret Service friends were also invited to assist the police in its investigation.

We listened intently to the discussions among the police investigators. Of course, my Secret Service friends and I knew about the connection between Charles and Coppelli. We had observed them for several weeks, tapped Charles's phone and we had been speculating about the plans of this unsavoury couple of misfits. But, at this stage, we refrained from communicating our suspicions to the police because there was nothing that could be proven.

Of course, the Secret Service was aware of the cryptic conversations between the two conspirators a few weeks before the massacre and now they understood better what might have been planned by Coppelli and Charles. But the details were still sketchy, with many missing parts. The evidence was merely conjectural, and much more was needed to arrest anyone.

The President would visit the University and he would meet Coppelli, the unlikely hero, who thus would have an opportunity to come close to the President. What, if anything, did he have in mind? There were still so many unknown angles to this story: was Charles prepared to sacrifice himself? Was his death planned or was it an accident? Was Charles shot by Coppelli, either intentionally or accidentally? If Coppelli was planning an attack on the President, how did he expect to leave the scene, if at all? Did Charles commit suicide? If so, what did he expect to gain from it?

'There are too many troubling questions, and the answers are speculative,' Hayden repeated.

'We need to pretend that Coppelli is indeed a hero, and this pretence will enable us to investigate the matter further. We need to take a step back and analyse the situation carefully,' he said.

When reviewing the audio and video tapes found in Charles's apartment, the Secret Service agents and the police came across a puzzling exchange between Charles and Coppelli about the use of email messaging, recorded just a few weeks before the massacre. It dealt with the first time that Coppelli became aware of the existence of email.

He told Charles that he heard about email for the first time in 1992 when a colleague took him to the airport in Florence on his way to Sydney where he would collaborate with Professor Paul Boscombe. In the car, his colleague indicated that he had just returned from the United States. 'Coppelli,' he said, 'when American academics come to their office in the morning, they switch on their computer, and they would see all the messages which have been sent to them during the night.'

'Well, I am certainly suitably impressed. But such a fad will never reach Italy or the country I am about to visit. However, if my views turn out to be wrong, I will discuss the advantages and disadvantages of the information explosion and the use of this facility in my lectures. Read my lips, Charles, I will leave the door of my lecture room wide open, so the entire world will be able to hear what I have to say on this topic,' Coppelli had remarked.

'In my lecture, I will discuss the communication explosion, generated by the widespread use of emails, with my students in the context of the demise of law and order in a Marxist society. It is certainly an interesting development which will create many problems, like loss of privacy, and a deterioration in peoples' ability to write letters. It will result in an education revolution and invite scammers to defraud the users of this email service. I can only guess what Marx would have been able to achieve if that facility had been available in his lifetime,' he had said at the time.

'Is this bizarre and cryptic exchange about the email revolution a coded message? Is this nothing else but a red herring or is there a hidden message in this exchange? What did it mean?' Lolita asked.

'Perhaps, it means precisely what was discussed by Charles and Coppelli,' I answered. 'That Coppelli did not understand the importance of emails in 1992. No need to dwell on this'.

'You know that a Secret Service agent never takes anything at face value. We always look for reasons that explain or justify the activities of people. We never interpret their statements literally. We have been trained to find clues in a person's conduct and expressions,' Lolita said.

It was well-known in higher education circles that, even in 2027, the University of Southern Kansas was one of the last institutions to embrace the advantages of a new, challenging digital world. The History of Ideas and Jurisprudence Department still prohibited students from accessing the Internet during lectures. They were expected to listen to the lecturer and to engage in stimulating discussions with classmates and the lecturer about some obscure, and irrelevant, issues that often amounted to not much more than exotic claptrap. Students were encouraged not to contact their lecturers and professors via email, but instead to approach them before or after the lectures, or to telephone them during work hours.

'Email is not an appropriate substitute for personal contact. The school promotes the free discussion of ideas which will enrich the lives of all participants and, to that purpose, face-to-face contact between students and the lecturer is necessary,' the school's brochure declared.

Of course, like any other institution, the school had to endure Internet teaching and prolific use of email, when Covid-19 devastated America only six years earlier. But now that the pandemic was over, a sign reappeared in every lecture theatre used by the Department. It said: 'There is no WIFI here. Pretend this is 1990 and talk to each other and discuss ideas with the Professor and your colleagues.'

'Why would he do a thing like this?' Jesper asked.

'Like what?'

'Conspiring with Charles to kill scores of people, at least potentially,' he said.

Why was Coppelli not targeted by the attacker? That was the main question. They could not find an answer because whichever way you looked at this, he was a hero who was willing to sacrifice his life for his students. He was lucky to be alive. But being lucky is not a criminal offence. They wanted answers to a considerable number of questions.

Was Coppelli really a person who would go into battle mode to protect his students and sacrifice himself? Is there anything in his past that indicates a different inclination?

Was it not the case that the death of Charles looked more like a suicide rather than as an accidental death?

If the massacre were staged by Charles and Coppelli, what would be their motivation? Is there anything in Coppelli's behaviour since the massacre that yields any clues?

*****

Charles was portrayed in the media as a frustrated idealist, who wanted to eradicate discrimination, despondency, misery and poverty and it led him to this dreadful murder spree, cutting short the lives of innocent university students, now the victims of a heinous crime.

Some intelligent commentators, however, were surprised that Charles would have wanted to attack students, who were renowned for their progressive and left-of-centre attitudes. They had all expected Charles to find another target, like the fat cats in the Administration Building, or senior public servants in a nearby building. But it never went any further than an opinion.

Kansas was the centre of the world for at least a few weeks after the shooting in Coppelli's classroom.

But Kansas was no longer the magical place of the Wizard of Oz that Dorothy wanted to return to in that iconic American movie. It was a place of unspeakable sorrow. A place of infamy.

13

'NOW WE KNOW THAT THERE IS A CLOSE LINK BETWEEN COPPELLI and Charles,' I said to the Secret Service officer.

'Richard, we already knew that. Remember that Charles had asked Martha to give an envelope to Coppelli, if something were to happen to him,' Hayden said.

'Yes, what was in the envelope?'

'A single sheet of paper. Charles asked Coppelli to take over the leadership of the DNA Movement if something were to happen to him.

'But it also requested Coppelli to take revenge on the President of the United States for the evil deeds for which he was responsible.

'Evil deeds? I do not know any evil deeds that the President has done in his life. It is strong language, isn't it?' I remarked.

'In retrospect, the envelope doesn't seem to help us very much, apart of course from confirming that there was a close link between these two comrades,' Hayden explained.

'The attack at the University was probably planned by both. It is likely that Coppelli, while pretending to wrestle with Charles, merely played his part in a well-rehearsed plot. He did not mean to protect his students. It would explain why he was not shot.'

'However, it still does not explain how Charles died, whether he was shot by Coppelli, either intentionally or accidentally, or whether Charles committed suicide, expecting to be shot by police anyway,' Jesper added helpfully.

'How Charles died is not even our most important concern. We need to know what they hoped to achieve. What was their endgame? What was their plan? If we do not understand their motives – that is Coppelli's motive since Charles is dead – there is nothing we can do,' Hayden remarked.

'So, what are we going to do? The President is visiting the University of Southern Kansas at the end of next week and he is expected to honour Coppelli, the unlikely hero, for his courageous and heroic exploits,' I enquired.

'As I said, we cannot detain him now because we are not able to prove anything at all. We do not know what he has in mind. There are merely unsubstantiated allegations, no evidence. But we need to protect the President all the same. If Coppelli intends to do something, it will be done during his meeting with the President, I think.

'The best way forward is to pretend that we do not suspect him at all and thus give the impression that, as a hero, he will be feted by the President at the Bravery Awards ceremony in the University's Conventions Centre. We need to proceed with the visit if ever we are going to find out the motivation behind the horrendous massacre in Coppelli's classroom. But we should inform the President and take measures to protect him against any attack,' I argued.

'Agreed, we need to inform the President. We do not seem to have another choice in the matter,' Hayden replied.

'I will talk to the President when I meet with him in a few hours for our daily briefing. May I ask that you and your colleagues, Lolita and Jesper, accompany me to the White House. I suggest I speak with the President alone and, if necessary, I will call you to join our discussion. Would that be suitable for your team?' I asked.

'Yes, we are ready when required,' Hayden responded.

*****

When I met the President a few hours later, he was in a bilious mood. The latest opinion polls disclosed a drop in the President's support in the heartland that voted for him. The drop appeared insignificant, but it was enough to worry the President. A small drop in his support, if not carefully managed, could easily become an unbridgeable gap.

'Ah, there you are, Richard. What could I do to beef up my ratings?' he asked.

'Mr. President, doing what you think you should be doing. Staying the course and be true to yourself.

'In any case, the only poll that counts, is the one on election day. There is still more than one year to go before the next election. By then, the electorate will eat out of your hands – I have no doubt about that. Our fellow Americans will all have fallen in love with you,' I said reassuringly.

I did not believe my own exhortation, but it had the desired effect of placating the President, for now, because I knew that he would return to this topic soon. The President started to relax a little bit, he looked around the Oval Office like a detective in a hotel lobby, waiting for a suspected criminal to step out of the elevator.

'Mr. President, I think we may have to deal with a potential problem. I emphasize the word "potential" because nothing is conclusive. But we need to protect you, nevertheless. We cannot take any chances,' I said.

'What is this all about, Richard?' the President asked worriedly.

'Next week you are scheduled to visit the University of Southern Kansas where the shooting took place. You will be meeting the survivors and their families. You also indicated that you want to honour Coppelli Colone for his bravery and courage, and you will embrace him, as a sign of support.

'Could we not dispense with the embrace?' I asked. 'You can always blame the Covid-19 virus which devastated this country just a few years ago?' I suggested.

'No, Richard, I want to be close to the people. I want to join them intimately in their grief, joy, expectations and be seen to be a part of their lives. It makes for exquisite television. And right now, I need to work on my popularity. You have seen the results of the straw poll, of course,' he said.

'Yes, Mr. President. But you need to know that I went to visit a hooker …

'A hooker, Richard, good grief. I did not expect you were into this kind of thing,' the President prematurely interrupted me.

'… who was a special girlfriend of Charles, and she told me

and my Secret Service colleagues that Charles and Coppelli were apparently good friends. Charles asked Martha – that was the name of the high-class escort – to give an envelope, with an enclosed letter, to Coppelli, if something were to happen to him. The letter merely asked Coppelli to take over the leadership of the DNA Movement if something were to happen to Charles. But, more interestingly, it also asked Coppelli to seek revenge for the evil misdeeds the President is responsible for. What is he referring to? So, why would he say that?' I asked the President.

'But, Richard, I only perform praiseworthy deeds. Do I look like an evil, wicked person?' the President said.

'Precisely my reaction, Mr. President. But it would explain why Charles targeted the Coppelli class and did not shoot at Coppelli. Of course, at this stage, nothing can be proven, and Coppelli is a hero, but the Secret Service is wary about this revelation and is visibly apprehensive. Can we talk about the plan designed by the Secret Service to protect you, Mr. President?' I asked.

'This is most interesting. Of course, we should talk about it. Let's invite the Secret Service team to take part in our discussions. Whatever needs to be done, will be done,' the President confirmed helpfully.

'I will ask them to join us, straightaway, Mr. President,' I hastened to add. This was important business that could not wait much longer. In anticipation, I had already invited the three Secret Service agents who were waiting patiently in the anteroom.

'Mr. President, this is what we recommend ...,' I started the conversation.

14

The President arrived in a convoy of limousines. In his own allocated car, he was joined by his wife, Catherine, the First Lady. I was sitting in the front of the car, next to the chauffeur, an affable, but discreet, Latino American who was the President's preferred driver. The President leaned over to his wife and whispered something in her ear. Although it would not be audible to the driver – the President was sitting behind me – I heard the President tell his wife to smile to the people who were lined up on the sides of the road leading to the University. Smiling is not something that came easy to the First Lady, and it was necessary to remind her of that duty which, undoubtedly, she found dull and challenging. A long fence, decorated with American flags and other paraphernalia, which looked like an expensive balustrade of a stairway of a pre-Civil War mansion, separated the people from the President's limousine.

'I do not quite understand why the President is waving at the spectators because nobody sitting in this car can be seen by the onlookers outside. The windows are dark-tinted as well as bullet proof – and so is the car – and it is only possible for people inside the limousine to look outside, but not the other way round,' I mumbled.

On either side of the car were grabrails and footrests to enable security agents and presidential guards to ride with the President. The President's car was in the middle of the convoy, with two limousines in front and two limousines at the back. The convoy started out from the airport where the presidential plane, Air Force One, had arrived from Washington DC an hour earlier. The plane was discreetly stationed in a remote part of the airport and guarded by an army of well-armed soldiers. The convoy was scheduled to drive to the University of Southern Kansas, which was one hour away from the airport, certainly at the speed the convoy was travelling. The President had instructed the drivers to proceed slowly, which meant that their speed should not exceed forty miles per hour. Kansas was a State that went for his opponent at the last election, so he saw this as an early opportunity to do some easy, and potentially, fruitful campaigning in the State which might help in swinging it his way at the next election.

All security measures were put in place by the Secret Service and the personal guards of the President. The University's security services were specifically ordered not to be involved in the security operation at all.

The University President, Professor Matthew William Meddleson, was not happy about this because the Service's decision implicitly indicated a lack of trust in the University's capabilities, but he could not do anything about it. It was completely out of his hands.

'You can't compete with the Security Service's operations,' he told his associates in the University's Administration Building.

His associates merely nodded. Most of them were aware that

their President was an incompetent and bumbling academic bureaucrat with grandiose ideas which were never implemented. They knew that he was afraid to have to work too much. He was at his best at night, with a glass of wine in one hand, and an attractive secretary on the other. As far as his associates were concerned, he had been appointed to his level of incompetence.

'He is a control freak. Unable to delegate, he is drowning himself in the minutiae of management which should be in the hands of his collaborators.

'Presumably, the University's Chief Executive is expected to manage his institution effectively and be seen to be active. But our President is taking all his actions to their illogical extreme,' they said.

There was one specific story that was told and retold over and again on campus. One day, the University President sent an email message to all staff. Communicating with staff, of course, is vital to the lifeblood of a university and a core activity of its management. But on this occasion, in dabbling in his own creation of futility and ignorance, he managed to win the Olympics of Mediocrity. In his email – and it was a long email, the equivalent of about five A4-sized pages – he explained that from now on staff would not be allowed to store their lunch sandwich and orange juice in the schools' refrigerator, because the school fridge cannot be used for private purposes. So, if it were possible to prove that the sandwich was school property and every member of staff could take a bite, then it could be stored in the fridge, but otherwise that would not be allowed!

The President of the University sent this email after receiving a communique from the government about corruption in publicly funded institutions. He saw the practice of using the fridge for private purposes as an egregious example of corruption which had to be stamped out. This issue was a high priority project for him, and it had to be dealt with immediately and ruthlessly. For him, using the school fridge for private purposes was a cancer that had to be eradicated from the University's practices.

Those who told the story always rewarded their listeners with a vulpine smile.

The sending of this email message provided Coppelli with an opportunity to tell his students what he thought about corruption in public institutions.

'The world has become mad. It is no longer possible to operate in a normal environment where human friendship and generosity are not described as examples of corruption. Last year, I was one of the keynote speakers at a conference here at the University of Southern Kansas. The organiser gave a bottle of an award-winning Californian wine to all keynote speakers, including me, to thank them for their presentations. However, a day later, in an email emanating from the President's office, I was directed to return the bottle to my School where it should be entered into a register of received gifts! All other speakers, who were not employed by the University, kept their bottle. I have no idea what happened to my wine bottle afterwards. Perhaps it sits in the University cellar until it is undrinkable which is presumably the only way to prove that the University is combating corruption effectively? It is an example of taking logic to its illogical extreme,' Coppelli told his students.

One of his students then told a similarly amusing story.

'Now that we are on this topic of wine, professor, I should like to tell you what happened to me. A few weeks ago, I attended a lecture organised by the students' union and the speaker was the local Commissioner Against Corruption. The Commissioner explained that, in accordance with the regulations of Kansas, all gifts must be entered into a register, even a bottle of wine. Following his lecture, I was supposed to thank the speaker for his willingness to speak to the students. In my reply, I mentioned that the speaker had made my task just a little bit harder because I had a gift to thank him for his splendid contribution: a bottle of wine!' the student said.

The students started to laugh uncontrollably. They enjoyed a delightful story, and it became better when embellished.

'Well, this is a good story, and it raises the question how far governments should go to regulate the lives of people. Are the current regulations affecting our freedoms?' Coppelli had asked. Coppelli then made a disclosure which made him popular even with students who did not like his strident criticism of capitalism.

'I have bought some undrinkable wine for a pittance and put a school label on it, giving the impression that it was produced just for me. I give it to speakers who I dislike. I praise it as the best wine ever produced by the school whereas it is not much better than vinegar. That is corruption, my friends, or at least deception. I get away with it because reasonable people can disagree about taste,' Coppelli said.

*****

The President took his wife's hand when he alighted the limousine and they left on the same side of the car. The car door had been opened by a guard, who saluted when the Chief Executive and his Lady exited the limousine. The Lady was clothed in a dark blue navy dress that was buttoned up to her neck and covered her knees. An expensive fur coat was draped around her shoulders.

She looks very Victorian, I thought.

The President wore an overcoat made from the finest American wool, and a shawl protected him against the wind which was blowing in from the steppes.

The University of Southern Kansas was fully prepared for this unexpected, sad, and at the same time uplifting visit. It was sad because all lectures had been suspended following the attack; the police presence was still clearly visible everywhere and television stations had transformed the University into a huge relay station. The University was the scene where this atrocity had taken place. It was a dreadful advertisement for the University that did not want to be regarded as a scene of devastation and infamy. But the visit was also heartening because there was an expectation that the visit of the Chief Executive of the United States would reinvigorate the university and lift it out of its misery.

It was obvious to all people that the Secret Service was in command. No detail was overlooked by the Service. A visit by the President was, of course, a huge logistical challenge that had been organized expertly by the Service. They clearly knew what they were doing – they had done it before, many times.

*****

In preparation for his big day, Coppelli had again taken a bath, the second in not much more than a week. He even bought a new suit for his meeting with the President. It was clear that he wanted to make a good impression. Coppelli also owned a car that reflected the philosophy of its owner. It was an old car, and from time to time, it would break down. The repairs would not be done if the car were still capable of being driven. Money was spent, very reluctantly, if it was no longer possible to drive it safely without repairs. The inside of the car was appalling and any description of it would do a disservice to its actual state. The car was effectively used as a bin, except it was a bin that could not be placed at the curb for collection by the Waste Management Department of Kansas. So, the filth stayed in the car, and over time, the remains of bananas, oranges and cookies became an infested and smelly imbroglio that gave the car a putrid concoction of horrible smells. Coppelli had a habit of buying coca cola drinks and chocolate milk, and each time a bottle or can had been emptied, it would be tossed into the car where it would stay for a long time, mostly until it nearly blocked the steering wheel. This drinking habit was very unhealthy because it contributed to obesity and Coppelli was beginning to suffer from it. His belly protruded from his stomach and already hung perilously over his ribcage, like a car that hovers over a ravine, as can be seen in some disaster movies. He had the appearance of a slouch. By age 62, if he were to continue his unhealthy eating habits, he would be suffering from a heart attack or obesity-related illnesses, like diabetes.

Perhaps this is an additional reason why Coppelli did not have any girlfriend willing to share his life and vision? I thought.

When he was behind the wheel, he was literally sitting in muddy surroundings.

'When you sit in the mud, you get dirty. And mud usually becomes a swamp. That is precisely what is happening with Coppelli's car,' I mused.

However, when the President's visit was announced, a university cleaning company moved in to clean the car thoroughly and wash it professionally. A mechanical engineer checked the dials on the dashboard and examined the operation of the car. A new set of quality rubber tires was fitted to the wheels. The car was also sprayed with a nice glossy paint. After that, it looked like a new old car, at least for a few days!

On the day of the President's visit, Coppelli proudly arrived at the University in his rejuvenated sparkling car. He had wanted to use public transport, but it soon became obvious this was not going to be an option on the day of the President's visit. The buses were overloaded with people who wanted to see, and wave at, the

President. They did not run according to their schedule, and they moved slowly like a tortoise because they had to stop often to pick up people who wanted to join the pilgrimage to the University of Southern Kansas. There was no room for them to sit down, so they were standing in the standing-only areas, treading on the toes of people who sat down. Social distancing was a distant reminder of the past!

When Coppelli arrived at the University's entrance checkpoint, the guard saluted the hero whose reputation had already become formidable in the University. He directed Coppelli to a reserved car park for which he did not have to pay, at least not today. The parking place was still about one kilometre away from the Conventions Centre where the ceremony would be held. Coppelli wanted to park his car in the car park of the Centre, but the guard told him that the spaces were reserved for the President and his entourage of secret agents and guards. Even the University President could not park his car there on the day of the visit. Coppelli tried to argue with the guard and even used his exalted position as Hero of the United States as a lever, but the guard was not for turning. Defeated, Coppelli drove away from the entrance and parked the car in the allocated reserved parking space on campus.

'At least, it is better than parking the car a few streets from campus on private property, the owner of which charges $30 as a parking fee. He is making a large profit on the day of the President's visit,' Coppelli mumbled to himself.

He then walked slowly to the Conventions Centre where he would be seated in the front row but would still have to wait, for at least thirty minutes, before the ceremony was scheduled to start. All attendees had been asked to be seated at least half an hour before the start of the proceedings.

The ceremony was to be held in the newly built Conventions Centre of the University. The reference to 'new' is perhaps not warranted because the building had been built five years ago and was often used for student theatre performances, concerts, musicals, and graduations. Sometimes, the Centre was used for major conferences and could also be hired for community events. The Centre was in a dilapidated part of the campus which the University was seeking to rejuvenate with new buildings. Most other buildings adjoining the Centre were still decayed – it was the least appealing part of campus before the construction of the Centre – but during the last week, there had been frantic activity to invigorate the surrounding buildings, inside and outside. Outside the Conventions Centre, new pot plants had been positioned and bushes had been planted; a few new walkways had been rapidly constructed, and the lawns were cut immaculately. Clay statues of gods and goddesses dotted the lawn and dreamily watched people who arrived at the Centre. The inside of the huge auditorium, with seating for over 2,000 people, had been hastily repainted in the week before the President's visit, and ducted and zoned air conditioning units had been serviced. The windows were surgically cleaned.

The Centre was last used as a theatre venue for a student performance of the musical *Rent*. It played to sold-out audiences over a period of fourteen days. The Centre contributed to the cultural life of the University and local communities, but now it was the epicentre of deep mourning and sadness. America's inability to address the gun problem that had been responsible for so much misery and violence only increased this sense of sadness and impotence.

The President's promise to produce a plan to curb the use of guns in America within a week, did not materialize. His good intentions may have been thwarted by the Second Amendment to the Constitution which unequivocally states that, '… the right of the people to keep and bear Arms, shall not be infringed.'

'Perhaps the right to carry weapons was justifiable in the early days after independence when the erstwhile colonies were still fearful of a British invasion to snuff out the gains of the War of Independence. Also, the police forces were not that strong in the latter part of the 18th century and in the 19th century and may have been inadequate for the purpose of servicing such a large country. But was such a dangerous, albeit constitutional, luxury viable in 21st century America?' I asked myself.

The invitees who were waiting for the President anticipated that the President would say something about the topic of gun control in his speech.

Half an hour before the event, the Centre was already full. It was an event by invitation. For one reason or another, the first five rows had been dismantled, so the first row now started with row six, increasing the distance between the audience and the podium.

'This is obviously a safety precaution,' Coppelli thought.

The first three rows of the reconstituted auditorium were reserved for the survivors of the massacre with the middle seat of the first row going to Coppelli, the Hero who would be honoured today by the President. Next to him, on the left, was the University President, and on his right, the Secretary of State, Murray Pompo. A place of honour was reserved for the First Lady. The Governor of the State of Kansas, and the local Mayor had also been invited and had a reserved seat in the front row. I was allocated a seat in the second row behind the First Lady.

Security guards were unobtrusively posted on the sides of the Centre and were also stationed at the entrance and in the driveway leading to the auditorium. Four snipers were on top of the building and an adjoining building. They were partially hidden by a chimney and plastic glass dividers, and their presence could hardly be seen from below.

At 10 in the morning, the President of the University entered the auditorium and occupied his reserved seat. There was polite applause but nothing extravagant. After all, this was not a joyous occasion, but a sombre, and suitable remembrance of those who sacrificed their life for a better America. Television crews were discreetly positioned at the back and in the main hall, to record the event which would be televised live throughout the Nation.

The minders of the American President were aware that this was an important electoral event that would cement the reputation of the President. His speech writers had made a special effort to ensure that the speech would have a profound impact. However, the event's program indicated that no questions at all could be asked of the President. He and the Secretary of State would leave immediately after bestowing the Medal of Bravery on Coppelli Colone. The Medal, in its case, was displayed on a separate table at the opposite end of the stage from the lectern, some way away, where one person could be seen standing next to the table, though indistinct due to the darkness in the auditorium.

The Master of Ceremonies, the Deputy President of the University, invited people to stand for the national anthem which the University orchestra would perform. The attendees rose to attention and placed their right hand on their breast when the orchestra started to play the anthem. The orchestra had practised during the previous week in the proscenium of the auditorium while it was hastily repainted. I could imagine that everywhere in America, people who watched the ceremony on television, would stand up and salute the anthem.

'Be seated,' the Master of Ceremonies said. 'I would like to welcome you to this event this morning. Today we are remembering the fifteen students whose lives were ended by a vile and brutal murderer in one of the University's lecture rooms, where students have a right to learn in safety. I would like to invite the President of the University to come to the lectern to say a few words. He will also introduce the President of the United States who, following his speech, will be joined on the stage by the Secretary of State who will confer the Medal of Bravery on Professor Coppelli Colone. This will be followed by a rendition of the 5th Symphony of Beethoven, performed by the University orchestra. Please join me in welcoming the President of the University,' he said.

The University President raised himself up and slowly covered the distance between the first row and the podium and climbed up to the floor of the theatre. He looked down on the proscenium where the musicians had been assembled. He looked forward to listening to the rendition of the 5th Symphony which would conclude the event in the Conventions Centre. He went to the lectern and took his place behind it; he took a piece of paper from the inside pocket of his coat and placed it on the lectern in front of him - his speech. He took reading glasses out of his other inside pocket. The reading lamp was already lighted, and the audio people of the University had tested the microphone only half an hour ago. His voice would be amplified throughout the hall, and, indeed, the University, and in the living rooms of Americans everywhere. Speakers had been placed strategically on campus so that all students and staff would be able to listen to the proceedings. The lectern covered his feet and torso, only his head was visible from the auditorium. He put his readings glasses on his nose. They were wide-rimmed, black framed glasses, suitable for the occasion. They adorned his nose which must have been operated upon a long time ago – probably because of a sporting accident when he was young – it still appeared fractured on one side, the right-hand side from where Coppelli was seated. *He must have been a rugby player in his youth, and his fractured nose may be the result of a serious tackle on the field during a game*, I thought.

'Secretary of State, Mr. Murray Pompo, Governor Marcel Delacy, Mr. Gerald Osborne, Mayor of Kansas City, Professor Coppelli Colone, Colleagues, Students, Parents and Friends.

'Only ten days ago, this University was the scene of unspeakable evil, when a shooter burst into one of the classrooms where students expect to be safe. Their lives and futures were ended prematurely by a murderer who wanted to inflict great harm on America. The relevant authorities are looking into the motivation of the murderer. But today, I do not want to speculate on the reasons which prompted an obsessed and sick mind to carry out such a heinous crime. Instead, I propose to talk about the magnificent efforts of our university community, our people, volunteers, police officers, and friends to make the University a safe place for all. Their work needs to be celebrated today,' he said.

He went on for fifteen minutes. Hardly anyone listened to the platitudes of the University President because his mannerism disclosed that he did not believe in the message he preached. Finally, the moment everyone had been waiting for, arrived.

'It gives me immense pleasure to invite Mr. Desmond Raymond Clarkenson, President of the United States, to come to the lectern to address the assembled audience. Following his address, the President will then invite the Secretary of State, Mr. Murray

Pompo, to bestow the Medal of Bravery on Professor Coppelli Colone. May I please ask you to stand when the President arrives on stage?' he asked.

The lights of the auditorium were dimmed, and the attendees stood in semi-darkness, but the lectern was well-lit. The President of the United States walked onto the stage, surrounded by a few minders. The thunderous applause was deafening and could be compared to an airplane flying overhead, so loud it appeared to be. The long-awaited moment had finally arrived, and the President slowly made his way to the lectern. His gait was a bit wooden, but otherwise he looked fine. His body was shielded by the lectern, only his face was visible, and his arms mechanically waved at the people in front of him. The image of the President was reflected on a huge screen on the wall. Nearby, but out of sight, a legion of guards and Secret Service agents had been stationed. As the auditorium was a school type auditorium with some depth, the Secret Service personnel were in the wings. However, they would be able to spring into action at the slightest threat to the President.

The President looked up to survey the surroundings and started to speak. Coppelli thought that the President looked fatigued; his speech pattern was automated, and the usual vibrancy associated with the man was somehow missing. *It is because of the trip from Washington DC and the solemnity of the ceremony today*, he thought.

The President was a good storyteller. He explained that he was sad to hear about this disastrous event. He wanted to console the victims' families. His government would assist in any viable way. In the next couple of weeks, he would unveil a proposal to curb the use of guns in the United States. So, it went. The speech certainly endeared him to many people.

He tried desperately to appeal to the older generation because his likely opponent at the next election, who was much younger, and more urbane, certainly appealed to the younger generation – he had a comparative advantage there. The President sometimes told his audience – but not today because the occasion did not lend itself to it – that older Americans vote for him because he is familiar with, and sensitive to, their needs. A standard tale he told them related to his time in Florence, in Italy where he spent one year as an exchange student in his student days.

'I opened an account in a local bank in the *Piazza della Signoria*. The bank was housed in a magnificent medieval building with views on Michelangelo's *David* – which however is a copy of the famous sculpture. The door leading into the bank was a heavy metal structure like those used in a vault. A huge dog, with outstretched paws, discerning eyes, big ears, and sharp teeth, always rested quietly in front of the bank without ever threatening anyone proposing to enter the building. I never found out whom the dog belonged to, but I assumed it was owned by one of the officers of the bank, or it could have been the bank's mascot. But it was certainly a daunting sight the first time a customer wanted to use the bank's facilities.

'When I went to the bank to withdraw money, I was asked at

one teller to pay a commission of 5%, another time at a different teller, it was 10%, and yet at another teller nothing had to be paid. Over time, I had discovered that when presenting myself at a specific teller, no commission was charged whereas a fee would have to be paid everywhere else. I could not understand how this system worked and did not know whether it was legal or whether the tellers were involved in some illegal scheme to increase their meagre banking salaries. So, I devised a scheme which would see me loved by seniors, while securing an opportunity to visit the teller of my choice. This is what I did: when I came to the head of the queue, I would usually be expected to go to the next available teller. However, if it wasn't the teller of my choice – which did not charge a commission – I would look behind me and if the person were an elderly man or woman, I would say in heavily accented Italian: "I have a lot of time. Why don't you go first? I will be happy to take your place in the queue",

Seniors were delighted with the generosity of this foreign gentleman.

'They don't come along like this anymore,' they would say.

Of course, they did not realize that the future President of the United States was cynically killing two birds in one throw. He would make friends for life, and still get to visit his favourite teller which he would visit as soon as it became available to him in the queue.

The President looked at the paper on the lectern and continued to speak.

'My fellow Americans, I was extremely saddened when my Press Secretary informed me of the shooting at this University. As your University President has said, a lecture theatre is a place where students should feel safe and protected. It is a place of light and learning. But ten days ago, the lives of fifteen students, who had their futures ahead of them were abruptly ended by a madman. We have experienced too many shootings in America this year, and it needs to stop because it affects the fabric of our civilized society and the right of people to live peacefully and safely. I commit my government to the task of gun control. I will be able to give you more details once a proposal has been sent to Congress,' he said.

'Well, this will probably never happen. When it comes to the crunch, he will plead the Second Amendment to the Constitution and the political challenges and Congressional roadblocks associated with gun control,' I commented to myself.

The President continued:

'I now invite the Secretary of State, Murray Pompo, to join me on the stage for the purpose of conferring the Medal of Bravery, also known as the Award for Heroism, on Professor Coppelli Colone.

'The Medal is an Award for Heroism. The Award consists of a sterling silver medal and a certificate signed by the Secretary of State.'

Murray Pompo immediately stood up and briskly climbed the stairs to the stage and took his place next to the lectern. The person who could be seen standing next to the table at the opposite end of the stage brought the case to the lectern where the Secretary of State was waiting.

The President waited a few seconds before continuing:

'It is with great gratitude that I would like to call upon Professor Coppelli Colone to come to the stage, to the lectern, to be presented with the Medal of Bravery, the Nation's highest bravery award, by the Secretary of State,' he intoned.

This invitation was followed by a tremendous burst of applause from the congregation. It was as if Jesus Christ had descended from Heaven to congratulate the Pope on a job well done. Coppelli's face was flushed with pride, his cheeks started to gleam. He turned around to accept gratefully the adulation of which he was the recipient. He shook hands with the President of the University, who was seated next to him, and with the First Lady, who was sitting a few chairs away from him in the first row. He straightened himself and walked slowly to the stage, all the time receiving the adoration of the public.

According to the Protocol, an explanation of which Coppelli had to endure numerous times during the previous week, he was supposed to stop about three metres from the lectern, with his face to the President. The correct place had been unobtrusively indicated by a white mark on the floor. When he arrived, he would bow and wait while the President read the testimonial.

The President looked at his paper on the lectern and started to read.

'The Bravery Medal of the United States is the highest bravery award in this Nation. It can only be bestowed on an eligible American, and in some cases, a foreign citizen by the Secretary of State. The awardee is expected to have demonstrated exceptional as well as unusually brave behaviour in challenging situations. These actions must have resulted in the saving of lives or property. People who are worthy of this Medal went out their way to help other people regardless of the effects of their actions on themselves. It is a Medal that honours those who unselfishly were ready to sacrifice their own life for the greater good.

'Today this Medal will be bestowed on Professor Coppelli Colone, a Professor at the University of Southern Kansas, by a grateful Nation, represented by the President of the United States. The Medal rewards Professor Colone for his exceptional courage shown during a sustained physical attack, while disregarding his own personal safety.

'Professor Colone, please advance to the lectern to receive, from the hands of the Secretary of State, the Bravery Medal of the United States for your brave and unselfish action which saved many lives. This Medal is a symbol of the gratitude of this Nation that forever will embrace you in its bosom,' the President said. The Secretary took the Medal out of its case and waited for Professor Colone to advance to the lectern.

Coppelli advanced, but his gait was shuffling, and it felt as if he was unsteady on his feet. Suddenly, as the Secretary of State was about to drape the Medal around the neck of Coppelli, inexplicably, Coppelli stumbled and turned his ankle and he crashed onto the floor. In the process, he appeared to grasp at the head of the President, attempting to soften the blow, but somehow his hands could not hold on to the President. It was as if his hands went through the President's body, precisely what would happen if he were trying to embrace a ghost.

A roar of anguish could be heard in the auditorium and pandemonium broke out.

Immediately, Secret Service agents and guards appeared from nowhere and they hustled the President and the Secretary of State off-stage to protect them. They also guided the First Lady, who was speechlessly watching the proceedings from her seat in the first row, to the exit door of the auditorium. The agents shoved them in a car and drove off at great speed in the direction of the airport, where Air Force One was waiting for their guests to return to Washington DC. There were no hindrances or delays on the way to the airport because most people thought that the ceremony was not yet finished. Or they were glued to the television set to see how the dreadful situation unfolded.

Some Secret Service agents assisted Coppelli, who had a broken nose, and bruises all over his face, and a trickle of blood was oozing out of the main wound. His knees were also bruised, and his new pants had split at knee level. It was an ignominious end to the Bravery Award ceremony.

The Master of Ceremonies quickly returned to the lectern to apologize for the accident, while congratulating Coppelli on his award and wishing him a speedy recovery. All attendees were thanked for their attendance and asked to vacate the building. The musicians in the proscenium were dismissed without playing the 5th Symphony of Beethoven.

On board the plane, the minders were feverishly drafting a few statements, which would be read by the President upon his return to Washington DC. It became clear that the President had to address the country following the unfortunate mishap at the University of Southern Kansas. One of his speech writers drafted a statement in record time, which read like this.

'My fellow Americans, yesterday I was at the University of Southern Kansas to console the victims of the atrocious crimes committed by a horrible criminal whose name I do not want to mention. I also wanted to honour one of the Heroes of this Nation, Professor Coppelli Colone. As you know by now, he single-handedly confronted the attacker who invaded the sanctity of his classroom where he was teaching his students. He prevented an even bigger bloodbath from taking place because he audaciously struggled with the armed attacker. When I finished reading the testimonial which Coppelli listened to, I invited him to come to the lectern to receive his Bravery Medal which the Secretary of State proceeded to place around his neck. However, most unfortunately, when advancing to the lectern, Professor Colone stumbled badly, he crashed to the floor, and he hurt himself. I would like to offer my support to him and wish him a speedy recovery.'

It was big news, and it would have been even bigger news if

the media had been aware of the suspicions raised by the Secret Service. As far as the media was concerned, it was just an unfortunate misstep by a man who was anxious to receive his Bravery Medal – it had happened before, many times.

The evening newspapers and the television news gave top billing to this tragedy that occurred at the University of Southern Kansas, the stumbling of the Hero Coppelli when he was about to receive the Medal from the hands of the Secretary of State. The papers did not publish the President's speech and did not cover his hasty retreat from the Conventions Centre. Instead, they concentrated on the unfortunate accident that left a stain on what otherwise would have been a sad, but most dignified, commemoration.

Coppelli was still a Hero of the United States and of the University of Southern Kansas.

PART THREE
The Unravelling
chapters 15-22

15

THE DAY AFTER THE ABORTED CEREMONY AT THE UNIVERSITY, Hayden sent an email invitation to summon me, Lolita and Jesper to a meeting which would be held in his office in a building close to the White House. I still felt tired after the excitement of the day before followed by an early morning return flight from Kansas City to Washington DC.

'I hope you are able to make the meeting. It is necessary to discuss what happened yesterday, especially the unfortunate incident during the Bravery Medal Award ceremony,' he explained in his invitation request.

'Yes, Hayden, I will attend the meeting. But please do not chastise me if I fall asleep. You will need to keep me awake with lots of coffee,' I said, when I accepted his invitation by sending a return email. Of course, I realized there was a job to be done and any postponement of our meeting would be time lost.

The three officers and I assembled in Hayden's office at 11 in the morning. The office was not much more than a dusty cubicle with a ceiling and a door to provide privacy. There were three chairs in the room, an office swivel chair behind the desk and two chairs fronting the desk.

It is abundantly clear that the office would not tolerate more than two visitors at any time, thought Jesper.

A window provided the occupant of the office with good

views of the building's atrium. A portrait of the American President was the only decoration on the wall. The L-shaped desk had a laptop on its bottom side, and a telephone and a few photos on its long side. One of the photos depicted Hayden and his wife on their wedding day. The other photo was a memento of their daughter's graduation from the University of Texas. She was smiling and looked stunning in her black robe, interspersed with red strips. A crimson bonnet covered her head, and a long red ribbon attached to it flowed seamlessly by her side. An ancient metal drawer sitting in a corner behind the desk with copious files sticking out of its compartments completed the picture of chaotic order.

Lolita and Jesper occupied the vacant chairs. I borrowed a chair from the office next door.

'Good morning, Mr. Hayden, I hope you had a good night's sleep. We all needed this after yesterday's disaster,' they almost said simultaneously, slightly facetiously.

'Could have been better,' Hayden mumbled incoherently. He retrieved a kettle from the bottom compartment of his drawer and a tin of Nescafé.

'I think we can all use a cup of coffee.' Without waiting for a comment, he started to boil some water.

'I don't have fresh milk. Just powder milk. It will have to do,' he said dismissively.

'Let's review yesterday's events,' I prompted him.

Hayden sat down in his swivel chair which he pushed back,

and he crossed his legs. He looked at the portrait of the American President and nodded. For a few moments, he gathered his thoughts and he looked around the room to ensure that he had everyone's attention.

'Well, when Coppelli arrived at the Centre, he was X-rayed like everyone else; no exceptions were allowed – except of course the President of the United States. Even his entourage, Press Secretary – that is you, Richard – guards, security officers like us, passed through the X-ray machine which had been installed by officers of the Secret Service the day before the Ceremony – it was not the property of the University – and it was tested and re-tested. The machine operated impeccably. When Coppelli went through it, it could not find anything suspicious, apart from a wallet with $50 in it, a few coins, a car key, a house key, and a dirty handkerchief. There were no weapons, and nothing that could have been converted into a weapon was found,' Hayden explained.

'But we know that Coppelli had something in mind. In our opinion – *his use of the word "our" indicated that his views were widely shared by us* – the massacre in his classroom was instigated for the purpose of engineering a meeting with the President. He must have planned this with Charles on their long walks. They may have reviewed the outcome of the slaughter of the parishioners in the Episcopal Church in Durham, North Carolina. Coppelli and Charles foresaw, accurately as it turned out, that the President would want to visit the scene of the massacre and embrace our unlikely hero. And Coppelli knew that Charles was willing to sacrifice himself during the attack on his classroom.

'Thus, my view is that Coppelli predicted that the President would visit the University to console the victims and embrace him at the ceremony. He would thus be able to meet the President and come into close physical contact with him. I think I can only speculate what he was planning to do,' he continued.

'Obviously, the entire event at the University was videoed from the beginning. The video recording is a permanent depository of everything that went on before, during, and after the ceremony. We should have a look at it now. I invite you, however, to concentrate on what happened on stage,' he said.

The video recording came alive when Hayden switched on the recorder. The three agents and I relived the excitement of yesterday. We looked at people arriving in taxis or limousines, dressed in tuxedos and some with gloves on their hands. The women were exquisitely dressed, sported stylish hats, and carried expensive handbags. One could have been mistaken for thinking they had arrived to view a prestigious horse race. We witnessed the arrival of the President of the University, the Secretary of State, the Governor, the Mayor, and the survivors of the massacre. We also watched, with great interest, the arrival of Coppelli, who was panting, having walked one kilometre from his reserved parking spot, and saw him disappear for a few minutes in the rest room, where the recorder observed him freshening up and checking the zipper of his pants. He took out a comb from the inside pocket of his vest and quickly flattened his hair to make it presentable. *He had obviously paid a long visit to the hairdresser before the Awards ceremony*, I thought.

Hayden decided to forward the recording to the moment Coppelli was invited by the President of the United States to come to the stage to receive his Bravery Award.

'Richard, Lolita and Jesper, you can see that Coppelli, having been invited by the President to come to the stage, climbs up the six stairs to the stage followed by the thunderous applause of an appreciative crowd. He stops about three metres from the President and bows to him, as instructed by the Protocol Officer. Then the President starts to read the testimonial. When he finishes his reading, he invites Coppelli to come to the lectern to have the Bravery Medal placed around his neck by the Secretary of State. Next, you can see that Coppelli, when advancing to the lectern, stumbled. This is strange because Coppelli had a steady gait when he climbed the stairs, and the floor was flat, definitively not uneven. There was no obvious reason for him to fall but, of course, it does happen occasionally.

'In my opinion, Coppelli was in a quandary when he reached the spot on the stage where he was expected to wait until asked to advance to the lectern to receive the Bravery Medal. He knew that he had to attack the President as soon as he mounted the stage. Indeed, if he waited until the person at the opposite table approached with the Medal, he would have lost his opportunity to attack. But, in a moment of indecisiveness, he waited until the

Medal was brought to the Secretary of State who was standing next to the lectern. It is possible that Coppelli expected to be embraced by the President once the Medal had been placed around his neck. If so, he may have thought that the embrace would provide him with the ideal opportunity to assassinate the President.

'I invite you to comment upon my suspicions. The video pictures reveal that Coppelli *deliberately* stumbled. If you look carefully, you can see that he somehow engineered for his right foot to be turned, so he then fell but, in the process, he desperately tried to grasp the neck of the President. The intention was to pin the President to the floor and strangle him. He would have had the strength to do that because, in his Macerata days, he was an amateur boxer, and a good one.

'But, to the surprise of Coppelli, his hands glided through the head of the President, and it was as if he was embracing a ghostly figure. He crashed to the floor, and he hurt himself badly. You know what came after the fall. Pandemonium. The Secret Service went into action to hustle the President and the Secretary of State from the lectern, and others helped Coppelli, who was seriously bruised, get up from the floor.'

Hayden purported to rest his case, but suddenly he remembered a detail which he also wanted to communicate to his assembled friends. He felt like a writer who places a postscript after his completed story.

'There is something else. If a person stumbles, their hands are usually stretched out to cushion the fall. But in Coppelli's case, his hands were clasped in a monkey-like grip. Coppelli's hands were ready to strangle someone,' he concluded.

'But, surely, Coppelli must have anticipated that the Secret Service agents would be there in a flash. Trying to strangle a person takes some time. It may well take a minute and the Service would have pumped a few bullets into Coppelli's brain well before then,' I reasoned.

'This may well be the case. However, Coppelli may have thought that he could finish the job in a matter of seconds. Also, as Coppelli appeared to stumble while trying to catch the President's head, the Secret Service agents may have thought that this was not an attempt to harm the President, but a genuine case of misadventure. If so, they would not have reacted immediately, thereby giving Coppelli some added time to complete his dastardly deed. And we also need to consider the possibility that Coppelli did not care whether he was killed. He may well have been willing to sacrifice himself, like Charles in Coppelli's lecture theatre. He may have wanted to become a martyr,' Hayden said.

'Your analysis, Hayden, appears to be compelling. You have persuaded me of the validity of your analysis. It certainly has merit,' I said.

The other Secret Service agents nodded and did not ask any questions. Obviously, Hayden's explanation and the video recording had told them a persuasive story.

'However, what do we do about Coppelli, now that we think he intended to assassinate, or at least harm, the President,' I asked.

'Nothing, because we cannot prove anything that would stand up in a court of law. Yes, in our opinion, the video reveals that Coppelli was grasping at the President's neck, but that could have been the normal reaction of a human being, to seek support to break the fall.

'So, there is nothing we can do.

'When Coppelli was in the University clinic to be treated for his injuries – there were many scratches, wounds, broken ribs, a broken nose – we asked him to submit to a DNA test, but he did not consent to it, giving his right to privacy as a reason. In any case, we have everything on video to revisit this event at any time.'

'Why did you want to extract Coppelli's DNA,' I asked.

'Coppelli was obviously a *de facto* leader of the DNA Movement. It would have been useful for the Secret Service to have his DNA in the investigation of any crimes committed by the Movement or its leaders.

'Of course, if we desperately wanted to have his DNA, the Service could have resorted to alternative strategies to achieve its purposes. However, we decided to let the matter rest, for now at least.

'My advice is not to do anything at all. What could be gained by a prosecution which we can't win?

'He is a Hero of the Nation. Even the victims' families would victimize us if we were to prosecute him – sorry for the pun.

'It is better to leave it and to keep an eye on Coppelli from now on,' Hayden concluded.

The matter was settled, at least for now.

I went along with this conclusion, but I would still inform the President about the events that took place at the University of Southern Kansas. This is my job, as the President's Press Secretary.

16

WHEN I AWOKE THE NEXT DAY, MY HEAD WAS SWIMMING AROUND me, as if it had separated from my body and barely able to keep itself above water. I felt dizzy and a rotten headache, which started after the meeting with the three Secret Service agents, had worsened during the night. It had got gradually worse the more I was thinking about the events at the Bravery Award Ceremony. Really, I do not think there was anything wrong with me, but the challenges and revelations of the last couple of days were taxing my brain. Memory flashes stuck to me like lichens on a person's breast. I flattened the imprint of my head on the pillow, and I raised my legs to my chin. After a few minutes of meditation, I eventually managed to get up, showered – a refreshing experience – and ate a good breakfast of cereals, croissants, and percolated coffee. Somehow, the headache subsided, and I was ready to face the day, the President, and the media.

When I reached the White House, the three Secret Service agents were already waiting for me in the President's anteroom. We were invited to see the President in the Oval Office and, as soon as we stepped in, he said:

'Well, the deception seemed to have worked well. Nobody in the media has picked up any problems. Normally they are so critical of me. Even if there is a small stain on my shirt, it would be publicized widely,' the President grinned while looking at his shirt. His eyes then darted to his pants, and he found that the zipper was securely in place.

The grin became a smile.

'It is good to see the President happy and alert to the world around him,' I mumbled to myself.

'But on this occasion, even though the deception was right in front of their noses, they did not notice anything,' the Chief Executive said contentedly.

'Yes, Mr. President. It was a perfect optical illusion. The media representatives did not realize that the person behind the lectern was a Hologram President,' I confirmed.

'I realize that the hologram technology is still in its initial stages of development, but it already seemed to have worked well during the visit to the University of Southern Kansas,' the President said.

'The technology did indeed work very well on this occasion, Mr. President.

'Do you know that there already is a booming new hologram touring industry, Mr. President? Spectres of Frank Zappa, Roy Orbison and Elvis Presley are attracting huge audiences, with many admirers returning repeatedly to listen to, and to gawk at, the shows,' Jesper butted in.

'It is certainly the new frontier in the development of the music industry,' I reinforced Jesper's comment.

'Yes, and it appears that it is also the new frontier in the protection of the President of the United States,' the President remarked.

'Of course, the hologram technology still has a limited application. For example, it would not have been possible for the Hologram President to take the Medal from its case and drape it around the neck of Coppelli. So, it became necessary for the Medal to be brought to the Secretary of State who would be the official to confer the Award on Coppelli. We were helped by the fact that, in America, Awards for Heroism are typically awarded by the Secretary of State. Thus, the involvement of Mr. Pompo in the ceremony was not unusual and adhered to the procedural requirements.

'In addition, the image of the real President was reflected on the wall behind the Hologram President. The audience would have believed that the image on the wall was the true reflection of the person behind the microphone and lectern. The greatest challenge was to synchronize the words spoken by the Hologram President with the lip movements of the image on the wall. Lip synching is also a developing science,' I explained.

'Of course, the hologram industry is nothing else but a moneymaking endeavour, a gimmick really, but it gives the fans of deceased musicians a feeling of belonging, of being close to their idol.

'There is still a lot of work to be done in this space, but we cannot complain because it worked at the University. I wonder how many people would have noticed the deception,' I speculated.

'It is, however, amazing that the "apparition" – because that is what it is, it is not a real person – has the ability to walk on stage and interact with the Secret Service agents, the guards and the audience,' the President said.

'The Secret Service did not rely only on this technology. We also used a doppelganger who accompanied the real First Lady in the limousine. When he got out, he waved assuredly to the assembled well-wishers like the real President. During the ceremony, he was kept in an adjoining room and was whisked away by Air Force One immediately after Coppelli's tragic fall,' Hayden added to the discussion.

'I assume the First Lady realized that the doppelganger was not her husband,' the President asked.

'Yes, she knew because I briefed her. She played her role as an accomplished actor. In any event, she would have worked it out soon,' I said.

'How?' the President asked.

'Mr. President, when the First Lady shares a ride with you in the presidential limousine, you usually take her left hand in your right hand, but this obviously did not happen on the ride through the centre of Kansas City to the University. An astute presidential watcher would have noticed this point, I think. And the First Lady did too,' I explained.

'You are very observing, you lot,' the President said. He continued to praise his minders.

'Your Secret Service agents did an outstanding job, Mr.

Hayden. Please accept my congratulations on a job well done. I would also like to commend my doppelganger, who did a tremendous job too. He must have trained for more than six months to be able to copy my mannerism, emulate my language and master my accent. By now, he knows more about me than I know about myself, the President said.

'Of course, we could not use the doppelganger for the Bravery Awards ceremony because the chance of the President – that is your doppelganger – being harmed by Coppelli was too great. In retrospect, we obviously made the right choices, Mr. President.

'But the doppelganger performed admirably in everything else we asked him to do. If I had not known about it, I would have sworn that the person who alighted from the limousine, was really you. Even your way of speaking and accent were mastered by the doppelganger. A doppelganger could not possibly have done a better job even if he had practised for months, to perfect this persona,' I said.

'One day, I would like to meet my doppelganger. I might learn a few things about myself by talking to him,' the President said jokingly.

He does not seem to realize how accurate his statement is, I thought.

'We will keep this I mind, Mr. President, that it is your desire to meet him one day', Lolita confirmed in a non-committal way.

'It was a clever idea to have involved you intimately in the preparations, Mr. President,' Lolita said. She had been silent until now, blown away by the opportunity of being in the presence of the most powerful man on Earth. At this moment, she felt that she had the best job in the world. Her parents, if they had been alive – they died a few years ago – would have been proud of her achievements.

'I assume the Secret Service officers, the guards, and the doppelganger are under a legal obligation to maintain total confidentiality and privacy? They are aware of this, and they would have signed a declaration to that effect?' the President inquired.

'Sure, nothing could possibly go wrong. In any event, if something were to leak, we have compelling evidence that the person at the Conventions Centre was really *you*, of course. The meeting has been listed in your official diary. Many people have seen you getting out of the limousine, albeit from a respectable distance. But you were securely secreted in the Oval Office, no doubt solving the problems of the world, and nobody was aware that you were here, because they all thought you were at the University of Southern Kansas at the ceremony to award the Bravery Medal to Coppelli. There is no doubt that the Secret Service did an excellent job; everything has been taken care of,' I commented.

'In any event, there is no need even to pretend that I was at the University, Richard. If we are pushed, we could always admit that the person behind the lectern was a Hologram President. We could easily justify this on grounds of public security, without implicating Coppelli. So, this Administration need not worry about anything at all. And if the story were to come out, I could even boast about America's burgeoning hologram industry. We are the world's leaders of this innovative technology,' the President said.

Hayden decided to add some further information for the benefit of the President.

'When Coppelli was called upon to advance to the lectern to accept his Award from the hands of the Secretary of State, he jumped out of his allocated, reserved chair as if some nail thumbs or a poisonous snake had been placed on it. Before reaching the lectern, awardees had to wait silently three metres away from the President while he was reading the testimonial. Coppelli was visibly overwhelmed by the occasion and by the time he reached the lectern, he may not have known what he would do. However, his instinct took over and he obviously decided to strangle the President. But we do not have proof that would stand up in a court of law. In any event, if something had happened, the Secret Service would have been able to deal with it. So, at the first available opportunity, he would have been unmasked as an idealistic and mis-conceived domestic terrorist. Now, we have neutralized him in another, more humane, way, by giving him a coveted Award! It is a terrible blow to this DNA Movement, is it not?' Hayden commented.

'Do you think that Coppelli, after receiving this Bravery Medal, will resume his advocacy for, and involvement in, that Movement?' I asked.

'Almost certainly not; this is a reasonable conclusion to draw,' Hayden opined.

I looked at the President's face and noticed a faint, slightly mysterious, smile – a smile of satisfaction and gratitude, but also concern.

17

'MAY I COME IN?', ASKED JESPER.

'Sure, what's up?' I answered.

'Yesterday and today, I have twice been contacted by the Concierge of the Willard InterContinental Hotel. There is a male guest staying there for six days and he would like to meet with you, rather urgently. Perhaps, it is more accurate to say that the guest is insisting on seeing you'.

'There are many people who want to talk to me urgently, Jesper. Is he a Republican?'

'No, he is an Italian.'

'Some Italian Americans are also Republicans, Jesper,' I said.

'He is an Italian from Italy, from a village near Florence. The name of the village is Barberino di Mugello. There is a formula-1 racetrack nearby.'

'He says he has some interesting information about Coppelli Colone that he wants to share with you'.

'Does he know Coppelli?'

'Not personally, but he has read about him extensively following his exploits at the University of Southern Kansas. Coppelli is a celebrity in Italy too. The street in the village where he was born has been renamed the National Coppelli Colone street, the Via Nazionale di Coppelli Colone. The street name sounds better in Italian, don't you think so?' Jesper said.

'He is the principal of the high school of Barberino di Mugello, which is on the road to Bologna and some twenty-eight kilometres north of Florence, but in his spare time he is a genealogist.'

'A genealogist is a person who …'

'Yes, I know what a genealogist is. You haven't told me his name yet.'

'His name is Mauritio Andrea Fabbri. Just to be sure I did some basic investigative work, and he is the person he claims to be. I even have a picture of him, in colour. Would you like to have a look at it? He was photographed when he addressed his students during a high school assembly.'

'And I went to the Willard InterContinental Hotel to ask staff – not one but four staff members, mind you – whether the person on the photo was Mr. Fabbri. They all confirmed without hesitation that it was indeed Mr. Fabbri. They remembered his flamboyant swagger, his green trousers and red overcoat with a small Italian flag superimposed on his coat pocket when he arrived at the hotel. He was dressed like Michael Portillo presenting an episode of "Great British Railway Journeys". And he speaks accented English. He is legit,' Jesper concluded proudly.

'He has something interesting to tell me about Coppelli. Well, that certainly triggers my curiosity. Yes, I think I can spare a few minutes to meet with him.'

'We should not ask him to come to the White House, Richard. After all, we don't know him that well and I cannot think of a reason we could give to the Protocol people to invite him to the

White House. We can see him in the lobby of the hotel, later to-day, say at 6 in the afternoon?' Jesper suggested.

'This is a promising idea, Jesper. But you never know, it could still be an elaborate set up to entice me into a trap. To be on the safe side, would you and Hayden be prepared to come with me, just to keep an eye on him, and ... me, of course. You could sit at an adjoining table, consume a beer, and pretend that you are totally engrossed in your own little world?'

'I am happy to do this. I will immediately contact Hayden to ascertain his availability, and I will ring the concierge of the hotel to organize the meeting, Richard. We will pick you up at 5.30 in the afternoon. Would that suit? Jesper asked.

'Yes, unless of course there is a political earthquake which would see me contained in my room at the White House or the Oval Office. So, see you later this afternoon, then,' I said.

After Jesper left, I considered what Mauritio could tell me about Coppelli that I didn't know already, but I was willing to keep an open mind and to give the meeting a chance.

I was collected at the appointed time by Jesper and Hayden. Hayden did not appear too thrilled about the assignment. He had tickets to go to the opera which was scheduled to start at 8.30 at night and he hoped to be leaving the hotel sooner rather than later. It would be the first time that he and his wife would attend a live performance of Bizet's *Carmen*. He explained that his evening meal would be waiting for him at home, prepared by his wife with whom he had been married for 29 years. He would still want to take a shower, dress in a tuxedo, and hail a taxi. They would only make it just in time for the performance.

'Well, if it appears that Mauritio is legit, you might return home immediately after 6 at night – I am certain that Jesper will capably look after the President's Press Secretary,' I said.

'I am sure he is a very capable officer; he is an ambitious guy. He is after my job,' Hayden said jokingly.

When they arrived at the Hotel, a concierge drove their White House limousine into a reserved parking lot and they went into the lobby, where Mauritio was already waiting anxiously.

'Good evening, Mr. Bentleys, thank you for seeing me tonight. I have some information for you about Coppelli Colone that you may find interesting,' he said.

I motioned to my two Secret Service agents to withdraw, without completely losing sight of me. They ordered a beer. Hayden was constantly looking at his watch. He would be leaving as soon as his glass of beer had been drained.

'Let's sit at that table, Mauritio, pointing to a table positioned close to the Secret Service agents' table.

'Would you like a beer? Let's say it is payment for the information you are going to give me,' I said facetiously.

'Why are you in Washington DC, Mr. Fabbri?' I asked.

'Oh, well, I have been here often in the past. Every second year my school organizes a trip to the Eastern part of the United States for our senior students. It has been scheduled for early next year. I am here to arrange the tour, check out the hotels, select meal plans, and talk to people who will be involved in the trip's preparations.'

'Will your students be accommodated in this hotel?' I asked. 'I am curious because the hotel is very pricey. It is one of the finest in the capital and has a long history of achievements. It is used by Presidents who want to get away from the Oval Office,' I said.

'Oh, no! It would indeed be too pricey for my students. But whenever I come to Washington I stay here. It is a little luxury I give myself.

'It really is a showcase of luxury. Some parts of the hotel may be a little bit dated but the indoor swimming pool, gym, roof garden and restaurants still offer unrivalled service to the discerning traveller.

'Mr. Bentleys, I am the principal of a school in a village not too far from Florence. The name of the village is Barberino di Mugello. For six years, I also served as a municipal counsellor in the village, representing the Forza Italia party. For about two out of these six years, I was the only opposition counsellor because the other counsellors all represented the Communist Party. Can you believe that? However, my real love is genealogy. I am an accomplished genealogist. I am well known in the Florence region for tracing the ancestors of people, sometimes even going back to the 14th century. Normally, I do not charge for my services, but I expect people to pay for my expenses.

'During the last couple of weeks, Coppelli Colone has been in the news in Italy, almost daily. He is feted as an American hero. In Italy, we claim he is an Italian hero. As he comes from the Florence region, I decided, just out of curiosity, to trace his ancestors, and I produced some revealing and interesting data. One could say that the information is startling, to say the least, perhaps even explosive,' he said.

'To cut a long story short, Coppelli is a direct descendant of – he stressed the next words – Christopher Columbus.'

Richard could hardly hide his surprise. If that information were correct, he had just won the jackpot because he would have a compelling weapon to wean Coppelli away from the destructive DNA Movement. He decided not to say anything, for the time being, because he did not want to spoil a good story. He refrained from asking questions of Mauritio because he wanted to hear the full story first. He nodded, encouraging Mauritio to unveil the details of his investigation.

'As you know, Columbus was born before 31 October 1451, in Genoa. His name in Spanish is Cristóbal Cólon.

'I started my search, as I always do, in the *Piccolo Museo del Diario*, which translates in English as the Little Museum of Diaries, a delightful museum in *Pieve Santo Stefano* in Tuscany. It is a goldmine of information. On this occasion, I struck gold because I discovered that the great-great-grandmother of Coppelli, a woman by the name of Dora Perestrino Collone, had kept a diary over an extended period. Her diary ended up in the Museum, but I do not know when, or by whom, or how it came into the possession of the Museum. However, I discovered that Dora had obviously been a keen amateur genealogist and had completed the job I wanted to undertake. In her diary, she reproduced a family tree that goes back to the middle of the 16th century, to the daughter of Christopher Columbus's son, Christopher's granddaughter.

'Over the next fortnight, I endeavoured to verify the information in the diary, as much as possible, and concluded that Dora's work was impeccable, certainly believable, and that her family tree was accurate. That would mean that Coppelli is a direct descendant of Christopher Columbus.

'I managed to make a copy of the relevant pages of the diary, if you would like to see them,' Mauritio said.

'Nevertheless, a definitive conclusion could only be reached if it were possible to do a DNA test. It is always conceivable that mistakes were made, either by Dora or me,' he concluded.

If this story could be confirmed, it would be the coincidence of the decade, I thought.

*****

My mind started to wander, taking in the enormity of Fabbri's revelation. I remembered that, soon after I finished high school, I had looked up the definition of 'coincidence' in an encyclopedia. A 'coincidence' was defined as 'a remarkable concurrence of events or circumstances without apparent causal connection'. My encyclopaedic search was a consequence of a remarkable coincidence which happened in my own life when I was a student in my final year of high school.

My high school had organized a joint speaking competition with the girls' school next door. It involved an improvisation where one is given a topic and you have five minutes of preparation time before you are expected to speak about the topic for five minutes. Public speaking was about the only thing I was good at in high school – a point I have made earlier. However, as it was a boys' high school, most of the students did not understand the mysterious world of girls. We were afraid to intrude in the enigmatic domain of the elusive creatures next door because we were afraid even to talk to members of the other sex. We did not understand how their brain worked. But when this joint speaking competition was organized by the boys' and the adjoining girls' school, I was expected to represent our school because I was the school's top speaker. The organizers hoped that the competition would enable boys to become comfortable in the presence of girls. It was a pipedream, dreamt up by the unimaginative leaders of these institutions, who wanted to do something about the quarantined life led by the students in their own schools.

My assigned topic was: 'What should society do to protect its historical statues and monuments?' But when the topic was given to me, I completely lost the plot. It was as if my life had been taken over by anxiety, and stress invaded every bone in my body. Surrounded by girls, it was impossible to concentrate on the topic and when I was finally expected to speak, I made a fool of myself. I was completely incoherent, and I started to stammer. There would have been no way for anyone to discern what topic had been assigned to me. I felt that, in a matter of minutes, I went from best public speaker in a boys' high school to a moronic stutterer in this joint competition.

Some six months later, when I was already in College, I returned to my high school to pick up my diploma and I strolled into the girls' school next door which was deserted because it was holiday time. Suddenly, I saw a piece of paper fluttering through the air; sometimes it would rest undisturbed on the ground, and at other times fly away when the wind swished through the trees, like a bush turkey or peacock who, when approached, simply goes a few steps further to tease you endlessly. I was finally able to pick it up. To my great surprise, it was the original scoring sheet of one of the judges at the competition which had taken place six months earlier, and I discovered that I had scored 0 out of 10. It certainly affirmed that I had been a disastrous speaker on the night. I made an impact, but not as a proficient speaker but more as a bumbling fool.

But what was even more stunning is that this paper fluttered up to me more than six months after the competition had been held when I was taking a stroll in the girls' school. It was as if the paper deliberately stalked me on that day and challenged me to seek revenge on the referee. The score sheet certainly encouraged me to seek excellence in everything I did. I was determined not to receive this score again, ever.

*****

Suddenly, I was awakened from my ruminations by the voice of Mr. Fabbri.

'Mr. Bentleys, is there anything wrong with you? I hope I have not upset you?' Fabbri inquired.

'Certainly not, Mr. Fabbri. I have been trying to digest your unexpected revelation. Yes, I would be happy if you were to give me a copy of the relevant pages of the diary. I would like to thank you very much for disclosing this information. The Administration is grateful to you.

'May I have your postal address, Italian telephone number, and email address? I would like to send you a personalized gift from the President to thank you in an appropriate way for your help,' I said.

'And Mr. Fabbri, if you would like your students to visit the White House when you tour the United States next year, please contact me, and I will organize it for you, and perhaps I might even engineer a private meeting with the President,' I told him gratefully.

'Thank you very much, Mr. Bentleys. I will certainly avail myself of that opportunity. I assume I can contact you by email?' he responded.

'Sure,' I said. My mind was already working overtime, deciding how I would communicate this information to the President.

'Have another beer, Mr. Fabbri. But unfortunately, I can't stay. I have to return to the White House,' I said.

I shook hands with Mauritio, who gave me his telephone number, postal address, and email account details.

'Have a good night, Mr. Bentleys. I hope to see you early next year with my students,' he said.

Jesper and I unobtrusively observed Mauritio until he finished his second beer. Mauritio then went to the reception desk to check for any messages. We waited until we saw him disappear in a spacious elevator which took him to his room.

The concierge retrieved our car when we were ready to return to the White House. He opened the passenger's door for me and Jesper took the driver's seat. On the way back to the White House, many thoughts swirled around in my head. Jesper realized that I was absorbing and analysing the information that I had received, so he kept quiet on our return to the White House. It was that time of the day when it was neither dark nor light, but the gloominess of the early evening was already invading Washington DC when people become mere shadows in the street.

My mind dissected Mauritio's information. I replayed our conversation several times in my mind, like the needle of a broken record that plays the same song. Specifically, one comment worried me. Mauritio had said that he did not know when, or by whom, or how the diary came into the possession of the Museum.

Surely, the Museum must have a set of rules with regards to the receipt of diaries? I pondered that, if the diary's provenance cannot be verified, it is possibly a fake. Perhaps, the provenance of the diary could be ascertained if I had more information about Dora Perestrino Collone? I also noted that Dora's surname had a double 'l' whereas Coppelli's surname only had one 'l'. My ruminations led me to conclude that, before informing the President of this development, I should travel to Italy to view the diary myself and satisfy that it was an original document. I hate to provide the President with hypothetical, tentative, or untested information. In my opinion, a visit to the Museum was the only approach capable of avoiding potential problems for the Administration.

I had not realized that Jesper was driving me back to the White House, so engrossed I was in my own thinking!

I came back to my senses when we had to wait for a minute for a red traffic light to change to green.

'Thank you very much, Jesper. This was excellent work. Also thank you for driving me back to the White House,' I finally managed to say.

'It is all part of the job, Richard. I hope you are able to use the information that Mauritio disclosed to you,' he responded.

I did not tell Jesper that I had second thoughts about the provenance of the diary and that I would ask the President for a few days' leave to go to Italy.

*****

The day after our meeting with Mauritio, I told the President that

I wanted to travel to Italy for three or four days. He was surprised and his reaction to my request indicated that he was slightly dismayed.

'But Richard, I need you here. You are indispensable. What are you planning to do in Italy? Do you have a love interest somewhere in Italy?' he asked.

'No, Mr. President, but something came up yesterday that I would like to check personally in Italy. Once I have the information, I will be able to brief you on the reasons for my trip. The information will either be momentous or trivial. Either way, I need to go there,' I answered.

'You cannot delegate the job to someone else? Is it really that important?'

'It is a search I have to do myself, Mr. President. May I suggest that for the next four days my Deputy stands in for me? He is an intelligent level-headed young man, who will serve you well. He has a degree in political science from the University of Southern Sydney, majoring in American politics,'

'All right then, Richard, but I hope to have you back in your role by the end of the week. I look forward to listening to your debriefing. You certainly have tested my levels of curiosity,' the President said.

✶✶✶✶✶

The next day, I was on my way to *Pieve Santo Stefano*. The plane landed in the international airport of Pisa and a taxi, which charged me a fortune, drove me to Pieve, more than two hundred kilometres from Pisa. I had forgotten to ask the driver for a fixed charge for the transport which cost me as much as the return flight to Italy. I would not be able to recuperate the full amount from the White House travel fund because the accountants always insisted on the cheapest transport mode, even for me.

Pieve Santo Stefano is a delightful, typical Tuscan village. It is a sleepy town, steeped in history and tradition, with medieval houses, some of which are painted in yellow, dreamily overlooking a peaceful car-free piazza, surrounded by cafés and restaurants with tables placed on the pavement. A church with a steep church tower which housed a bell to round up the faithful stands in the right corner of the piazza. The piazza is ornately decorated with colourful balloons and festive lights that surrounded an illuminated Christmas tree erected to celebrate the season – it is the third week of December 2027. The village is richly surrounded by crumbling Roman monuments, including ancient bridges, one of which is dedicated to Tiberinus, the God of the Tiber.

I picked up an information leaflet in the visitors' centre in one of the side streets of the piazza. It described the history of the village, the centre of which had been mined and destroyed by retreating German forces in the Second World War. However, the churches and the *Palazzo del Comune* survived the destruction. Lately, the village became known in Italy as the 'Diary City' because it accommodated the *Museo del Diario* set up in 1984 by journalist Saverio Tutino. I had come to Italy to visit this Museum.

Before leaving the United States, my office had organized a meeting with the current curator of the Museum, Alma Costrino,

'How nice to meet with you, Richard,' she said in a charming manner extending her hands to me. Alma spoke impeccable English.

'How come your English is perfect? I can hardly trace an accent,' I asked.

'My parents live in the United Kingdom where my father works for an international company. I went to school there, followed by university studies in librarianship,' she explained.

'I have seen you on television many times and I am delighted you decided to visit our museum, which is unique in the world. It contains thousands of diaries, donated by people from around the world. It is a veritable goldmine for people who want to do research about their ancestors and our ancient heritage.'

'Thank you very much, Ms. Costrino. I very much appreciate your help. I have come all the way from the United States to have a look at the original diary of Dora Perestrino Collone, who was born around 1867 in this village.'

'Oh yes, you are already the second person who is interested in this diary. A local genealogist came by a few weeks ago to inspect the diary.

'You will find it in the collection of unverified diaries,' she said.

'What is an unverified diary?' I asked.

'These are diaries the provenance of which we do not know.

In other words, we do not know when, by whom, and how they came into the possession of the museum. We have more than four hundred unverified diaries. They were not endorsed as authentic, and therefore they could be fake diaries, dropped here by people apt to disrupt our work which is the maintenance and preservation of our cultural heritage.

'The diary looks more than a hundred years old but a sophisticated dating machine – we have one right here – seems to indicate that it is only about 30 years old. It has been made to look old,' she explained.

'So, does it mean that Dora never existed?' I enquired.

'No, Dora Perestrino Collone is a real person. If you look up the register of births and marriages in the main church, you will find an entry for the year 1867 which is when she was born. What is interesting is that nowhere is there an indication that she attended school, not unusual in those days, and it is likely that she could not read nor write. However, the diary is beautifully written and could only have been drafted by a person who, at least, finished a primary school education plus a few more years of high school. In my view, it is highly unlikely she could have written this diary, although she could have been self-taught.

'So, as we do not know where the diary came from and it cannot be verified as legitimate, it has been placed in the box of unverified diaries,' she told me.

'You are sure that the diary, even though it looks old and worn, is likely to be a fake?' I asked.

'That much is certain, Mr. Bentleys, nevertheless we keep the diary here because the mystery surrounding the diary will one day be resolved, I hope. And there are people like you who want to have a look at it. I too am curious to find out what is so special about this diary. Perhaps it contains valuable information?'

I inspected the diary because I had come to Italy for this purpose. I could not see anything wrong with it, but to the initiated, it was nothing more than a clever forgery. I wondered why anyone would want to deposit this fake diary in the museum, if indeed it was a fake. If the diary had been legitimate, it would have been possible to trace Coppelli's ancestry back to Christopher Columbus. Whoever placed the diary in the museum may have wanted to create the impression that Coppelli was a direct descendant of Christopher Columbus. I was disappointed that the diary was likely to be a fake. I had hoped fervently that the diary would provide proof of Coppelli's ancestry and that I would be able to convey such momentous information to the President.

The curator gave me a quick tour of the museum. She also asked me to pose for a picture, which would be framed and placed in the museum with a caption: 'The Press Secretary of the 47th President of the United States, Mr. Richard Andreas Bentleys, visiting the Museum on 19 December 2027'.

After visiting the museum, I wandered over to the church to have a look at the register of births and marriages. The curator had been kind enough to give a call to the parish priest to alert him to my visit. When I arrived, the priest had already opened the book to the right page. I took a photo of it and thanked the priest, an elderly man in his early 80s who had been the priest for the last 45 years and was a church fixture like the many statues that adorned the church.

'If all these statues were to be smashed, as some people in the DNA Movement would like to do, Italy would be converted into a desolate desert, deprived of its rich history and traditions. A rich history would be replaced by physical and emotional poverty.' I said to myself.

On my way back to Washington DC, I dreaded the moment I had to confess to the President that my trip to Italy did not yield any benefits. I did not enjoy the meal and the drinks that the cabin crew offered to me. Eventually, I fell asleep and only awoke when the captain, speaking on his intercom, informed the passengers that the descent into Washington DC had commenced.

18

It was already late at night when I arrived at the White House. I noticed that the lights were still on in the Oval Office. The President had told me that, as his Press Secretary, it was not necessary for me to make an appointment to see him. At all times, as I was his most trusted advisor, I could simply barge in and see him to discuss matters of State or even to make a social call. I decided to knock on the door to the Oval Office to have a chat with the President.

'Come in,' I heard the President say. As soon as I entered the Office, the President's eyes lit up like a Christmas tree, so happy he was to see me.

'Ah, Richard, I hope you are a messenger of good news? I'll pour you a whiskey.

'How was your trip to Italy? I am sure you have some revelations to make which will shock my conscience,' he said facetiously.

'Mr. President, I hope I am not disturbing you at this late hour of the day. But as you were still working in the Oval Office, I thought I would bring you up to date on the Coppelli matter. You need to be familiar with a few interesting developments in this story,' I said.

'Yes, what is it, Richard?'

'You remember I told you that the Secret Service wanted to

take a DNA sample of Coppelli? However, he did not consent to it when we patched him up after his dreadful accident in the Conventions Centre. He relied on a nebulous right to privacy to reject our request.

'But five days ago, I received an urgent request from the concierge of the Willard InterContinental Hotel to meet with an Italian guest. His name is Mauritio Andrea Fabbri, a principal of a high school in Barberino de Mugello, near Florence,' I said.

'Yes, I know that village.

'Really, how come?' I asked. I was genuinely surprised because I did not know anything at all about this.

'Do you recall that I spent a carefree one-year sabbatical at the University of Florence during my undergraduate days? I remember visiting that village several times to buy ice cream. The village is near a formula-1 racetrack, I think.

'When I was there, the village was governed by the local Communist Party. Can you believe that, in Italy?

'Apparently, it still is,' I said.

'The municipal council adopted some weird rules. For example, you could only buy ice-cream in a one-litre pot in the headquarters of the Communist Party that occupied the grandest house on the piazza of the village. The ice-cream was not available at, and was not sold in, the local co-op. I assume the taxes on the ice-cream were high and spiced the treasury coffers of the Party. Every week I went to pay my respects to the Comrade-in-Chief because I wanted to buy their delightful ice-cream. It was the best in the world!' the President exclaimed. He was smacking his lips when reminding himself of these ice-cream episodes.

When is he going to stop interrupting me and listen to me, for a change? The information I want to communicate to him is important, I thought.

When there was a short lull in the President's tale, I took the opportunity to continue with my briefing.

'Mauritio is a keen genealogist and he visited Washington DC, staying in the Willard InterContinental Hotel for six nights. He was here to organize a tour for his senior students who are scheduled to visit the Eastern part of our country early next year.

'But listen to this. As Coppelli hails from a small village near Florence and is feted there as a local Hero, Mauritio decided to trace Coppelli's ancestry. He found a diary in the local Diary Museum, written by Coppelli's great-great-grandmother – Dora Perestrino Collone was her name – which contains a family tree of the Colone family. Dora had traced her ancestry back to the middle of the 16th century to Christopher Columbus's granddaughter. Her work alleviated Mauritio's task because she had completed most of the research for him. The diary revealed that Coppelli is a direct descendant of Christopher Columbus. This also explains his surname, Colone. Columbus's surname was Colón in Spanish. Dora's surname was Collone, with a double "l", so sometime during the last 150 years, someone decided to drop one "l".

'Wow, that's a significant piece of intelligence, Richard. We might use it to weaken the DNA Movement, by "decapitating" its leadership?'

The revelation stunned the President, and he could not find the words to describe his surprise and anticipated joy at 'decapitating' the Movement.

'Yes, Mr. President, this is precisely what I had in mind. However, it was necessary to travel to Italy, to the village of *Pieve Santo Stefano*, to confirm the accuracy of that information. You see, Mr. President, I was not altogether confident that Mauritio's information was historically accurate. I was concerned when he told me that he could not ascertain when, or by whom, or how the diary had been deposited in the museum. It appeared to me that, in relying on Mauritio's tale about Dora's diary, we were destined to embrace a solution which was as simplistic as it was inaccurate.

'After viewing the diary and talking to the curator of the Diary Museum, I realized that the diary was a fake, since carbon dating made it approximately 30 years old, even though it looks ancient. What is equally concerning is that my visit revealed that Dora Collone could not read nor write and therefore, could not have written the diary. It is thus possible that some charlatan produced the diary to create the impression that Coppelli Colone is a direct descendant of the great navigator,' I reported to the President.

'So, you wasted your time in Italy, Richard?'

'Not entirely, Mr. President. Mauritio's revelations might still enable me to find out whether Coppelli is a direct descendant of Christopher Columbus.

'I propose to invite Coppelli to a meeting with me and my three Secret Service friends. I will recount Mauritio's story, but without telling him that the diary is likely to be a fake.

'I think Coppelli will be greatly surprised by the information that we will feed him.

'I will also tell him that it is just possible that Dora or Mauritio made a mistake or misinterpreted the relevant information. Not likely, but mistakes are always possible in this space. I will then ask Coppelli again to submit to a DNA test. I can't see how he would be able to rebuff us on this occasion because he is probably as curious as we are about his ancestry.

'In my opinion, Mauritio's revelations can thus be used to convince Coppelli of the necessity of settling the matter by submitting to a DNA test, which he previously refused. I assume that his curiosity will make it impossible for him to refuse a test. Do I have your permission to proceed along these lines, Mr. President?'

'Sure, Richard, and please keep me informed,' the President answered.

'Once we have his DNA, we will be able to compare it with other known descendants of Christopher Columbus, or with a DNA sample that we could take from Columbus himself. He is interred in the Cathedral of Seville in Spain. I think the Spanish government would sympathetically consider our request to take a sample of the remains. What do you think about this proposal, Mr. President?' I asked.

'What kind of government does Spain have, Richard? Is it a conservative or a socialist government? The Spanish never seem to have made up their minds as to how they want to be governed,' the President asked.

'At the moment, it is a socialist government, but that could change quickly, Mr. President,' I answered

'Well, in that case, Richard. I do not think the government would allow us to disturb the remains of Columbus. These politicians are always in favour of what we are against, or vice versa.

'When the socialists came to power a few years after the death of General Francisco Franco, they introduced legislation to remove Franco from his purpose-built tomb and they started to rewrite history. Isn't that another example of the desecration of monuments and the subversion of history?' the President asked.

'Mr. President, there is a qualitative difference, I think. The removal of Franco's remains from his tomb was sanctioned by a government of a different persuasion, of course, in a calculated attempt to legislatively change history. What we are experiencing now in the United States and, indeed, throughout the world, is a spontaneous – well, I am not sure about that because it could be orchestrated – movement led by people, not governments to destroy monuments and statues,' I explained.

'In any event, I think it would be possible to establish conclusively that Coppelli is or is not a descendant of Christopher Columbus, if only we were to obtain his DNA,' I concluded.

'Noted,' the President said.

'You have my blessings, Richard. But please inform me as soon as the results of the DNA test are known. This is fascinating stuff; it could be interesting,' the President said.

'Yes, it is ironic that Coppelli agitates so publicly and loudly against Christopher Columbus, accusing him of heinous genocidal crimes, the Father of Genocide no less! And yet, he might well be a direct descendant of the great explorer and navigator!'

'If he is a direct descendant, he will probably see history in a different light?' the President suggested.

'This would be highly likely, Mr. President. But there is more, much more,' I indicated, thereby raising the President's curiosity.

'The Secret Service is now firmly of the view that Coppelli did not accidentally stumble, but actually engineered it so he could assassinate you, the President of the United States.

'Why? I was about to give him a Bravery Medal, and he received it in the end after the fracas,' the President said.

'Do you recollect I told you about the envelope that Martha gave us? It contained a single sheet of paper in which Charles directed Coppelli to seek revenge for the "evil misdeeds" which he attributed to you. So, I assume that Coppelli was merely implementing this directive when he tried to assassinate you during the Bravery Awards ceremony.

'I should also tell you about our discussion we had with Professor Colone soon after the unfortunate events at the Awards Ceremony.'

'Mr. Coppelli, how come you stumbled?' we had asked him.

'I was extremely nervous. It was a great occasion for me to be honoured by the President. I tried to prevent the fall by holding on to something, to break the fall. So, I instinctively grasped at the President, to prevent me from falling, but I somehow could not get hold of him. It was as if my hands glided through his body. It felt as if the President was simply not there at all. As if he was a ghost. It was as if a knife smoothly went through a block of creamy butter.'

'This is how he described the incident to us, Mr. President.'

'He will probably never realize how accurate his assessment of this situation was,' the President said.

'By the way, knowing you, I assume you invited Mauritio and his students to the White House when next they are in the United States.'

'I did, Mr. President, and I also indicated that I would be able to engineer a private meeting with the President himself!' I responded.

'Are you not getting ahead of yourself, a little bit?' the President retorted.

19

Hayden extended an invitation to Coppelli to attend a meeting in Washington DC with him, his two Secret Service colleagues and me. The meeting was planned for the Friday of the first week of January 2028.

'We want to congratulate you on receiving the Bravery Award. And we also like to use the opportunity to debrief you,' Hayden had told him when arranging this meeting.

When Coppelli's plane arrived from Kansas City – the airline ticket was purchased by Hayden's office – he was picked up by a driver from the White House pool and taken to the headquarters of the Secret Service. He was asked to wait in a nice office with a picture of the President on the wall. The sofa had been arranged to ensure that visitors sitting in it would necessarily have to admire the Chief Executive's picture. A coffee table with a glass top full of daily newspapers, a travel magazine, and a recent copy of *Newsweek* was placed in front of the sofa. However, Coppelli decided to sit in the sole armchair which was placed in a corner of the room from where it was difficult to view the President's picture. A conference table was strategically positioned on the right-hand side of the room, underneath an enormous light bulb that illuminated the whole place. The office boasted a minibar with drinks waiting to be consumed by visitors to the office.

After about ten minutes, the door to the office was opened and Hayden, Lolita, Jesper and I entered the room.

'Would you like to have a drink, Coppelli?'

'Perhaps some Italian limoncello?' Hayden suggested.

'Yes, that is awfully nice of you. I would like some limoncello.'

'And it comes with a sumptuous and humongous cheesecake,' Hayden continued.

He had decided to sweeten him up before revealing the information he wanted to discuss with Coppelli.

Hayden placed the delicacies on the coffee table and waited until Coppelli was comfortably seated and in the process of devouring the cake.

'Coppelli, we are in possession of a letter which Martha was supposed to give you if Charles were to perish, which he did. However, instead we convinced her to surrender it to the Secret Service.'

'Who is Martha?' Coppelli asked.

'Martha is a VIP hooker who regularly serviced Charles. He obviously trusted her with the envelope which he expected her to give to you upon his demise.'

Coppelli didn't flinch. 'What was in the letter?' he asked casually.

'Not a great deal. There were two messages, requests really. Charles asked you to take over the leadership of the DNA Movement if he were to die. He also directed you to take revenge on the President of the United States to punish him for his "evil deeds". Do you have any idea what were these "evil deeds"? What exactly did Charles mean?'

'Well, as to the first request, I have to consider my options. I am inclined to take on the challenge of leading the Movement, but I am afraid that these demonstrations are getting out of hand. I do not like the destruction of property and the uncontrolled gratuitous violence. But when there are one million people on the streets, there is not much that I would be able to do to control the crowd.

'As to the second request, I have no idea what Charles wanted me to do,' Coppelli said.

'You and Charles never discussed anything at all with regards to the President? Did you ever talk about any "evil deeds" which arguably had been committed by the President?'

'Nope," Coppelli shifted uneasily in his chair and his eyes started to dart from one person to another. He picked up some cheesecake crumbs with a finger to put them in his mouth, and he casually looked at the picture of the President but turned his gaze away almost immediately. The picture reminded him of that fateful accident when he crashed to the floor of the stage, trying to grasp the neck of the President.

The Secret Service officers had decided not to confront Coppelli with their suspicions that the fall was orchestrated deliberately and that he tried to grasp the President's neck to wrestle him to the floor. There was nothing to be gained from such a disclosure and a lot to lose. In any case, nothing could be proven conclusively.

'Coppelli, we have asked you to come to our office today because we have a most interesting piece of information to communicate to you.

'A few days ago, an Italian gentleman visited our city, from Barberino di Mugello, staying in the Willard InterContinental Hotel. He is a genealogist. He has traced your family ancestry because you seem to have built up quite a reputation in Italy as a hero. And his research revealed that you are a direct descendant of – he waited a few seconds before continuing – Christopher Columbus.'

The revelation exploded in Coppelli's body like an atomic bomb, sending plumes of disbelief in the sky. He felt silent, and any natural resistance to the "interrogation" by the Secret Service officers collapsed. His mouth dropped open revealing half-eaten pieces of cheesecake, and saliva was dripping down on the side of his cheeks. He wiped a few morsels of the cheesecake from his mouth with his left hand rather than with the napkin that laid undisturbed next to the limoncello glass. He looked with incredulity at me – speechless. He did not at first instance believe this piece of information because he suspected that the Secret Service could be duplicitous, and sometimes disinformation is the best information available to the Service.

'I guarantee that the information is *not* fake news, Coppelli. I suggest that we visit the gentleman later today or early tomorrow if you are interested in the details of his research. He has agreed to extend his visit by a few days and would still be available until tomorrow night for a follow-up meeting. His name is Mauritio Andrea Fabbri, and he has quite a reputation as a genealogist, especially in the Florence area. He discovered that your great-great-grandmother, whose name was Dora Perestrino Collone, kept a diary and made a family tree going back to the middle of the 16th century.

'I have made a copy of his research findings and I am happy to share them with you. It will make for interesting reading tonight,' Hayden remarked.

'Is it possible that Mauritio, if that is his name, has made a mistake?' Coppelli finally blurted out.

'No, we do not think that a mistake has been made. Mauritio is not a lummox. But a mistake is always in the realm of possibilities. We have checked the results of his research ourselves, as far as that is possible, and we are satisfied that the information is correct.

'Nevertheless, theoretically it is always possible that a mistake has been made.

'That's why I would like to suggest something, Coppelli. To clear up this issue, why don't you consent to a DNA test? We will then be able to compare your results with the DNA of known descendants of Christopher Columbus, and the mystery would be solved finally. I am sure you want to test the veracity of this information.'

'Most certainly,' Coppelli said.

'I am happy to submit to a DNA test.'

*****

The DNA test was done the next day before Coppelli was able to change his mind – an ever-present danger. The results were tested and retested. They were compared with the DNA results of a known descendant of Columbus, who had been flown in from Spain to make himself available for this test. The results were as clear as spring water: Coppelli was a direct descendant of Christopher Columbus. Perhaps, the diary's conclusions were accurate, after all?

'How is it possible? Could you explain a bit more?', Coppelli asked. when he was confronted with the results.

'I am not a scientist. I suggest that tomorrow we visit the Laboratory where the researchers will explain the results of your DNA test in detail; they will do a much better job than I can. I just communicate the result of their investigations to you.

'Now, how do you feel about this?' I asked.

Coppelli did not answer; he was dumbstruck.

Afterwards, when the meeting had ended, Hayden claimed that he saw a transformation taking place in Coppelli's demeanour. Although Hayden's claim was an exaggeration, it was clear that Coppelli had been struck by a devastating piece of information akin to lightning.

Naturally, my Secret Service friends or I did not tell Coppelli anything at all about the provenance of the diary.

'Of course, this does not clear up the mystery surrounding the unverified diary. But there could be reasons as to why the family tree, which may well be accurate, was found in a recent diary which was made to look old. The owner of the original diary may have wanted to keep it, but still endeavoured to make the information in it available for research by transcribing the content in a new diary? That may well be an acceptable explanation, but we obviously cannot be certain,' I said to Hayden, Lolita and Jesper.

But the diary was not needed anymore. A DNA test doesn't lie.

20

A FEW MONTHS AFTER RECEIVING THE MEDAL OF BRAVERY, when he was healed – in the spring of 2028, the week before Easter – Coppelli travelled to Italy where he was invited by the Mayor of Florence to receive the keys to the city. A tickertape parade was organized by the city's council. The streets were lined with cheering and clapping people. Some waved small Italian and American flags that fluttered in the wind on this bright sunny day in spring. Girls offered Coppelli some colourful flowers, and they kissed him on the cheeks. He rode in an open Fiat through the centre of the city at 10 kilometres an hour, an honour usually reserved for the top scorer in the Italian Seria A soccer competition who also made the winning goal in the World Cup. Like royalty, he waved at the people who were feting him as their local hero. He was inundated with confetti that was strewn on the streets in front of his car and smothered by the love of this beautiful medieval city. He received a few offers of marriage from local girls, who promised to look after him with unstinting devotion and everlasting love.

The parade ended in the *Piazza della Signoria* where a podium had been constructed and an audio system installed. The local television station had sent half a dozen journalists for a live coverage of the event. The Mayor, several city counsellors and Coppelli were seated like victorious kings on ancient chairs decorated with beautiful wood carvings and plush upholstery. The

Mayor explained to Coppelli that the chairs were once owned by the powerful Medici family, but later came into the possession of the city. The Mayor, realizing that this event would cement his reputation as a successful politician, gave a captivating speech in which he described Coppelli as a local genius who obtained a professorship in the United States and saved a score of students from certain death, while all the time disregarding his own welfare.

'Coppelli Colone is one of us. He is an Italian hero, and we are immensely proud of him. It gives me immense pleasure to invite him to accept the keys to the city of Florence,' he shouted to the crowd.

It was a week of feasting, adulation, and hero-worshipping for Coppelli.

✶✶✶✶✶

After one week in Italy, he returned to his American classroom to teach history of ideas and jurisprudence students. A late snowstorm had transformed Kansas City into a Christmas-like landscape, but the snow was melting now, and a few rays of sunshine started to warm the city. The wind billowed gently through the trees which had been planted around the ill-fated lecture theatre a few years before. Coppelli was not teaching in the lecture room where the tragedy took place. That room had been gutted by the University administration and been converted into a permanent shrine to the students who were murdered there in cold blood. It was never going to be used again for lecturing purposes. The room was permanently locked to prevent curious visitors from gawking at this place of infamy. Only when special permission was granted by the Provost, or the President of the University would it be possible to visit the scene of the heinous crime. Every year, a non-denominational memorial service was held in that room; the service could only be attended by family of the victims, survivors, and some invited guests.

Soon after Coppelli started teaching his students, they detected a change of staggering proportions in their professor's teaching philosophy, and personal behaviour. His appearance was no longer repulsive, and his dress sense was more conventional. It appeared as if he had bathed; his long hair had been cut, his teeth brushed, his goatee removed, and he did no longer smoke cigarettes. And his philosophical attitude was no longer stridently one-sided. He stopped imposing his preferred views on his class and he encouraged unimpeded discussion of ideas. The freedom of speech enjoyed by his students soon became a talking point on campus and revitalized its stale culture of compliance.

In his lectures, he talked about the importance of respecting history.

'Mankind could learn a lot from history,' he repeatedly said.

'Of course, racism destroys the soul and hearts of people and reduces their opportunities for no other reason than a biological accident of birth, but it is vital we learn from the events of the past because, soon enough, this generation will also be the past and will be judged like we judged our ancestors.

'History is a supreme teacher.

'Of course, when Christopher Columbus discovered the Americas, he committed many documented crimes, and if we test his activities in the light of modern standards, we can only be justifiably horrified.

'But it is possible to argue that the navigators and discoverers of the 15th and 16th centuries were enlightened people of their time. Columbus certainly thought he did God's work when he wanted to convert as many indigenous people as possible to Christianity.

'If we test past practices in the light of modern knowledge, then many actions of the past would have to be regarded as immoral and now also illegal, like slavery, child labour, corporal punishments, torture, and the imposition of discretionary punishments. We know that these practices are odious examples of violations of human rights, but it is also feasible that people in the 15th and 16th centuries did not realize this or understand the consequences of their actions.

'Or, in an Australian context, – I worked in Australia for a year at the University of Southern Sydney, *he reminded his class* – the government removed indigenous children from their parents and placed them with white families. This was considered as a humane, welfare act in the '40s and '50s. Now, of course, we know that such removal violates the basic rights of parents and children and was nothing else but an example of ethnocentrism. The Australian Government rightly apologized in 2008 to the indigenous people for this stolen generation.

'No generation has a monopoly on morality and righteousness?' he told his class.

'I predict that many of our opinions staunchly held now by most of us may be regarded as retrograde in 50 to 70 years from now.

'That is why it is important to learn from history.'

Some of his students wanted to know his views about the destruction of monuments and statues. They knew he had been an aggressive and assertive advocate of the DNA Movement, and the students were keen to find out how he regarded this Movement now. He was brutally honest when he told his students that his previous advocacy for the Movement was a mis-conceived and counter-productive exercise.

'I do not condone the racist actions and attitudes exhibited by the people who are immortalized on some of these statues and monuments. But, in their own way, they may have honestly contributed to the society they were living in. Take for example, General Robert E Lee, who President Lincoln invited to be the Chief Commander of the Union Army during the American Civil War. The General declined the invitation because he felt that his loyalty should be with the State he came from, Virginia. Loyalty is a positive trait but, in his case, it also involved the promotion, or at least acceptance, of some practices which later would be heavily criticized as egregious violations of modern-day standards. Does it mean we have to destroy his statues?

'Whether we like it or not, Lee is a part of American history, and we cannot just erase him from our history books. In doing so, we bury our heads in the sand like an ostrich and pretend that the past has never happened.

'Would it not be better to attach an explanatory note to the statue that explains the context in which the General worked? Also, the statue could be surrounded by other statues that extoll the contributions made by African Americans or Union soldiers who died in that terrible conflict, the American Civil War. Would that not be the better way to go?' he asked his students.

'Should we destroy all the remaining Roman statues and monuments in Italy and elsewhere in Europe because the Roman Empire's wealth and power was drenched in the blood of slaves?', he rhetorically asked his students.

Coppelli soon obtained a formidable reputation as an excellent, vibrant, and stimulating lecturer, a model for all other staff to emulate. He even became eligible to apply for the coveted Excellence in Teaching Award of the University which came with a prize of $20,000 and a Certificate of Exceptional Achievement. The University had decided that lecturers were eligible for the Award if nominated by at least ten students and two colleagues and provided they had completed the University's Tertiary Education Teaching Certificate. All staff could enrol in the Certificate course free of charge. The Certificate teachers were respected teachers in the Education Department. The brochure, in extolling the virtues of the course, indicated that education experts would teach participants how to teach courses at university level. Coppelli enrolled because he was interested in applying for the

Teaching Award. But to his great surprise, those who were supposed to tell other staff how to teach, could not teach. They had difficulty formulating educational philosophy; they could not properly convey their ideas to members of the class and exhibited an assertive and aggressive mentality which most participants disliked. They bumbled their way through the lectures; they were unimaginative, and not open to considering different teaching methods, and were jealous of those who succeeded as teachers in the University. Sometimes, Coppelli felt as if he was going to take control of the proceeding. Often the words, 'Get out of the way, I will show you how to teach', were on his lips, but he restrained himself because he was merely interested in that Certificate which he needed to be eligible for the University's Teaching Award. He told his students:

'Look, there are three types of academics. First, there are those who can teach and are good at it. These academics teach. Second, those who cannot teach will eventually end up teaching others how to teach – *he considered that this is what happened in the Certificate course.* Third, if academics cannot teach and they also fail to teach other academics how to teach, then they become education and teaching critics, which means they will criticize indiscriminately the teaching and research activities of every other academic. In my experience, most university academics here at the University are critics,' he said.

'Professor, surely this view does not endear you to your colleagues,' a student commented.

'Indeed not. However, what is most important: to be honest or to tell people what they want to hear?'

His assertion, of course, had been recorded and some of his colleagues had heard his disparaging comments about their inability to teach and their inclination to become 'critics'. His colleagues were incensed, and they sent vile and aggressive email messages to Coppelli to complain about his unacademic and uncollegial attitudes.

'You are giving all of us a bad name. In any event, you have just expressed an opinion. You have no evidence whatsoever,' was about the nicest message he received during the fortnight following his discussion of his comments in class.

These criticisms did not ruffle Coppelli. Instead, Coppelli read some of these messages to his students in class.

'In sending aggressive email messages to me, my colleagues have just demonstrated that what I told you is true. They have become critics, instead of devoted teachers who concentrate on their teaching.

'You now understand why, in our school, we have adopted a policy of discouraging the use of email. Email usage often results in the promotion of aggressive communication behaviour that is damaging to people,' Coppelli said.

He did not wait for a reply and the student did not volunteer a reply. But it led to a heated debate between Coppelli and two other students, who disagreed with the Professor's and the Department's discouragement of email usage. The students opined that the use of email had facilitated communication around the world.

Students were enjoying the discussion because the participants tenaciously defended their views and refused to admit defeat. But suddenly a stranger appeared at the door of the lecture theatre. Coppelli always kept the door open.

'We should allow the air to circulate,' he told his students. However, his students believed that Coppelli wanted any casual visitors to the University to hear him teach and admire his teaching prowess.

When the students saw the stranger at the door, muffled snivels of anxiety swept through the room, and it stopped Coppelli in mid-sentence.

'What is happening?', he asked one of his interlocutors. He had obviously not yet seen the stranger at the door.

The student pointed hesitantly to the door and remained silent.

The stranger at the door was the University President. He beamed a smile.

'Please forgive me for interrupting your class, Professor Colone. But I have some excellent news to share with you, and your students will also be delighted to hear the news,

'The University Senate has decided that the University's Excellence in Teaching Award will be awarded to you,' he said.

The class erupted in boisterous and sustained laughter. They thumped the table they were sitting at, and they started to congratulate Coppelli who could not believe what he had just heard.

'Thank you, Mr. President, I am humbled by the University Senate's decision. I am not sure I deserve this Honour,' he stammered.

'You most certainly deserve the honour, Coppelli. The Senate praised your innovative teaching, your ability to enthuse students and encourage them to develop logical and sustained arguments. You make students think! An ability to think is a rare quality these days, even in the Academy! The University's Senators thought that you were a model tertiary teacher, and not just a brave Hero! Congratulations, we are all proud of you.

'May I suggest that the class be disbanded for now, that is if the students are happy with this?'

The students did not reply. The President's question was rhetorical; it had only one possible answer!

The President told the class: 'I would like to take your professor back to my study where an excellent bottle of Bollinger is waiting for us, to celebrate his good fortunes. Afterwards I propose to take him to dinner in the finest restaurant in Kansas City.'

This sounds expensive, Coppelli thought.

'Yes, yes, *Viva il Professore*. He is the best of the best,' the students chanted.

Coppelli was quickly becoming a legend.

After the dismissal of the class, the President and Coppelli, walked back to the Administration building where the President had his palatial office. The President's suite consisted of various rooms. People gained access to the President's suite through an anteroom where two prim older secretaries were working on files and typing letters on laptops. They politely greeted Coppelli as he entered their domain but remained taciturn. The University President would look after Coppelli. A door led into the private office of the President. It was as big as a small apartment, around sixty square meters. To the left was a kitchenette and a large dining room where prominent politicians, businesspeople, selected academics, and movers and shakers would eat sumptuous lunches. To the right was a utility room, a shower, a powder room, and toilet.

It would be possible to live here comfortably for some time, Coppelli thought.

It was the first time that Coppelli visited the University President's office. On three sides, the President was surrounded by bookshelves that covered the whole wall, from the ceiling to the floor; books on psychology, political economy, and a myriad of other topics – the President was a political scientist and psychologist – his desk was located on the only side where there were no books. The desk was huge, as expected, it had a black laminated top with a laptop and a telephone on it, but nothing else. Behind it were a row of drawers, where some personal files of the President were kept.

'I can see that you are admiring my desk, Coppelli. Do you know – of course, you don't – that it has three secret compartments that can only be opened by me using a bespoke remote. There is another remote which enables me to hermetically close the door leading to my suite. It is a safety issue,' he explained proudly.

'The President of the United States has his bunker below the White House, and I have my magical remote,' he said jovially.

'Well, you certainly have many books, Mr. President,' Coppelli said slightly amused. 'Have you read them all?' he asked.

'Of course, I am an avid reader. I know the contents of all my books,' he responded equally facetiously. 'Why don't you take a seat on the sofa? I will fill our glasses with Bollinger. I have a few more bottles in the fridge. I assume you like champagne. It is better than your Italian prosecco,' the President said.

After a few minutes, they were joined by the Deputy President of the University and the Senate committee members who recommended Coppelli for his Excellency in Teaching Award. They would all join the President and Coppelli for dinner later that evening. There was pleasant banter all around.

'It is good to see that you have completely recovered from your fall at the Bravery Awards Ceremony,' the President said.

'Yes, I tried to cushion the fall by holding on to the President. It is just an instinctive reaction, you know, but it was as if the President was a chimera, and my hands went through his head as a knife in butter. There was nothing there to hold onto. I am still wondering about this,' Coppelli disclosed.

'Well, in situations like this, a lot is unreal,' the University President remarked.

'Let's go to the restaurant, have dinner and enjoy ourselves. Celebrate the achievement of our brave Professor, whose name is now a household name in the United States.

'I have organized a few limousines that will take us to the restaurant. It takes about 20 minutes to get there.

'I hope you will all enjoy the menu I have selected for this occasion. The food is Italian, the wine is Australian from the Margaret River area, and the coffee and company are American,' he said contentedly.

'I am British,' the Deputy President reminded the President.

'*Viva il Professore*,' they all chanted.

*****

When Coppelli arrived at his home around midnight, he took a shower and brushed his teeth – his hygiene standards had been raised after the Bravery Award Ceremony – and then he went straight to bed. He would still be reading a chapter from a book. After such an exciting day and night, it would be impossible anyway to sleep well.

He arranged his body comfortably in bed, he propped himself up with a cushion, poured himself another drink and took the book from the bedside table. The title of the book was *The Science of Holograms* and Chapter Three advised on *How to Create an Optical Illusion without Anyone Noticing*.

Half an hour later, Coppelli put the book down and, half sleepy, vowed, 'His day will come, one day.'

He was still determined to achieve his objectives, but without the violence associated with the destruction of statues and property.

'An Italian is never defeated,' he mumbled, exhausted but happy.

21

THE SECRET SERVICE HAD ALSO TAKEN A DNA SAMPLE OF Charles Roderick Dudley during his autopsy. The Forensic Pathologist had not yet released the results of the autopsy to the media, but the Secret Service had obtained an advance copy of the results.

Following the autopsy, the President recommended the cremation of Charles's remains, but the Service thought it would be better to bury him, in case it was necessary to exhume him in connection with the calamitous attack in Coppelli's classroom, and the destruction of property during the DNA Movement demonstrations.

A day later, in May 2028, Hayden requested an urgent meeting with me.

'What is so urgent, Hayden?' I asked.

'Well, I do not know where to start, Richard, but I have a piece of information that will change the history and course of this country,' he said.

'That is a wide and sweeping claim. What do you have on your mind?'

'You remember that Charles's autopsy took place yesterday. The autopsy revealed that it is likely that Charles committed suicide. The hole where the bullet penetrated his skull, is consistent with Charles holding the rifle in his right hand to shoot himself.

The trajectory of the bullet is also consistent with this theory. As Coppelli is left-handed, it would have been impossible for him to inflict the wound that killed Charles. Our view is that Charles, knowing that police officers were in the corridor and fast approaching, decided to commit suicide to prevent him from being shot by the police,' he explained.

'That is certainly interesting, but it will surely not change the course of this Nation.'

'Indeed not; suicide has always been one of the theories considered by the Service and the Police. It will change nothing,' Hayden agreed.

'Yes, that much is true. But Richard, you have not heard the real reason I wanted to see you urgently.

'It was discovered that the DNA of Charles is a complete match with the DNA of a powerful and influential person,' he said.

'Who is it? I am already trembling with trepidation. You are raising my curiosity levels.

'Is it the Pope, or the President of the People's Republic of China, or the Dalai Lama, or perhaps our Australian friend, Benjamin Adhemar? I asked sarcastically.

'Don't be facetious, Richard. Charles's DNA completely matches the DNA of the President of the United States.'

'You mean, Desmond Raymond Clarkenson?'

'Aha.'

Hayden briefly waited for this message to sink in. For quite some time – it could have been five minutes – I could not formulate a reply. What I just heard was unbelievable; it was as if a missile targeted at me, had sparked my brain.

Hayden did not wait for me to respond and continued his story.

'I am saying that there is incontrovertible evidence that Charles is the son of the President of the United States.

'Obviously, when we found out we ensured that the pathologists were under a duty of non-disclosure. They were told that very heavy fines and long jail sentences would be imposed on those who disclosed this information to anyone. They understood that – I hope for their sake.

'Naturally, we immediately looked into the background of the President. The President is 57 years of age, and Charles was thirty-one on the day he died. That would make the President 26 years old when he had an affair with Charles's mother, who unfortunately died a few years ago, after suffering from cancer. It also means that the President had an affair when he was already married to Catherine, the First Lady,' Hayden explained.

I immediately saw the consequences of these revelations. The President would find it difficult to campaign on traditional family values if these revelations were true. But worse, his request to cremate the body of Charles would be interpreted by vicious media vultures as a clumsy attempt to hide forever the affair of 31 years ago. There is no doubt that the President was justifiably concerned about Charles's terroristic attitudes, but he may have been equally concerned about his own secret past.

'Was Charles aware that he was the President's son?' I asked.

'We cannot be certain, but we think that he knew. There are two reasons for this. First, when he visited Martha for his weekly "check-up" he asked her to contact the President of the United States if something were to happen to him. She promised she would do that, but obviously never had an intention to act upon this promise. We assume that this request indicates that Charles knew, or at least suspected, that he was the illegitimate son of the President. Second, there is an indication that Charles may have told Coppelli that he was the President's son. We found a note, addressed to Coppelli, in Charles's derelict apartment in which he discloses that he is the illegitimate son of the President. In the note, Charles also encourages Coppelli to seek revenge. The note is a final testament, not unlike the one made by Hitler in his bunker the day before he committed suicide. But there is no hard evidence that Coppelli knew of the existence of this note,' Hayden said.

'If Coppelli knew about this secret, this would explain why he has abandoned his militant ways to change the country. Because he knows that, at an appropriate time of his choosing, he would be able to expose the President of the United States as an adulterer and hypocrite. There would be no need any longer to assassinate the President. Such a disclosure would be a more sophisticated, and cruel, way of inflicting untold misery on the President,' Hayden concluded his explanation.

'What would you like me to do?' I asked.

'I do not know. This is a political issue and that is your department. You need to make the decision what you propose to do about this information,' Hayden answered.

'Are you able to guarantee that the information you have given me is completely accurate?', I asked for confirmation.

'There is no doubt that the information is accurate, Richard. I leave it to you to consider the consequences of this information for the present Administration. For now, we will classify the information. It will disappear in a thick file. In 50 years, a diligent researcher will discover it and will become an overnight sensation,' he said.

I had a job to do, and I did not look forward doing it.

22

'MR. PRESIDENT, SOMETHING CAME UP THAT I HAVE TO DISCUSS with you. and it cannot wait,' I said.

'You are not going to resign, are you? You are indispensable in my Administration. You are convicted to stay here until the very end,' the President retorted.

That probably will be sooner rather than later – the end, that is, I thought.

'Hayden, the Secret Service agent, visited me in my office. He provided me with details on the demise of Charles. The autopsy took place yesterday, and some interesting things were revealed,' I started gently.

I could see that the President became uneasy and shifted his body in his presidential swivel chair. He clasped his hand and then he lifted one hand to massage his eyes. He looked at the desk and removed a few specks from the surface. Stretching his legs under the desk, he was waiting for me to continue.

The outside light filtered through the huge windows of the Oval Office, and I could see the expanse of the White House lawns. A detail of maintenance officers and gardeners were working in the garden to beautify the bed of roses and rhodo-dendrons and remove a few patches of weed which had miraculously arrived after the rains from a few days ago. The gardeners even discovered a few mushrooms that had appeared overnight, but they could not tell me whether they were edible or poisonous.

'There is no point inviting a mushroom expert to come to the White House, only to inspect a few mushrooms. Just remove them from the lawn,' the Chief Gardener had instructed.

'Mr. President, you remember that during the autopsy, forensic pathologists extracted Charles's DNA, and the Secret Service circulated it through their sophisticated machines and a perfect match came up.

'Charles's DNA is a perfect match to *your* DNA, Mr. President,' I announced.

'Charles is your son, Mr. President,'

I expected him to say that the results were inaccurate, but instead and to my surprise, he admitted that Charles was his illegitimate son.

'Yes, Richard, it is true. Mind you, it was a youthful indiscretion. I was already married to Catherine,' he admitted.

'I met Charles's mother, who was also already married, on one of my campaign trips when I was a candidate for the House of Representatives. She attended one of my rallies and came to see me after my speech. She said that "I was a man on the way up" and she indicated that she wanted to get to know me better. I was stupid enough to invite her to dinner, and afterwards …

how could I be so imprudent? At that time, I was 26 years of age, I had not yet been elected to a political office, but I was very much involved in the affairs of the Republican Party in Massachusetts,' he clarified.

'How come Charles's mother never revealed the affair?' I asked.

'It wasn't really an "affair". It was merely a one-night stand, Richard. Anyway, it was enough for her to get pregnant. When she found out, she arranged for me to see her in a coffee shop, and I pleaded with her not to divulge the information to anyone. If it had become known that I had been unfaithful, my career as a politician would have ended before it even began.

'Fortunately, she was willing to accede to my request, but she asked for financial assistance.

'So, I secretly gave her a yearly stipend which would be terminated, if she were to disclose that I was the father of Charles. Even her husband was not aware of the deception. Until this day, he believes he is the father of Charles,' the President said.

'Where does it leave me?', he asked.

'Yes, what are the options? You could own up to the deception. This would make your wife extremely unhappy, and your chances of re-election would be severely damaged. The electorate and your opponent would describe you as a hypocrite and you would no longer be comfortable campaigning as a social conservative on family issues. Or, alternatively, you could carry on as if nothing has happened, in the hope that your secret will not be revealed. However, numerous people already know about this affair, which is in addition to the people who did the autopsy,' I stated.

'In fact, Charles may even have told Coppelli about it in a sort of testament that he left behind in his apartment. In it, he claims to have told Coppelli that he is the illegitimate son of the President. So, if Coppelli wants to harm you, he does not need to assassinate you anymore. He can simply disclose this sordid affair – or one-night stand, as you would call it – to the world at a time of his choosing and harm your electoral prospects.

'I suspect that this is what he may well have in mind,' I said.

The President was honestly contrite.

'I was saddened when I learned that Charles was behind the DNA Movement. This Administration has done a lot of work to facilitate the equal treatment of all races in this country. I was even more saddened when the members or supporters of his Movement started to destroy businesses, loot shops, and demolish our historical statues and monuments.

'The achievements of this Nation are the envy of the world. We should protect and nurture them. It is our historical destiny and duty,' the President said.

'But I have to take responsibility for my mistakes.

'I think I will resign my office as President of the United States.

I will address the Nation tomorrow night to announce that I am stepping down at 12 noon the next day and that our Vice-President will be sworn in as the 48th President of the United States,' he told me in confidence.

The President's statement gripped me by the neck as if a rope had been placed around it before the hangman opens the plank on which a condemned person is standing.

'But, Mr. President, surely there is no need to resign. An American President would not waste his re-election chances because of a sexual dalliance? There is a lengthy list of former American presidents who, at some point in their lives, were involved in sexual indiscretions, and yet went on to do great things for the country.'

'That is correct, Richard, but I have a different moral compass, my friend,' the President retorted.

'There is no need to resign the presidency. What will you tell the people? What reason will you give? It cannot be health reasons because your health is still robust,' I stressed.

'The truth, Richard, the truth. The truth sets you free.'

*****

The following day, at 6 in the afternoon, the President addressed the Nation.

'My fellow Americans.

'During the last three years, I have overseen an Administration that has substantially improved the lives of American people. I am proud about our human rights legislative agenda which aims at achieving real equality of opportunity for all Americans. My Administration capably and successfully returned the country to prosperity following the disastrous Covid-19 period that devastated this country and killed more than 600,000 of our compatriots, just a few years ago.

'Much more needs to be done. I am so sorry that our "law-and-order" policies did not result in the outcomes I had hoped for. I am sad that the DNA Movement, while well-intentioned, facilitated the destruction of property and the removal of many historical statues.

'As a Nation, we need to protect our heritage. In destroying our statues and monuments, we are denigrating our history and depriving ourselves of the opportunity to learn from history. I hope we do not see such destruction again for a long time, if ever.

'I have decided to address you tonight because I promised when I took the oath of President that I would always be honest with the American people, and right now, it is important to be honest.

'To my great shame, I must admit that, when I was 26 years of age and already married to Catherine, I had a sexual encounter with a woman who has since died. That woman was the biological mother of Charles Roderick Dudley, the domestic terrorist who invaded Professor Coppelli Colone's classroom and killed at least fifteen students. You will recall that the Secretary of State and I travelled to the University of Southern Kansas to award the Bravery Medal to Professor Colone.

'Yesterday, I confessed the affair to my wife of 36 years and, fortunately, she has forgiven me, which I am so happy about. Earlier this afternoon, I talked to the father of Charles Dudley, his stepfather, and I explained the situation to him, honestly and fully. He was understanding and most supportive and he, too, has forgiven me. He brought Charles up as his own son. He often mentioned to people that his son looked a bit like the President of the United States, and he hoped that he too would achieve high office. He even told me that he voted for me at the last election.

'However, I know that this episode, regrettable as it is, will burden my Administration. Some people will question the integrity of this Administration and my moral ability to lead this great Nation. They may even think that I recommended the cremation of Charles Dudley as an attempt on my part to hide the existence of my sexual indiscretion. I can guarantee that this is not the case. I merely wanted to ensure that his grave would not become a shrine for extremists.

'Therefore, I have decided to resign the Presidency as from tomorrow at 12 in the afternoon. At that time, the Vice-President will take the oath to become the 48th President of the United States. I wish him and his Administration the absolute best. I know that the country will be well cared for.

'Finally, I would like to ask the media to respect the privacy of my family to allow a process of healing to take place.

'It has been an immense privilege to have served as your President. God Bless America,' he said.

*****

As far as people knew, the President was happily married, and he had never been accused of adultery. Any scandals, if they existed, were carefully hidden in the closet. Until a few days ago, I certainly had not been aware of anything in the President's personal history that could affect his election fortunes. Indeed, he was a perfect advertisement for the maintenance of traditional family values. The First Lady, Catherine Alma, was devoted to her husband and to the many charities of which she was the Patron. The President referred to her as 'Cathy'. Their lives were busy and exciting.

Cathy and the President met 37 years earlier in college, when the President was 21 years of age, and she was nineteen. They were immediately attracted to each other. Most times, it would be a platitude to say that it was love at first sight, but on this occasion, it was an accurate assessment of their relationship. He was in his Senior Year in College and would add a few more years of study to gain a Master of Business Administration degree at Harvard. Before he left for Harvard, they married in an Episcopal Church built in the early 18th century, where they were surrounded by history, beautifully painted windows, a granite altar, a splendidly crafted wooden pulpit which was more than two hundred years old, handcrafted pews, a bronze baptism font, and some sculpted statues of eminent pastors of the past. Their parents were of the view that the couple married too soon after having met, but they could not, and would not, stop the intended marriage. Of course, since then, they became very fond of their successful son and son-in-law, the President, and their daughter and daughter-in-law, the First Lady. They even changed their allegiances to the Republican Party, something they had claimed they would never do. But they did.

*****

For at least one hour after the President's address to the Nation, almost nothing could be heard in Washington DC. There was hardly any traffic and no music emanated from the houses. The children did not play in the streets and squares of the city. The only noises that could be heard were the frantic telephone calls made by journalists to their papers and stations and the humming sound emanating from television sets in peoples' homes.

I was out of a job, unless the Vice-President, soon to be President, decided to keep me on, which was unlikely because I suspected that he wanted to appoint his own man or woman to this demanding job. Like the President, I could proudly say, 'It was an immense privilege to have served' as the President's Press Secretary.

*****

Coppelli watched the President's resignation speech with great interest in Kansas City.

He had opened the envelope, which contained Charles's political testament. Charles had made two identical envelopes, one he left in his apartment and the other he gave Coppelli. The envelope contained a single sheet of paper in which Charles beseeched Coppelli to take over the leadership of the DNA Movement after his death. Charles also disclosed that he was the illegitimate son of the President of the United States. His mother had told him the day before she died. She was visibly relieved when she had told him. It had been too much for her to keep this a secret for so long. She had asked Charles to keep this information a secret because nobody would believe him anyway, unless of course a DNA test were to confirm the veracity of this potentially explosive story. She was still in love with the President.

Coppelli now understood why Charles had been talking about 'revenge' when he ensnared him in his work. Not only revenge on American society for continuing racial policies and maintaining a society where benefits are determined by one's race, but also 'revenge' on the President for seducing his mother.

Following the resignation speech, Coppelli realized that it was no longer necessary to assassinate the President because he had been removed from public life anyway, a self-imposed punishment.

Coppelli went for a walk to order his thoughts.

PART FOUR

The Revelations

chapters 23-26

23

A FEW YEARS LATER, WHEN COPPELLI TURNED 66 YEARS OF AGE, his grateful students decided to organize a memorable party for him. They thought that, as Coppelli would soon retire from active teaching, it would be a well-deserved and appropriate celebration of a brilliant career and of a remarkable professor, who left a legacy of heroism, self-sacrifice, and scholarship. For several months, they frantically convened meetings of interested students to make plans for the spectacular event which would be billed as the grandest soiree ever held on campus. They asked the University for permission to use the quadrangle's expansive lawns of the University as the venue. The application revealed that they were planning to build a temporary platform, where the speeches would be held and Coppelli be granted life membership in the students' union. One of the highlights of the evening would be a speech by the professor himself, who had been asked to reflect on his life's achievements. There would be stalls displaying the publications of Coppelli, some of which would be for sale, and the best food and drink, and a banquet would be offered to invited guests.

The University's President signed off on the students' application, although some parts of the proposal had to be revisited, especially the students' proposed plan to restore the venue to its original state, after the festivities. But in the end, all disagreements, or misunderstandings between the Administration and the students were ironed out, and the light was set to green. According to the students' union, Coppelli would get what he so richly deserved.

At the time of the students' application, the person who announced the conferral of the University's Teaching Award and enjoyed a bottle of champagne and an exquisite dinner with Coppelli was no longer the President of the University. The University Senate had sacked him two years previously because the IT Director had discovered that, over an extended period, he had accessed hard porn sites on his university computer. Also, the University's auditor revealed that the President's expenditure almost equalled his salary and was spent on expensive overseas trips, flying First Class, and staying in the most exquisite hotels. He had also surrounded himself with apparatchiks of dubious quality and reputation and paid them a fortune for little work of value. However, he crossed an imaginary red line when, in an interview to a local station, which the President thought was not recorded, he described the Senate as a 'bunch of stupid, uninformed troglodytes who couldn't even speak properly'. After that outburst, it was just a matter of time before he would be summoned by the Chancellor to receive his marching orders. His position was in limbo for about three months, during which he threatened the University with lawsuits and 'spectacular' revelations. He claimed that he had confidential information about some University Senators that would expose their incompetence and gross mismanagement. But, in the end, his threats amounted to mere puff because, eventually, he meekly handed in a formal resignation.

A new University President had been duly selected by the Senate. He was a competent financial manager who considered the consequences of his actions on the university, the staff, students, and the wider community. He was an excellent communicator with impeccable connections to government and policymakers.

The new President of the University of Southern Kansas was me!

Following my departure from the White House, I received lucrative offers to serve as a director of public companies. Two universities approached me to accept a professorship in the history of ideas, offers which I rejected. I found it more lucrative to charge a lot of money on the speaking circuit. People wanted to hear about the President I had served for more than three years as Press Secretary; they were interested in the Administration's policies, achievements, and failures. Some people wanted to hear about the President's "affair" with the mother of Charles Dudley. As could be expected, there were many requests to comment upon the shootings at the Episcopal Church in Durham, North Carolina and at the University of Southern Kansas, among other atrocities.

I imagined that my erstwhile high school friends, and enemies, would be blue in the face from jealousy. Not unexpectedly, I started to receive invitations from my posh Chicago Catholic high school to speak to their students and their newly reconstituted photography club. I was held up as a model citizen, and an example of what could be achieved with diligence and the wise application of one's talents. I was described as a person of high morals and integrity, bent on exposing corrupt practices in schools, universities, and government circles.

There is no such thing as successful as success itself, I thought.

When the offer to assume the Presidency of the University of Southern Kansas was made, I could not refuse it because it represented a once in a lifetime opportunity to make an impact on the higher education sector. It did not matter that I was not even an American citizen and had maintained my Australian citizenship. The University Chancellor had explained to me that I was a citizen of the world, and at that time, I was the person the University wanted to appoint.

'I even expect you to take your holidays in Australia, Richard. I know that once people have heard the laughing of the kookaburras and the thud of hopping kangaroos, they will want to hear these sounds from time to time. No problem there, my friend,' the Chancellor had stated.

The Chancellor's reference to laughing kookaburras reminded me that, at our Australian home in Sydney, a kookaburra always sat on the railing of our deck, waiting for me to get up in the morning. I would feed the beautiful bird; it gratefully accepted the leftover cheese, fish, and meat I gave him for breakfast, and sometimes lunch. The bird had brown feathers speckled with white patches; it had inquisitive eyes and a long pointy beak. I could stand next to it, and it would not fly away. It would sit on the railing until we finished our breakfast and then it would start its daily adventures – but it would return the next day.

'I very much appreciate your sentiments, Chancellor. And yes, I intend to visit my home country from time to time. My roots are still there,' I confirmed.

Even my membership in the Republican Party was not a bar to becoming President of the University. It helped when, in discussions with the Chancellor, I discovered that he too was a fellow traveller of the Republican Party. I decided that my presidential career at the University would involve a revolution in the world of ideas and the battle of cultures – I was going to appoint more conservatives to weaken the progressive framework of the University. I have now served in this position for a little more than one year.

*****

I was luxuriating in the President's office – the office with the huge desk and the bespoke remote – on campus when the students first came to explain what they had in mind to celebrate the life and times of Professor Coppelli Colone. I listened attentively to their grandiose and turgid ideas, most of which could not be implemented. Their requests presented me with a moral dilemma.

Whichever way I look at it, there is no right solution which offers itself to me, I thought.

The application worried me greatly and I sat on it for more than a week. Students were becoming restless, and the first inklings of discontent appeared in the students' campus newspaper which was unimaginatively known as *Campus News*. A few articles had already been published in which the Administration – the students did not yet dare to target me personally – was described as 'indecisive' and 'un-cooperative'.

So, when I finally decided to give the students permission to organize the event on campus, their preparations accelerated frantically. They gave visible expression to their enthusiasm by building an impressive platform, providing seating for many hundreds of guests, printing programs, and allocating stalls to vendors of food, drink, and books. The students' excitement was infectious and palpable when one entered the previously sedate cloisters of the University's main quadrangle.

Coppelli's stature and prestige had only risen during the intervening years. He was a Hero of the University, and of a grateful Nation. He had received the highest Bravery Award from the hands of the Secretary of State, – no mention was made of the unfortunate incident at the Awards Ceremony – and the University's Teaching Award which is the most prestigious award on campus. He was constantly feted during his many overseas trips, not just in his native Italy, but in other countries as well, receiving numerous citations and medals for bravery and scholarship. I could not deny the students' requests because otherwise I would have been described as miserly, uninformed, and even vicious.

Some staff members joined the planning committees that organized the event, which was scheduled for late spring of 2031, the year before Coppelli's planned retirement. Preparations were on schedule. When the day arrived, it was foggy in the morning and the mist spread itself as a veil over Kansas City. It heralded a beautiful, sunny day. Later in the morning, the weather became truly glorious, proudly exhibiting a blue sky without a single cloud, no rain had been forecast, and the Bureau of Meteorology had predicted warm temperatures of around 75 degrees Fahrenheit. The campus looked festive with flags flying everywhere, the American flag, the Italian flag, the Kansas flag, the University flag, and the Students' Union flag, and it felt as if the campus's quadrangle was converted into a huge fun fair that had forgotten the solemn nature of the event, the celebration of the life of a great man.

Of course, as President of the University, I was invited to give a speech. I had decided to keep it short. I was uncomfortable with the request to glorify the achievements of Professor Colone. Doubts gnawed at my conscience which still battled dark memories planted there by Coppelli during the massacre in his lecture theatre, and the battle was still raging unabated. Of course, when I became President of the University, I was aware of the almost unrestrained adulation on campus of Coppelli; it was nothing short of a Coppelli cult.

Apart from Coppelli himself, I was the only one on campus who knew his secret, that he was not a Hero, but a calculated serial killer, whom I could not expose without causing untold upheaval and misery for all.

*****

The President of the Students' Union invited me to say a few words. I slowly climbed the few steps to the podium to give a short address.

'Good evening, Professor Coppelli Colone, friends of the University. I am pleased to welcome you all to the main quadrangle of the University for this commemoration. I have known Professor Colone for a long time since the disastrous attack in his lecture theatre five years ago. I know that the University and wider community hold him in high esteem. I am pleased to be part of this celebration. On a day like this, I should not make a long speech, because the day really belongs to Professor Colone. I will yield the floor to him and to his students to do the talking,' I said.

Some of the attendees were surprised that I failed to glorify Professor Colone and thought that I had demonstrated a spectacular lack of gratitude. But their views remained unexpressed opinions. Some other people believed that I had struck the right balance and my decision to let the Professor speak for himself was the right decision.

'After all, it is the Professor's Day,' they said.

The moment of glory had arrived! Coppelli would address the assembled crowd before the feasting would commence.

As he did a few years before when he accepted the Bravery Medal, Coppelli slowly walked up the six steps to the platform, where he assumed his place behind the lectern. He cleared his throat and started to speak.

'Mr. President, students and friends. I am standing between

you and dinner and therefore, I too will not impair your sanity by speaking for a long time,' he started his speech.

This is a line that I had heard many times before. Not very imaginative, I thought.

As it turned out, Coppelli's speech did not reveal any new insights into his life. It was a superficial account of his activities. Surprisingly, he spent little time on the University attack, concentrating on his teaching and research achievements. A good observer would have concluded that Coppelli too was fighting an unresolved battle within himself.

There was one more fabulous surprise planned before the assembled crowd would be invited to feast on fresh oysters, lamb, barramundi from the Northern Territory in Australia, freshly cooked vegetables, rice, and red potatoes, followed by an Italian-style tiramisu. The organizers had also ensured that copious amounts of Chianti wine from Coppelli's region of Tuscany would be available at the feast.

The Master of Ceremonies, a history of ideas student, announced that a life-sized statue of Coppelli would now be unveiled. This announcement sent a frenzied wave through the already hypnotized crowd. They chanted, '*Viva il Professore. Long may he live*.'

The statue had been sculpted by a local artist and it would be permanently positioned in the middle of the quadrangle. The location of the statue had been the subject of intense debate in the Senate. I argued that the statue should not be displayed in the quadrangle, but instead kept in the University's Museum, which was poorly patronized. On this occasion, the Senate did not follow my advice, and gave in to the students' demand. Of course, I was determined that, at the first available opportunity, I would remove the statue.

The statue was an excellent image of Coppelli. There was general agreement among the students and staff that Coppelli must have sat for it while it was sculpted. He had an outstretched hand as if he wanted to protect those under his control which, according to the official reports, is precisely what he had done during the attack. Everybody admired the statue which was regarded by the assembled crowd as an almost God-like creation. It was cordoned off to prevent admirers from jumping on it or touching it. Coppelli was moved to tears when he saw the statue.

24

FOLLOWING THE CELEBRATIONS AT THE UNIVERSITY OF SOUTHERN Kansas and the unveiling of his statue, Coppelli was invited to visit Cadiz in Spain, which is the place Christopher Columbus sailed from on 2 April 1502, on his last journey to the New Indies. The Cadiz Chamber of Commerce had built a replica of the *Santa Maria*, the sailing boat commanded by Columbus on his last trip. A hundred people had been randomly selected to join the celebratory expedition to the New Indies and to serve as sailors on the vessel. Coppelli was the Chamber's guest of honour on this recreation of the maritime exploits of his ancestor.

*****

After the DNA test had confirmed that Coppelli was a descendant of Christopher Columbus, he had studied the life and the career of his illustrious ancestor. He considered himself an authority on Columbus. Coppelli realized that, although his ancestor was known as the discoverer of the Americas, the Columbus adulation was unwarranted because the Norse people, even 500 years earlier, had almost certainly discovered the New World. Around 1000 AD, a Viking warrior, Leif Eriksson, visited what is now Canada. President Lyndon Johnson signed an Executive Order that proclaimed 9 October as the Leif Eriksson Day to honour the legacy of the Viking explorer.

Nevertheless, Columbus became a truly imposing historical figure whose discovery is celebrated in America on 12 October, Columbus Day. It commemorates the landing of Columbus, on that day, in the American islands. Although the two dates, 9 October and 12 October are close to each other, this closeness is a mere coincidence. Apparently, 9 October was chosen as the Leif Eriksson Day because on that day in 1825 the ship *Restauration* arrived in New York, carrying Norwegian immigrants to the United States.

Christopher Columbus had been trained for a life of sailing, discovering, and marauding. He took to the seas when he was 10 years old. Even at a youthful age, he visited lands far away from his native Genoa in Italy. His voyages took him to the British Isles, Iceland, and present-day Ghana. He did not know another life. His formal education was limited, but he was a gifted, intelligent person who read widely and was familiar with developments in geography, astronomy, mathematics, literature, and the arts.

Columbus undertook a first voyage to the Americas, leaving Spain on 3 August 1492. He did not anticipate finding a new continent but merely a convenient route to Asia. He called the lands that he discovered the New Indies, and the inhabitants, Indians. Columbus was able to embark on his first voyage following arduous and persistent representations to King Ferdinand II and Queen Isabella I of Castile, and previous approaches to European royalty as well. He was commissioned to return to Spain with gold and spices, and if successful, he would be showered with largesse. Following his return to Spain in early 1493 with captive natives, he had been made the Governor or Viceroy of the New Indies, in accordance with the agreement reached with the Crown of Castile. But by 1502, after completing a second and third voyage, his Commission as Governor was withdrawn because he had been accused of heinous, atrocious crimes and cruelty against the indigenous population and Spanish settlers. He was accused of gross negligence, incompetence, and brutality. These accusations of alleged atrocities had reached the ears of the royal sponsors of his voyages. He had been briefly imprisoned after his third voyage but released soon after. He was preparing for his fourth, and last, voyage to the Americas and would be leaving from Cadiz, Spain on 2 April 1502.

Columbus still exuded a powerful influence on all those who were selected to sail with him on this fourth voyage. He was commanding an impressive fleet of seventeen ships, and he was in charge himself of the main vessel, the *Santa Maria*. Preparing for this trip was a huge logistical exercise. Food, medicines, and especially fresh water had to be loaded to last for at least six weeks before they would be able to restock or reach the North American continent. Christopher had seen too many failed voyages because sailors started to rebel when their provisions were in short supply or no longer available. The selection of suitable, loyal sailors was a major and constant headache for the commanders of his vessels.

Columbus had no sympathy for, or patience with, complaining sailors who questioned his authority and were involved in rebellious or seditious activity. He was known as a harsh and uncompromising commander. His brig on the *Santa Maria* was always full of sailors. Most of these would be executed by hanging, without mercy. This was the way of the 15th century and the early part of the 16th century. There was no other way.

On 2 April 1502, Christopher Columbus was barking orders as if he were a seasoned dictator.

'Load the provisions on board the vessels – immediately', he instructed Ludovico who was responsible for this onerous task. Ludovico Castello Mare had been with him for all his voyages and was one of his most trusted sailors. It was for this reason that he placed him in charge of the provisions. This was a delicate and sought-after job that carried great prestige with the other sailors.

'I want to talk to the commanders of my ships in my cabin – immediately', he barked to some people who were still loitering on the wharf. They looked up to him and took off their hats in a sign of respect. They walked up the gangplank in a straight line like a group of rowdy schoolchildren under the direction of a tyrannous teacher. They would receive their instructions which would have to be implemented without fail.

The *Santa Maria* was the biggest and most beautiful of all the ships in his convoy. It was a 4-masted vessel powered by sails and its beam was 20 metres. It had a long bow with a glorious statue of a Greek Goddess that ploughed through the waters of the deep ocean, heaving, and raising. The vessel was able to achieve a speed of 5 knots per hour and complete, on average, 120 kilometres per day. It was a two-story vessel. The cabin of the Commander-in-Chief was on the upper level, not unlike the location of a modern-day executive suite, which one would find on the higher or highest levels of a commercial building. The sleeping quarters of the more than hundred staff, bakers, cooks, butchers, cleaners, sailors, soldiers, farmers, doctors, even a priest were below deck, in the bilge, where the berths were located. The priest had his separate alcove below deck where he could communicate without hindrance with the God of Christianity and plead with Him for an uneventful but fruitful trip to the New Indies. He would provide the sailors with the blessings of the Almighty God, and he would hear the sailors' confessions every day.

*****

Coppelli was excited to retrace the steps of his ancestor. As the guest of honour of the Chamber of Commerce, he was assigned a nice cabin and he enjoyed dinner with the captain, every night. He provided the sailors with useful information on Christopher Columbus to ensure that the voyage accurately reflected the navigator's last trip.

The journey on the replica *Santa Maria* was uneventful during the first four weeks of the celebratory voyage. The vessel anchored in Gran Canaria, in the Azores which was a dependency of Castile in Columbus's day, for some maintenance and replenishment before continuing the journey westwards.

Disaster struck on 18 May 2032, three weeks after leaving Gran Canaria, when Coppelli's vessel sailed into a hurricane, which the sailors had never experienced. The vessel could not avoid the storm because it was not fast enough to circumvent the perilous event. At first, the ocean was quiet and enjoyed the warm rays of sunshine which converted its surface into a giant cobalt expanse. The stillness and the absence of wind, which made sailing difficult, were alarming omens that a storm was brewing. Dolphins and whales, which had amused the crew even a few days before, were nowhere to be seen, as if they had been alerted that a calamitous event was on the way. The usually noisy ocean birds had fallen silent which was a harbinger of the coming disaster. It must have been like the day before Mount Vesuvius erupted and covered Pompeii with a blanket of ash in 79 AD.

The storm arrived around three in the afternoon. The hurricane's explosive force tossed the *Santa Maria* around, from left to right, from right to left as if it was a paper ship dancing precariously on the water's surface. It shuddered like a leaf that desperately clings to a tree branch. The ocean turned into a revengeful paroxysm, angry, and unforgiving. The vicious storm started with thunder far away but in less than half an hour it had reached Coppelli's sailing vessel. Every bang was preceded by lightning that boiled the ocean, becoming a terrifying furnace. A cocktail of white foam and gigantic waves rammed into the vessel and threatened its integrity. Its wooden planks creaked and screeched and croaked like a pig taken to the slaughterhouse.

The Heavens opened their sluices and dumped their total supply of water, worth several months of precipitation, on the sailors who desperately tried to pump the water out of the vessel. The torrents of rain, sometimes accompanied by hail, became a torrential stream, and grew into a deluge that relentlessly lashed the decks of the *Santa Maria* and flagellated the sailors.

*****

Coppelli, when studying the celebrated career of his ancestor, had come across a detailed description of a storm which had battered Columbus's convoy of ships on his last voyage in 1502. The storm had refused to surrender even when the crew invoked the help of the Almighty. Most of the sailors were still superstitious and regarded the storm as a punishment from God. They professed their belief in the Almighty and promised loudly to lead a virtuous life, if only they would be spared. They called out to the priest because they wanted to confess to some minor, and sometimes, appalling, sins in a futile attempt to secure their admission to Heaven. It was the busiest day of the priest's life on board. He hardly paid attention to the screams for assistance because he was concerned with self-preservation.

'God only helps those who help themselves,' he proclaimed.

Instead of helping themselves, some sailors wanted to die rather than be struck down by lightning. A few sailors could not stand it any longer and they jumped overboard. Others were swept overboard when monstrous waves as high as modern skyscrapers attacked the ships.

'This is a message from God. God is punishing you for maintaining a sinful lifestyle, swearing, stealing, cheating, and fornicating,' the priest intoned, still trying to do the job for which he was paid a pittance.

*****

Coppelli thought that the hurricane he was experiencing was worse than the one described by Columbus. The captain of his vessel had great difficulty keeping it afloat. Like Columbus before him, he desperately barked orders which most of the time could not be heard.

The deluge lasted for three days. Towards the end of the third day, the vengeful God showed mercy and compassion, and granted the sailors some respite. By then, the sailors were exhausted and ready to return to Spain, but the captain decided to continue this journey of discovery and retrace Columbus's steps, just like Columbus had done in his time.

Throughout the ordeal, Coppelli's body was shaking uncontrollably. He looked like a corpse that made a gargantuan effort to blow some life into itself. He had difficulty focusing on the objects around him. He touched every piece of furniture in his cabin to seek support from these inert objects. As he was suffering from ophthalmia, his eyesight was fast deteriorating. His gout was excruciatingly painful and severe arthritis tormented the bones in his body. He suffered from a persistent headache. Irritating rashes appeared all over his body, and he had vascular disease. He was certain that this recreation of Columbus's last voyage would not end well.

'The process of ageing is not for the faint-hearted,' he reminded himself.

He took his head into his large hands and started to cry when no one could see him. As Columbus would have done, he kneeled in front of the cross of Christianity and asked God for forgiveness for his terrible crimes, the murder of innocent students, and the indiscriminate destruction of property and historical statues and monuments throughout America.

He then sat in his chair to meditate and contemplate, for several hours. As he was meditating, he was no longer sure that his defilement of Columbus's statues and his involvement in the students' massacre were legitimate responses to the endemic problem of racial discrimination. He had told the captain not to allow any visitors into his cabin for a few hours. He needed to have some time for himself to prepare for what inevitably was going to be a tense, but hopefully, fruitful meeting of the ship's sailors. It was necessary for him to show leadership; he needed to inspire the people around him. He was their idol and they all looked up to him. He was respected as a father figure who looked after the welfare of his family. If he showed weakness, the recreation of Columbus's voyage would crumble like a dilapidated wooden house, the foundations of which have been attacked by hungry termites. He sat in his chair for a long time, at least a few hours, thinking about the past and the present. It was the chair that

Columbus had occupied during his last voyage. The Chamber of Commerce had been able to borrow it from a museum for the celebratory journey. It is the same chair that had been displayed during the Columbian Exposition in Chicago in 1893. It was always destined to become a museum piece, a part of the Columbus adulation culture. Coppelli was its present occupant. He liked this chair because it was comfortable; a mighty ship with two masts had been imprinted on its upholstery. It was part of the antique furniture in his cabin that also boasted a chaise longue, but Coppelli preferred to idle in this priceless Columbus chair.

When the hurricane's destructive force abated, the captain of Coppelli's vessel took shelter in the mouth of the Rio Jaina River on the island of Hispaniola, the eastern part of which is now known as the Dominican Republic. The vessel was heavily damaged, and it ran dangerously low on water, and food too was in short supply.

As part of the recreation, when the vessel arrived in Hispaniola, the indigenous people were waiting for Coppelli and the sailors with spears and other projectiles. They did not have hostile intentions; the sailors were welcomed by a friendly crowd that organized a delightful feast for the sailors. In contrast, when Columbus arrived on the island in 1502, the indigenous people were unfriendly and aggressive. Coppelli had read about Columbus's arrival on the island when studying the life of his ancestor. The commander of one of the other ships in Columbus's convoy, the *Verona*, had provided Columbus with an opinion:

'Christopher, after the second voyage, you established a settlement with 650 Spanish settlers. Perhaps some atrocities were committed by the local tribes or the settlers. Anything really could have happened to make these savages brutally hostile.'

'We will eventually find out what happened. If there have been atrocities, those responsible for them will be punished. In the meantime, take up your arms and wrestle control over the island from these savages,' Christopher had commanded.

The savages' primitive weapons were no match for the muskets of Columbus's soldiers. He did not give them any warning but simply shot his way onto land. The indigenous population fled in fear afraid for their lives. Columbus established a beachhead and systemically started to explore the island, murdering the population as he advanced inland. He did not show any mercy. As he did not know the island, he was afraid of traps. He was also mindful of his sponsors' expectation that he would return to Spain laden with gold and a few savages, who did not appear to have a religion and therefore could easily be converted to Christianity. He could display these primitive natives as exhibits to his Spanish benefactors. They were museum pieces.

As he advanced into the interior of the island, he discovered that the Spanish settlers had been murdered and their tenements had been destroyed. From then on, Christopher became a monstrous tyrant who slaughtered the indigenous population, the Arawaks and the Taino People, and sold their females and males into slavery well before slavery developed in the Americas. He became a genocidal maniac whose statues adorn the squares and streets of the United States.

Of course, when he died in 1506, Columbus could not have predicted that these documented genocidal activities would be used in the future to justify the destruction of his legacy.

One keen participant in this destruction was a fellow Italian, Coppelli Colone who, during many DNA Movement protests, sought to demystify the alleged achievements of Columbus.

25

COPPELLI RETURNED TO THE UNIVERSITY OF SOUTHERN KANSAS in late June 2032. The retracing of the voyage of his ancestor initially worked as a cathartic tonic, at least for a while.

But the depression, already evident on the voyage, returned uninvited and clouded his judgment. A few months following his return, Coppelli went on a long walk after sunset. His walk took him to the centre of Kansas City and the City Park and back to the University. He walked and walked, more than 20 kilometres. As it was night, the heat of the day had retreated, and the sun would not get up for another six hours to start a new day. And still he kept on walking and thinking.

When the sun finally decided to make its ritualistic entry by shining its warmth on the City of Kansas, Coppelli suddenly felt that he was being followed by a stranger. He observed a shadow, not much more than a dark silhouette, in front of him and it accompanied him, wherever he went. If he decided to walk faster, the shadow also walked faster. Coppelli did not dare to look behind his shoulder because he was afraid that the stranger might wrestle him to the ground and strangle him, exactly in the same way he had intended to dispatch the President of the United States. He even thought that the person by whom he was shadowed might have a knife that would be thrust into his body at any time. Or the stranger would shoot him with a rifle? It was a most alarming development in the mental capacities of Coppelli because he had become afraid of his own shadow!

Over the next couple of days, Coppelli's depression became a debilitating illness which made it impossible for him to function effectively. But even in his dejected state, he recognized that, because of his involvement with Charles, fifteen students had died in his classroom. He was responsible for untold misery, and yet, he was awarded the highest bravery award for his actions, the Nation's Bravery Medal. In truth, he realized that he was a vicious, unrepentant, serial killer, not a hero, and he did not deserve the Bravery Medal.

Coppelli's behaviour became erratic and unpredictable. The depression developed into an unbearable burden and fatally affected his ability to perform his university duties. His teaching in the University became pedestrian and failed to inspire his students. His erstwhile formidable reputation as a champion of free speech lost its shine. He no longer received invitations to celebrate his life and achievements – it was as if the collective memory of his former friends, supporters and admirers had vanished. They had all deserted him.

Not long after, on Tuesday, 12 October 2032, which was still known as Columbus Day, even if there were no official functions to commemorate the navigator, Coppelli drove his car to the train station of Kansas City. He parked his car securely in the station's car park, leaving the key in the door lock. He placed an envelope on the passenger seat, and he removed his expensive watch which he deposited next to the envelope. A recently published book on the hologram technology which he had been reading was also placed on the seat.

Coppelli slowly, reluctantly, walked into the station. He looked up the schedule of trains coming from Washington DC. There was one that was scheduled to arrive at 4 in the afternoon. He then sat down on a bench, waiting for the train to arrive. By then, he lived in his own dream world, and he did not acknowledge any traveller who waited to board the train on its arrival in the station. When the train finally came into sight, Coppelli calmly walked up to the train, and he was killed instantly. The conductor later told the police that he saw Coppelli on the track when it was too late for the train to be stopped.

Coppelli's envelope, which he left on the passenger seat of his car, contained a letter explaining his actions. He wanted the world to know the real story of his deceit, deception, conspiracy, and serial killing. He also candidly admitted that he regretted his involvement with the DNA Movement. In his letter, he also decried the destruction of monuments and statues and implored students to respect history.

'History serves as a mirror which give us insights into the lives of our ancestors,' he said.

The DNA Movement had lost a potential leader.

26

After Coppelli's death, his estate executor found his testament in a drawer of the bedroom of his house. It was a detailed document that provided its readers with a lot of information on his life, achievements, and abject failures. The testament had been typed on his personal Dell laptop and printed out at home. It was a copy of the letter he had placed on the passenger seat of his car, which he had abandoned at the Kansas City station car park. An identical third copy was found in a drawer in the living room, so it was always going to be found – he made sure of that.

Coppelli's house was a small, two-bedroom detached house with a tiled roof in an affluent neighbourhood, close to his office at the University of Southern Kansas. He bought it twelve years ago, soon after the University confirmed his tenured appointment. He repaid his bank loan over three years, and he was no longer burdened by a mortgage. He also had bought a new car, a Fiat, which is the type of car he had driven in Italy when he was a student at the University of Macerata.

The testament revealed what had happened before, during and after the attack by Charles on that fateful day in 2026 when he was teaching Marxism and the Law to his students.

The testament described how he and Charles discussed extensively the possibility of assassinating the President, provided they could get close to him. Coppelli, having studied the movements of the President, was convinced that the President would always travel to the scene of a disaster to comfort the local community and embrace victims and survivors. Thus, the attack on his lecture theatre was planned to anticipate the President's visit to the University where he would embrace Coppelli, the hero, who would thus have an opportunity to assassinate him.

'I am sure that the President isn't really interested in the victims and survivors of a catastrophe. He is only doing this to boost his electoral appeal. He is a hypocrite,' he wrote in the testament.

The testament revealed that Coppelli was ideologically sympathetic to Charles. They both hated the society they lived in, and they wanted to take it back to year zero, to make a fresh start.

'It is not altogether clear where these views came from,' I explained to the three Secret Service agents, who had become my friends and were at the University to tie up loose ends.

'Coppelli's parents had been members of Mussolini's party during the Second World War and, therefore, their idea of a successful society would have been brutally snatched from them after the War. His parents' despondency and uneasiness with the Italian political regime coupled with the creation of the social welfare state may have fanned Coppelli's hatred of society.

'But it may also have to do with lack of opportunities. Remember that Coppelli was unemployed for a long time after graduating from the University of Macerata,' I reminded them.

However, in truth, Coppelli's views had been formed well before he became unemployed and even before he gained his law degree at the University of Macerata. The testament indicated that his views had been formed, not by first hand experiences, but by reading about the corruption, rapaciousness, and greed associated with capitalist societies.

Charles and Coppelli also deplored that African Americans were often denied the opportunities available to white people, all because of their race, an incident of their birth. Coppelli was naturally attracted to the DNA Movement which Charles established. But his assessment of this Movement in the testament paints a complex picture:

'The Movement's aim was to highlight the deprivations suffered by people on the ground of race, a trait over which they have no control. I was thus naturally attracted to the Organization set up by Charles, who attended many of my lectures at the University of Southern Kansas and my guest lectures in Chicago. It is, however, deplorable that most of the funds raised from sponsors were in fact appropriated by Charles for his own purposes and only a small amount of money, a pittance really, was used for the achievement of the objectives of the Movement, which the donors wanted to support. I nevertheless went along with Charles, because the need to confront the Nation with its discriminatory practices and past was paramount.

'It was unfortunate that the demonstrations in Washington DC and Minneapolis and other cities turned violent. Charles later told me that the violence, the destruction of property, and the invasion of businesses run by white supremacists was a planned objective of the marches. He had cleverly posted a few provocateurs in various parts of the demonstrations to entice the marchers into violence. Although I did take part in some of the violence, I now regret having participated in this illegal behaviour.

'Charles and I talked about nothing else but "revenge" after the President issued his Executive Order. By assassinating the President, we were going to revenge the deprivation, exploitation, and lynching of many African Americans. I volunteered for the job. The prospect of becoming an assassin appealed to me because I would be known, for eternity, as the person who contributed to a more egalitarian society by assassinating the chief representative of a thoroughly immoral regime. To that effect, I studied the profile of the President for months. I retraced the President's movements during his time in office and I carefully observed his responses to the disasters, especially shootings that occurred regularly in the United States. I correctly assumed that, once an atrocity occurred, the President would visit the site of the shooting and embrace victims and survivors. He would certainly warmly embrace and congratulate a hero who valiantly pretended to wrestle the attacker to the ground. Thus, the idea of becoming a "hero" germinated in these discussions which Charles and I had with each other on our long walks.

'Charles and I also practised wrestling and I taught him the basics of boxing. It was important to ensure that people would regard our struggle in my lecture theatre as a genuine, desperate, heroic attempt on my part to protect my students. In that, we were supremely successful. However, I was surprised that Charles decided to sacrifice himself because that was never discussed between us. I certainly did not shoot him. He lowered his gun as I wrestled him to the floor of the lecture theatre and he shot himself, to ensure that he would not be shot by the police. I am lucky that I was not killed by the police because when they burst in, they did not know whether I was an attacker or the professor. Fortunately, one of my students immediately identified me as the professor who saved scores of students from a certain death during the attack.

'I had earlier told Charles, when I discussed my first experience with email messages, that the door of my lecture room would be wide open, to communicate my views on digital messaging to everyone willing to listen. So, he would easily be able to find my lecture theatre. Also, Charles knew that every lecture theatre in my building bloc had a message which discouraged students from using the email facility and WIFI and, instead, to converse with their lecturers face-to-face. In that way, he would know that he had arrived at the right building.'

The Secret Service agents and I looked at each other.

'These confessions obviously reveal that Coppelli was a willing conspirator and that makes him a serial killer,' I said. My three friends agreed with my assessment. The testament continued:

'I secured an opportunity to kill the President during the Bravery Medal Awards Ceremony. I knew that I could not take any weapons into the Conventions Centre. However, this was not a problem because I used to be a boxer and I could easily strangle him in no time if I got him by the neck. However, when I advanced to the lectern to receive my Award, I stumbled. I did *not* stumble deliberately. I just accidentally turned my ankle. It had happened before because the ligament in my right knee and the cartilage are diseased. Nevertheless, I still went for the neck of the President, and I was surprised I did not catch him. I later understood that the apparition was not the President, but a hologram. I became quite an expert on holograms because I have read many books and articles on the subject since that time.

'Charles discovered the day before his mother died that he was, in fact, the son of the President, but he did not communicate this to me. When I finally found out when reading his testament, I realized that it was not necessary anymore to assassinate the President, because he would resign anyway, which is what happened. We had a President who was elected on the false pretence of protecting family values while hiding his affair with the mother of Charles. Yes, it happened a long time ago, but in my experience, a leopard does not change his spots and a tiger does not change his stripes – it may have happened many times during the last thirty years.

'The revelation that I was a direct descendant of Christopher Columbus was as devastating as the storms my ancestor fought on the way to the New Indies. And it was as devastating as the hurricane which I found myself in during the recreation of Columbus's last journey in 1502. It changed my life forever. I understood that everyone is a product of their time, and so am I, and that it is necessary to honour and protect history. I am now firmly of the opinion that we should not destroy monuments and statues even if they are of people who were later unmasked as genocidal murderers.

'The reality is that I am a serial killer. I deserve to die because the pain and suffering will only subside if I am gone. That is why I decided to commit suicide.

'I wish Professor Bentleys the best of luck at the University of Southern Kansas. He is doing an excellent job as the President of the University. I fully expect him to remove my statue from the main quadrangle of the University. Indeed, I will be happy if it were to find a resting place in the University's Museum,' Coppelli wrote in the testament.

*****

Coppelli's prediction of the fate of his statue was prescient. I recommended to the Senate that the statue be dismantled and reassembled in the Museum, with a long explanatory note, explaining to visitors the history of the statue and the events surrounding the shooting. The recommendation was accepted without any dissent.

Life slowly returned to normal at the University. I presided over the University with a firm hand, common sense, and competent management. I was able to increase the rankings of the University. It became the University of choice for thousands of students, who wanted to study in the State's premier teaching and research institution.

*****

In early 2033, I received a phone call from the recently installed 50th President of the United States, a Republican.

'Mr. Bentleys, I want to come to the point immediately. I am hereby inviting you to become my Press Secretary,' he said.

'But I am the President of the University of Southern Kansas. I just can't pack up and leave.'

'No problem, I will organize for you to take leave of absence without pay for four years. You will be able to return to your presidential job when you finish your assignment with me. Who knows, you might even be the nominee of the Republican Party in 2036? I only intend to serve for four years,' the President said.

'Not possible, Mr. President, because I am still an Australian citizen.'

'You could become a naturalized American citizen. The United States recognizes dual citizenship. So, you can be both an American and Australian. But, of course, as the Constitution requires American presidents to be born in the United States, you would be ineligible to become the Chief Executive of this country. I am sure we will find something else for you to do!'

'How come you thought about me for this assignment,' I asked the President.

'A few days ago, I visited, for the first time, the utility room of the White House and I found a few boxes on the table with papers destined for the incinerator. On top was a report about you, written by, or for, our 47th President, Desmond Raymond Clarkenson. The report describes you as determined, opinionated, obdurate, obstinate, argumentative, obnoxious, but extremely driven, ambitious, competent, communicative, and loyal. These are the qualities that I seek in the person I want as my Press Secretary, Richard,' the President explained.

'I will announce the appointment tonight. Can you start tomorrow?' he asked.

The invitation was extremely flattering. I could not refute the President's approach.

'Mr. President, it will be an honour to serve you as your Press Secretary,' I said proudly.

Another spectacular coincidence, I thought. It reminded me of that little piece of paper in the girls' high school that floated up to me and challenged me, never again, to score 0 out of 10.

'I think I will invite Martha to dinner tonight. It will be my only free night because, as from tomorrow, I will again be bound by the rules of behaviour applicable to a Press Secretary,' I said contentedly.

EPILOGUE

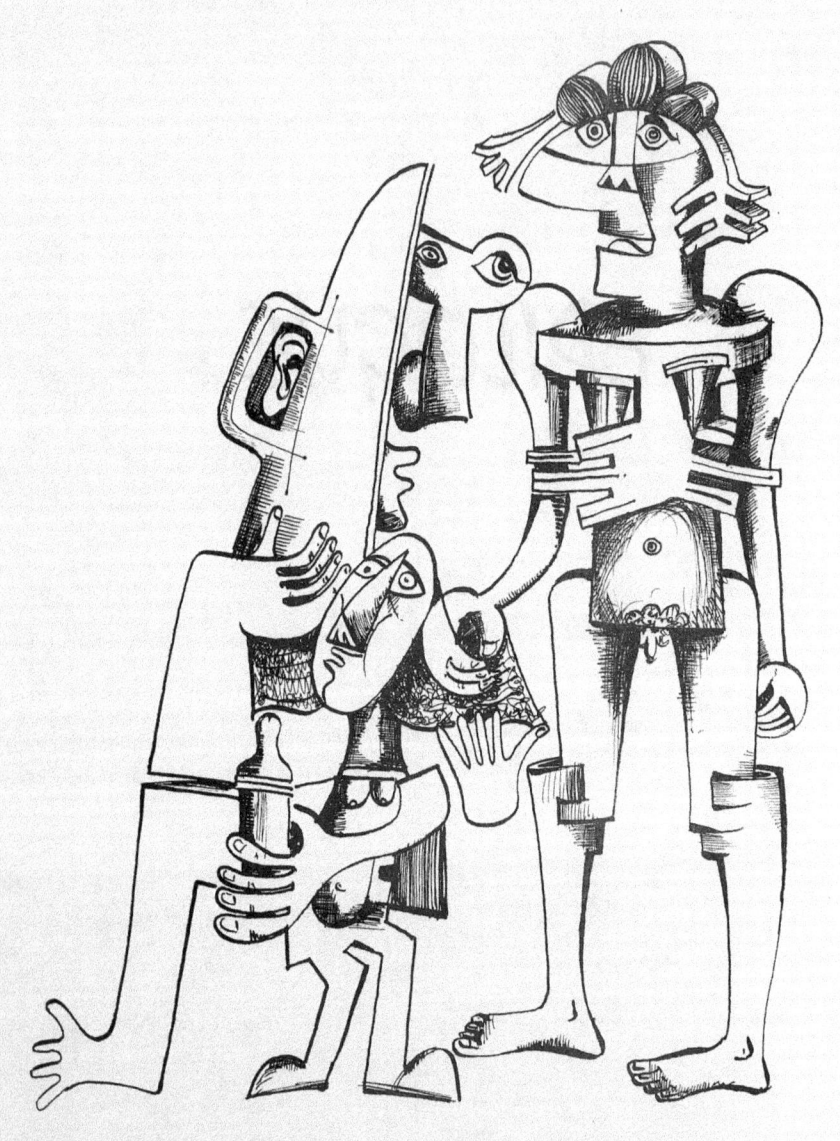

COPPELLI IN 100 WORDS

In his book *Tell Tale* Jeffrey Archer describes that he was invited to write a story of exactly 100 words in 24 hours. He managed to include two such stories in his book. This encouraged me to attempt to tell the story of Coppelli Colone, this novel's prodigious protagonist, in 100 words.

Here it is.

When working at the University of Southern Kansas, I befriended Coppelli Colone, a genial and famed teacher. He authored erudite books – fiction and non-fiction, every year.

But there is a fine line between insanity and geniality. Coppelli smelled like a rotting rat, that lay hidden in the attic, because he infrequently bathed or showered.

One day, I was window shopping in Florence. When I was about to turn a corner, a familiar smell wafted through the air. I exclaimed, 'It is him, Coppelli'.

Coppelli's blood-soaked eyes stared at me in disbelief. They were the eyes of an unrepentant serial killer.

AUTHOR'S NOTE

I enjoyed writing this novel. It is my second novel. Like my debut novel, *A Twisted Choice* (Boolarong Press, 2020), it focuses on a real issue that mesmerized the world community: the destruction of monuments and statues throughout the world, notably in the United States, the United Kingdom, but also in Australia and other countries. This topical issue provides the background for this tale of conspiracy, attempted murder, revenge, and redemption.

It is a novel about coincidences. Bill Bryson notes in his iconic book *Notes from a Small Island* that, although there are many scientific studies about the probabilities of coincidences, he did not have enough examples to complete an article on remarkable coincidences he was writing for an airline magazine. Consequently, he failed to submit the article on time. The day after the missed delivery date, he attended a book sale, organized by the literary editor of *The Times*. He recalls that the very first book he saw at the book sale was a paperback entitled *Remarkable True Coincidences*. It contains many examples of coincidences which he could have used in his article. This is certainly a coincidence, but on top of this, the 'very first coincidence it discussed concerned a man named Bryson.'

The late Australian Senator, Dr John Herron AO, used to say that 'coincidence is God's way of remaining anonymous.' Extraordinary coincidences always play a part in the lives of people.

Agatha Christie, the Goddess of the whodunnit, recognized this when she wrote in her book, *The Secret Adversary*, that, 'I've often noticed that when coincidences start happening, they go on happening in the most extraordinary way.'

The impetus for writing this novel was provided by a book that I had recently read about the history of Philips, the well-known Dutch electronics company. In 1986, the late former Managing Director of Philips Industries in Australia, Herman Huyer, had given me his memoir, entitled *As I Remember*. The book was not officially published; it was typewritten and duplicated, but it was bound properly in a blue cover, to enable his family and grandchildren and some other people to know the life's history of the Director. In his book, he recounted the story of his time as the Managing Director of Philips in Greece in the late '60s when that country was in the hands of the army, the Colonels. Philips had built a new telecommunications factory in Greece at the time with the permission and, indeed, support of the military junta. Consequently, Huyer was criticized for 'collaborating' with a dictatorial regime. When he visited the headquarters of Philips Industries in Eindhoven in the Netherlands, he discovered that a monument erected in honour of Anton Philips, the founder of the company, had been painted black by an unruly crowd. So, this type of protest has a long history, indeed.

The story in this novel is set in Chicago, Kansas City, Washington DC, in the United States, and in Sydney, Australia. I have lived in Chicago, and I have visited Washington DC several times, but I have never visited Kansas City. In the novel, some scenes occur in Italy – in Florence and Macerata. My wife and I lived in Barberino di Mugello, which is twenty-eight kilometres north of Florence, and we have visited the beautiful medieval city of Macerata in the Marches region of Italy, on many occasions. From time to time, I taught at the Law School of the University of Macerata.

The main protagonists of this story are Coppelli Colone, Desmond Raymond Clarkenson, Charles Roderick Dudley, and Richard Andreas Bentleys. Their tales are intertwined, and they will eventually result in the demise of Charles, Coppelli and Desmond. Richard is portrayed as a capable, ambitious professional who was destined to go far in his career.

I believe that people can learn from history. Historical monuments and statues are a mirror into mankind's past, and they provide us with an opportunity to reflect on the lives, achievements, and mistakes of our ancestors. It is for that reason that I bemoan the destruction of property, monuments and statues which we have witnessed during the last couple of years. Like in my first novel, the protagonists must consider the consequences of their actions for themselves and society when they are involved in destructive acts.

The rioters justify the violence and the destruction of historic monuments, which we witness regularly on our television screens, on the ground that 'equality' should be the overriding value in our society. Of course, I have always been in favour of 'equality', specifically 'equality of opportunity'. As an academic, I published various papers in scholarly journals and in popular magazines, in which I argued that impediments to participation in public life, based on a person's race, should be removed. But the DNA Movement and the pamphlets produced by the progressive intellectual elites reminded me constantly that my understanding of 'equality' is but an antique remnant of a bygone era. The Movement wants the destruction of the present system, no less. The facilitation of this objective is assisted enthusiastically by collaborating progressive university academics.

The description of the voyage of Christopher Columbus in this novel is based on real events, but it is not historically accurate. The narrative of his last journey in 1502 is largely fictitious. While he occasionally encountered storms, the storm described in the novel is the product of imagination.

Initially, I considered that the President's doppelganger would visit the University of Southern Kansas to drape the Bravery Medal around the neck of Coppelli. However, I was alerted to the existence of hologram technology which I used in this novel as it appeared a more interesting and novel way of developing the story.

I would like to emphasise that this novel is fiction and that all names used in this novel are fictitious. The University of Southern Kansas and the University of Southern Sydney do not exist, but are typical of academic institutions throughout the world.

I am indebted to my beta readers, who read drafts of the novel.

My first gratitude goes to my wife, Edith Moens, who is an avid as well as a critical reader of my work. This book is dedicated to her, for her patience, encouragement and incisive criticism. Edith's maiden name is Van der Mijnsbrugge. She is the sister of the artist whose drawings are reproduced in this novel. Joris Van der Mijnsbrugge, who died prematurely in 2003, and was a promising and much respected sculptor in Belgium. His futuristic drawings are particularly suited for this novel which is set in the not-too-distant future.

Various drafts of the novel have been read by Eric Sim from Singapore, Martin Klapper, Peter Gillies, Nicolet Mijnssen, Keith Thompson, Victor Goh from Malaysia, Rosemary Lucadou-Wells, Augusto Zimmermann, John McRobert, and other people, who prefer to remain anonymous.

Finally, I acknowledge the valuable editorial and formatting assistance of Michael Gilchrist of Connor Court Publishing. I am also grateful to the founder of Connor Court Publishing, Anthony Cappello, for his willingness to publish this novel. He has always been an ardent supporter of my work.

I would like to thank all of them for their willingness to provide feedback and offer assistance which has been invaluable during the writing of the novel. Their contribution has made the novel into a better and more enjoyable product, which I hope will give my readers many hours of reading joy.

BOOK CLUB NOTES

The writing of this novel was motivated by the systematic destruction of monuments and statues in the United States, the United Kingdom and Australia during the dark days of 2020 and 2021 when Covid-19 ruled the world, but also before that time. The theme of the novel is the importance of learning from history and the value of maintaining historical monuments and statues.

There are many sub-themes in this novel, for example, the importance of honesty in public life, reading and writing, and morality. Important sub-themes are the fight against racial discrimination, gun control, and the pursuit of equality of opportunity.

Here are a few questions that members of a book club might consider.

1. Do you find the description of the characters compelling: Desmond Raymond Clarkenson (the President), Richard Andreas Bentleys (the Press Secretary), Coppelli Colone (the Professor of the History of Ideas and Jurisprudence), Charles Roderick Dudley (the Leader of the DNA Movement), and Christopher Columbus (the Navigator)?

2. Do you believe in coincidences? Do you recall coincidences in your own life?

3. How many coincidences did you discover in the novel? Which coincidence is the coincidence that the title of the novel refers to?

4. What are we able to learn from history?

5. What place should the study of history have in high schools and colleges?

6. The novel suggests that past events should not be judged in the light of modern standards. Do you agree with this suggestion? Explain your view on this issue.

7. What are the advantages of hologram technology?

8. Is the development of DNA science a good and desirable development? Consider its consequences for medical science, privacy, law enforcement, data protection and information gathering.

9. What did you learn about the American system of government? Does the system reflect the democratic choices made by the electorate?

10. What does the novel tell you about electioneering and campaigning?

11. What is the novel's message on corruption in government?

12. There is quite an emphasis on university governance and the loss of freedom of speech in the academy. What is the role of free speech on campus and how should it be protected?

13. How do you view the actions of the President's Press Secretary when he became President of the University of Southern Kansas?

14. Can you relate to Coppelli's decision to commit suicide? What could he have done to redeem himself?

15. Do you believe that statues and historical monuments should be destroyed if they venerate heinous crimes?

16. If you believe that statues and monuments of historical figures should not be destroyed even if they venerate crimes, how would you address new evidence regarding the historical actions of these figures?

ABOUT THE AUTHOR

Professor Gabriël A. Moens AM is Emeritus Professor of Law, The University of Queensland. He served as Pro Vice Chancellor, Dean and Professor of Law, Murdoch University. He also served as Head, Graduate School of Law, The University of Notre Dame Australia; Garrick Professor of Law, The University of Queensland; and Professor of Law, Curtin University. In 1999, Professor Moens received the Australian Award for University Teaching in Law and Legal Studies. He is the Founder and Emeritus Editor-in-Chief of *International Trade and Business Law Review*. In 2003, the Prime Minister of Australia awarded him the Australian Centenary Medal for services to education. He was named the "International Alumnus of the Year" by the Pritzker Law School of Northwestern University, Chicago in 2019. In June 2019 he was appointed a Member of the Order of Australia (AM) for services to the law and higher education. Professor Moens is a Membre Titulaire, International Academy of Comparative Law, Paris; a Fellow of the Australian Institute of Management (WA); a Fellow of the College of Law; a Fellow of the Australian Academy of Law; and a Fellow of the Australian Centre for International Commercial Arbitration.

He is author/co-author/editor/co-editor of *Enduring Ideas*, Connor Court Publishing 2020; *Law of International Business in Australasia* (2nd ed), The Federation Press, 2019; *The Constitution of the Commonwealth of Australia Annotated* (9th ed), LexisNexis Butterworths, 2016; *Arbitration and Dispute Resolution in the Resources Sector: An Australian Perspective*, Springer, 2015; *Jurisprudence of Liberty* (2nd ed), LexisNexis, 2011; *Commercial Law of the European Union*, Springer, 2010; and *International Trade and Business: Law, Policy and Ethics* (2nd ed), Routledge/Cavendish, 2006. His debut novel *A Twisted Choice*, a thriller exploring the origins of Covid-19, was published in 2020 by Boolarong Press. He has published a short story, *The Greedy Prospector*, in an anthology of short stories in 2021. He writes opinion pieces and commentary for various magazines and newspapers.